Song

AN APPALACHIAN CRYPTID TALE
BOOK ONE

JAE DIXON

First edition

electronic: ISBN: 979-8-9875490-0-1

paperback: ISBN: 979-8-9875490-1-8

❀ Created with Vellum

Beloved, this was always meant for you.
From me,
with love.

February 14, 2010

Author's Note

Again, this novel is entirely a work of fiction. The names, characters and incidents portrayed in it are the work of the author's imagination. Any resemblance to actual persons, living or dead, is entirely coincidental.

The University, departments, and professors are fictional and archetypal. These are a collection of the best and worst traits humanity has to offer in academia. This novel does not represent any specific University or college town in Appalachia.

The rural Ohio town mentioned is a blending of several rural towns the author has lived in and is based more on legend than any historical fact.

Any and all legends, lore, or historical events mentioned should be researched by the reader and not assumed to be fact.

LANGUAGE AND GENDER

The author uses They/Them/Theirs as a singular pronoun frequently. Gray and Pooka are agender. Addison is gender fluid. When a character does not know someone's gender, that character will refer to that person as *they/them* until it is clarified.

APPALACHIA

The author grew up in Pennsylvania and Ohio in the 1990's and early 2000's. They learned a lot about legends and practices of those regions from close friends and their families. For this series they have done research to add to the setting. Out of respect, the author will not detail specific cultural components of the beautiful and varied Appalachia folklore and practices. Any magic related spell or practice in this book is fictional.

CONTENT WARNING

This dark fantasy novel contains; Adult language, Chronic Illness, Consensual Sexual Situations, Colonization, Drug and Alcohol Use, Death, Discussion of Mental Health/Involuntary Commitment, Emotional/Verbal Abuse, Grief and Loss, Mention of Historical Violence, Murder, Physical Assault, Mention of Parent Death (Cancer), Mention of Child Death, Mention of Execution, and *Monster Fucking*. The main characters' romantic and physical relationship does not contain abuse.

The Winged Folk do not tolerate abuse or any other non-consensual activities unless it's Indrid and murder.

Song

Prologue

A GOBLIN AND THE SENTINEL

T he wind of Fate rustled through the trees as winter faded into the spring. A young goblin scurried through the under-brush, searching for shelter from the impending last frigid storm of the year. Light slanted through tree branches, casting deep shadows among the fallen branches and rotting leaves. The goblin, a Pooka, nestled in the gnarled roots of an ancient, lone sentinel as old as the forest itself.

Pooka chirped softly, their fur matted with blood from a wound that sluggishly bled. Their nest, their family, had been torn apart by a larger Folk and finished off by a thin fox that would not live to see the summer. Pooka was a youngling, too young to live on their own. They chirped again as a single drop of blood rolled to the forest floor.

The parched Earth drank it in. The sentinel vibrated with the bit of essence that had been shed by the tiny goblin. It was enough pain and loss to rouse the Well into speaking. *This Folk is important to the mountains,* the Well thought. The sentinel, which looked like a decayed tree, opened its eyes. Slowly, its face shifted, looking down at the injured being.

"Greetings, my child," the Well spoke through its earthly form. A sound of cracking and groaning wood.

The Pooka hopped, startled by the sound and sudden movement.

"Do not fear Us, child." They smiled in the way an ancient power could in the rigid earthly form they took. "We are here because you called for us."

The Pooka simply squinted up at the talking tree. Pooka sensed this was an ancient being, some primordial power, even if Pooka did not have the language to describe this being. Pooka chirped, a greeting in their people's language. The Well beamed with light visible to only those of essence, a branched creaked as it lowered to scoop Pooka from the forest floor.

"We know your destiny, child. We know the destiny of all our children. Those who have passed. Those who are here. Those who have yet to come. We know you are essential to this valley's life, to our Keeper."

Pooka stood on their hind legs before crying out in pain as the ruined skin pulled, blood trickled out.

"Ah, sweet one." The Well ran a thick knotted finger down Pooka's flank, the Pooka's skin knitted together as if it had never been damaged. "Is that better, child?"

Pooka twisted to inspect the area, large black eyes taking in the miracle of the Well's essence, the magic that lived within the Earth itself. A tiny paw of seven-fingers messaged the area for several seconds before Pooka churred in thanks.

"You are welcome, child." The Well paused. "There is something I must ask of you. It will be difficult, perhaps, and not a task for one as young as you are."

Pooka chirped in slight defiance. The Well heard them grumble that they were young, yes, but not incapable of helping the old forest God. *That is what this being must be, a God.* The Well chuckled at Pooka. Pooka realized the forest God could hear their thoughts.

"Yes, dear one. We can and no, We are not a God." The Well tilted the Sentinel's head, a strange gesture for a tree. "We are something that has been here as long as the mountains. We were the first bloom. We were the first death."

The Pooka chirped. *Is that not a God?*

The Well thought on that. Perhaps that was what the young Folk believed now. It had been so long since the beginning of remembered time. So much knowledge had been lost in the years when there were no Keepers. A great migration had occurred over the last few centuries, the Folk's numbers dwindling.

"We are not a God, no. We are the flow of what connects us all, the Folk and the humans that are of essence. We are the magic of this world from the other worlds. We are the key to knowledge. We are the burst of light in life. We are the quiet of time ended."

Pooka chirped. *That does not make sense forest God, but you're old.*

The Sentinel made a wheezing sound, like a sharp breeze rustling leaves, as the Well laughed. "Perhaps you are correct, child. I am old."

Pooka pulled themselves up straighter, clutching to the oversized twig that served as the Sentinel's thumb. *My family's gone, forest God, but you say I'm important. Wasn't my family important, too?*

The Well sighed, a breeze rustled the Pooka's soft fur. "We do not value your family any less than you, and fate is a fickle thing. Your life bringers were tasked with producing a great guide in you. You will lead the valley and our forest into the next generation of peace. You will help heal what has been fouled. You are the Keeper's Cicerone if you agree."

The Pooka sat back on their haunches and whistled quietly. *Will the Keeper know it's me?*

"No, I imagine the Keeper will not understand this for some time." The Well's thoughts churned. They would have to impart a great deal of knowledge into the Pooka's mind before delivering Pooka to the Keeper's mate. Fate had whispered that the Pooka would be the chaperone to the bright human of songs through many of his chapters, to the end.

"Are you ready, my child? For what I must do may cause you more grief. Fate has not been easy with you. We cannot spare you the hurt you have already felt, the grief of the seasons to come. And sometimes, Fate's path is altered by our choices and that of others." The Sentinel drew Pooka in closer to its trunk as the Well began to pull from the roots.

Pooka snuggled closer to the bark that was not quite bark anymore, but a warmed, rough skin. The longer the Well stayed in this form, the more living it became. Pooka let out a long breath, a small cloud puffing out toward the gray sky.

I'm ready, forest God, they chirped softly.

Very good, the Well spoke in Pooka's mind. *In the time before, when this world was very cold and not yet molten, a great power flowed through the spaces. This is the original form of Us, essence. We were everything and We were nothing. Soon, the Universes began to take shape, and within them a multitude of worlds. This was a place, a world, where We-essence found home. The planet formed, as worlds do, and then came the Peoples and Creatures along with it.*

This world, Earth as the Peoples now call it, was different, though. There was a great, deep tear that connected Us to a thousand other worlds. In the beginning it acted as a window for Us to see. Then as a door as the beings of the other places began to come. Few stayed and even fewer as our home flowered into the mountains, oceans, and forests you see now. As nights passed, the doors closed. We could no longer see into the beyond.

There was one world, the world of the Folk, that remained open to Us. We watched as that world lived and died. Eventually, some Folk began to cross the barrier to live among us under the skies. Their door closed, as they always seem to do, but We are still connected to the origin.

We are still the web that everything is linked to or within. We drift among the thoughts of those that are living and those that are passed. We hold the knowledge that the Keepers must possess to balance this world. For that is how and why the other places crumbled. They had lost their balance. We are balance. We are order. We are chaos.

When a Keeper is chosen, they are tied to us. We give them the knowledge that does not exist in words, but in the places of the absence of sound. Keepers hear the lore on the breath of the wind. They read the history in the dewdrops on blades of grass in the civil twilight. This is not something that is spoken, it is something that is known.

Pooka shuddered at what the Well had given them. The young goblin blinked, realizing they no longer were in the forest but on the dingy carpet of an *efficiency apartment*. Unsure of how they knew those words, they noticed a sleeping human in the corner. A spider crawled up his face toward his mouth. Pooka charged across the floor, grabbing the spider and swallowing it whole. Perhaps the forest God was wrong. Eating spiders for the human did not seem like a hardship to them.

CHAPTER 1

Silence in The Trees

GRAY

I remember when the river had another name. The First Peoples here called it a gourd or something; I was still young then, and not as familiar with their language. It is gone now, or at least, I no longer hear it spoken in the valleys and the hills. It happens to us, the Folk—not remembering words like we used to. The New People, they change the words every decade or century, though it happens more quickly now. The changes.

The New People came and distorted everything. I remember when the flow of the river was altered, when the waters rose and were dammed. When the river was moved and all that was left was a dribble until the snow melted and the ice broke. When there was the smell of ash on the wind from the ridge. I can still hear the moans of the lost at night, under the stars. They are still up there, the dead, set in straight white stone lines among the trees and wild things. I used to visit to feed the deer and sit in the old tower. I have not done that since the New People opened the tunnels and tore down *his* home.

This is my *territory* to travel, following the river and roads. The New People only see me when I allow it. They do not remember the old world or the words and songs that connect us.

The night I found *him*, I had gone farther north than my usual route to see that curious place filled with the young New People. They did the most fantastic and confusing things. Reading out into the sky dramatically, drawing permanent pictures on their bodies, impaling their flesh, and drinking until they emptied the contents of their stomachs into the streets. The young ones lost their shoes, their virginities, and the old ways of understanding the world around them.

Perhaps it is my amusement with them that had doomed me to find him. Maybe it was Fate. At first, it felt like a hard line pulling me in his direction. It was a tether not so different from the one that bound me to the land and the Well.

And there he was. *Beloved*. He had the most precious face, and eyes the color of the deepest river, not blue yet not gray. Beloved's hair was as dark as the winter mud-stained hills with skin as fair as the old crow bones that have lain for seven seasons on the overlook. He gently spoke his songs to the moon at night when the others slept. That is how I found him that night, weeping so sweetly under the stars.

The air was finally starting to warm after months of languid, frosted nights. The nights were not as long, but that darkness felt like an embrace against each wing. The bugs were not singing as loudly as they would be in a few weeks' time. There are fewer of the young New People by the time the frost leaves for summer heat. Those that stay are not as recklessly entertaining. The ones that remain seem preoccupied and less aware of the world around them. They bump around the grounds while strangling cups filled with what smells like fire heated rot. They are not taking time to notice the foliage, or the bugs, or the ghosts.

Tonight, Beloved was sitting behind his house with papers strewn across the dark emerald lawn. He did not have a mug of that foul smelling tar. There was a bottle of something clear labeled with a wolf howling at the moon. The young, New People called it *moonshine*. It is made somewhere in the hills nearby. He was drinking liberally from it, muttering under his breath. I watched from the taller trees. I did not think he would be happy to see me. The tears in his eyes made me think he would not be happy to see anyone.

He picked up the closest piece of paper and started reading the lines. I swayed to the rhythm as he hummed out his song, verse by verse. His words were a little slurred and angry. He violently tore up the lined sheet he was holding. I do not know what the paper did to him. All it had on it was his song. Beloved's beautiful song was now tiny scraps among the tall blades of grass. Words mixed up with worms and dirt. My wings twitched, I wanted to hold him tight.

"Goddamned, fucking chair," he hissed. "That fucking bastard wouldn't know nuance if it fucked him in the face." Beloved waved his hands to no one in particular. I was not sure why he was angry at a chair. I also did not know the young people gave genders to furniture. Perhaps that was something new. Each generation seems to be more enlightened than the last.

"Allen can sss...suck," Beloved hiccuped, "my di...ick." He stood up, lurching forward and almost falling face first into the ground. The muscles in my arms flexed, wanting to go help him to his nest. I would have to follow him during the day to find out who or what Allen was and why Beloved would want him to suck his dick. I do not want another being touching my precious human.

Beloved twisted too quickly and listed to the left like a boat taking water. He caught himself but was much closer to falling. He leaned over far enough to grab the bottle and staggered across the patio to the door. He fumbled with the knob before stepping into his haven. His back foot missed the step and he tripped, falling hard. From across the yard glass shattered and a pained grunt echoed. I held my breath and waited. No other sounds came from within.

No longer able to wait, if Beloved was hurt, he needed me. Jumping down from the branches, I landed without a sound. No one would see me cross the lawn. He was inside the door far enough that no one would see him *float* through the room as I carried him concealed behind essence. As I approached the back step, he was laying on the ground unconscious and thankfully uninjured. The only casualty was the alcohol he had been holding. He had simply done what the other young ones did: drink too much and sleep deeply.

Scooping him up in my arms, I walked him to his nest, which was by the far wall under a casement window that was glued shut. The room was dingy, carpet stained and old. The walls were painted white brick with cracks running parallel to the places where the foundation had settled. The floor had sunk a little into the ground, causing an unevenness. The furniture was mismatched and in poor condition.

There were empty cans lying all over the space and on every flat surface. The label of the drinks said they were made of *monster*. Purring to myself; the subtle rise of arousal not felt in recent memory stirred. Perhaps Beloved would want to drink me down since most young New People considered what I was to be a monster. His tongue in and on me would be pleasant.

With one arm wrapped around my precious little mortal, I pulled back the blankets in the nest. The linens were cleaner than the rest of the cave he lived in. His home and nest seemed lacking. This place was empty. I would have to bring Beloved gifts for his subterranean cave, maybe some leaves or branches. The ground would look better with moss and some black trumpets. Maybe I should give Beloved some spiders for the windows.

He grunted as he settled into his nest. He looked so small and cold. I wanted to snuggle in with him, but I would not. It would not be right. He had to invite me into his nest. I would never force myself or assume he even felt the same appeal I did.

Pulling the covers up to his shoulders, I made sure my claws were retracted. I did not want to scratch that soft skin or ruin his nest. He shifted again, no sign of waking up for hours, most likely. Moonshine had that effect on the young New People. The Winged Folk needed far more to sleep so lazily.

Slowly I backed away, gazing upon such gentle slumber. He would be my life and my death if I could show him my face. I wanted him to touch my wings. Closing my eyes, I inhaled deeply and then breathed him in again. What would that skin feel like under my claws? What would his heat feel like against my cold in this wet air?

I sighed as my desire grew for his companionship, his touch. It had been too long since I had wanted the company of anything more than a sunlight fly.

After cleaning up the glass and poison water off the floor, I walked outside. A soft chirp startled me, it was coming from the crack under a door leading to another room in Beloved's home. *Ah*, there was a

Pooka here, too. That would explain the lack of spiders. Such a lovely little Folk to have living with you.

Walking outside, I collected the sprinkling of papers, leaving a stack under a rock by the door. I could not collect the shredded words, those belonged to the Earth and grass spiders now. I do not think they understood the New People's words; the enchantment of Beloved's songs would be lost on them.

I shut the door. I would be back. I did not want to leave.

CHAPTER 2

Weed and Beer

EZRA

J esus Christ and all the Saints," I mumbled as I held my head. How much did I drink last night and how in the hell did I make it back to my bed?

I looked around the room with bleary eyes. Somehow, I managed to get inside and shut the back door. The door that I rarely used except when I needed to sit outside and get wasted after a bad meeting with Professor Allen, overlord of my thesis project.

The last thing I remembered was ripping up some of my poetry and... falling on my face. I must've blacked out. I hadn't been this drunk since the high school bonfire parties in the woods. I burped, tasting the moonshine. *Am I still drunk? Ah, fuck.*

I drug myself out of bed, stumbling over to the mini fridge I kept downstairs. I pulled out a shitty IPA to chug. Thank God and above I didn't have to play teaching assistant today.

I paused mid-swallow. If I had office hours, I would need to cancel due to an "illness." I couldn't take a bitching freshman today. They're always complaining about how hard being a freshman was. I'm in no mood for 19-year-old sorrows when I clearly am a hack, hemorrhaging financial aid on a degree I'll never finish.

Allen had been brutal last night. He'd handed me my portfolio with instructions to revise my "disappointment."

It'd been that way every Wednesday meeting for the past six months. He hated my work and saw no true value in it. He *warned* me that if I didn't start to show more of the initial promise that got me admitted to the program, I could bet on a life of self-publishing to four people until I gave up. He added insult to injury by reminding me that no university is going to hire an unpublished professor.

I sat there quietly, taking the weekly abuse, nodding my head with a vacant look on my face. At least, I was going for vacant. I didn't want to give him any more ammunition. He was abusive, but I was terrified to go to the department head to ask for a change. At the time, Dr. Everhart was sure that asshole would be a perfect match for my work. All Dr. Allen accomplished was destroying my will to write and my desire to stay at the university.

I finished my beer and thought about waking up my roommate for some weed. Addison worked overnight shifts, and either were on their way to bed or already tucked away in the garage bedroom.

Nothing about this home was normal. It was over 100 years old. The two of us that still lived here had picked the remodeled garage and basement for our rooms. There were two perfectly *normal* bedrooms left, both empty. One was still covered in the dust from a dance major roommate who'd kept chinchillas. It had been that way since they graduated two years ago. We left it for posterity and to remind us why we no longer had other roommates.

Addison had been in the same MFA program with me and graduated a semester before I did. Instead of teaching undergrads or moving toward a PhD they became a youth counselor at a local residential program for kids who'd difficulties in "traditional" school settings. They loved the kids, even the ones that punched them in the face and called them names. I listened to see if they were awake, watching TV or smoking. I couldn't hear or smell anything but that didn't mean I was out of luck.

I walked up the stairs to find Addison slumped at the fading red Formica laminated table. They'd a bowl of cereal in front of them. It was what was sitting next to that cereal that had Addison's undivided attention. They were rolling a pile of joints, probably for the week. This was the first shift of five and Addison had a bad habit of staying up later that first day. It caught up to them, which is why they spent so much time food and drug prepping.

"Hey, Addi." I sank into the chair across the table from them.

"Ezra." They nodded, not looking up. They paused mid-roll and slowly pushed a finished joint from the pile across the table.

"That obvious?" I chuckled.

"You're drunk at eight a.m., so I'm guessing that's from last night." They continued to roll, not making eye contact. *Bless them.*

"Yeah. I got into the moonshine Mick brought over for solstice."

"Jesus." They looked up to assess the situation that was my disheveled state. "The meeting was that bad?"

"It's always that bad. It got to me more yesterday." I looked away, not wanting to talk about why. It was a day that never had a chance of being good. I was fated to end up at the bottom of a bottle regardless of Allen's words.

"Okay, well. Get high and then get some sleep. There's some electrolyte water in the fridge. Take a bottle with you. I don't need my favorite roommate getting sick downstairs." They'd gone back to rolling as if I hadn't appeared to be the fucking mess that I was.

"Thanks, friend. I appreciate the tender loving care." I chuckled softly as I lifted myself out of the chair.

"Hey, Ez. Did you call your sister yesterday?" They quietly asked, attempting to not disrupt the calm.

"Uh, yeah. She was okay." I shifted a little on the spot.

Addi looked up at me. "Are you okay? I didn't forget. I..." they trailed off. "I didn't know if you wanted to talk about it."

"I'm good. Thanks." I nodded as I backed toward the fridge. If I had a personal narrator to my story, this is the part where they would say, '*But Ezra was, in fact, not good at all.*'

I WAS SITTING on the back porch again. The summer heat wasn't as oppressive during the day and the nights were still cool enough to need a hoodie. The light pollution was low in this town, so I could see the larger constellations from my yard. Not bad for a rural Ohio town sitting in the Allegheny Plateau.

When I woke up well after noon thanks to Addi's joint, I was hungover, but I needed to feel it. Yesterday was abysmal. I should've taken the day off. I should've rescheduled my weekly torture session with Allen. I'm fairly certain I shredded half of my portfolio into mulch. Luckily, it's all digitally backed up.

I ran my hand over my face, trying to wipe away the tiredness that'd been creeping up on me over the passing few months. I was having one of those doctoral student existential crises where I didn't know why I was doing this anymore.

I did it to impress *him* and he's dead. Dad's dead. The poet laureate. The prolific writer. The intellect. The greatest husband. The best dad. The very dead man. At least he'd lived long enough to see me get an acceptance letter. Mom was gone before that.

"I wish you were here." I looked up at the sky for a response. "You could've helped me with this fucking portfolio or maybe told me to stop while I wasn't in as much debt."

I sighed and leaned forward, my head hanging. I heard a rustle from the trees between our house and the neighbor's. I looked up, expecting to see a bird or other wildlife, but there was nothing there. The yard was deep, surprising in such a packed neighborhood. It had something to do with the houses being built into the hills probably.

Something rustled again. Odd, it sounded kind of big. Maybe the neighbor's cat was climbing up the tree. Last summer, the little fool got stuck and it was a huge ordeal for the fire department to get the tiny hell-beast out. Apparently, firemen shouldn't be called for pets stuck in trees, but since they were already there, they still helped.

"Here kitty, kitty." I stood up, crossing the yard to the trees. "Come on, kitty, the hot firemen don't want to crawl up there again to get you."

I made that weird human kissing sound humans reserved for pets and cute animals. I heard the rustle again but when I got closer, I noticed a large branch sagging a little underweight. It was a thick branch that shouldn't be sagging unless something human-sized or larger was on it. I froze; the leaves blocked the rest of the branches enough that I couldn't see in.

"Hello?" I could feel my shoulders tense. "Uh, is someone up there?" I needed to go back inside before whoever or maybe whatever it was decided to jump down and have a conversation. I took a few steps back; feeling the tension building throughout my core. I was a runner during danger, certainly never the fighter.

I quickly reached the concrete porch without any more incidents of moving or noise. I could feel my heartbeat in my ears. *Jesus Christ, what is that?*

I went back into the house, closing the door and locking it tight. I thought about calling the police, but I didn't have a real reason to call. I got startled by shadows and a breeze.

I texted Addi to let them know I thought I saw a large animal or ex-boyfriend in the backyard and to be careful when they got home. I was standing in the hallway that led directly into my little "cave" of a gutted efficiency apartment when I heard a loud *thunk* outside. I froze.

"What the fuck," I whispered to myself and the basement ghost Charles. We had joked for years the place was haunted, but over the past few months I was seeing things move in my apartment. Sometimes the door to the basement would open and shut on its own. I would swear on a stack of Bibles that the spiders moved out and someone was taking my trash.

I blinked at the back door like an asshole, frozen in fear. There wasn't a peephole but if I went up to the kitchen, I had a clear view from the large window over the sink to the backyard. I snuck through the basement, climbing up the wooden stairs that were at an angle more suitable for a ladder. When I got to the kitchen, the lights were out. I left everything off to save on our electricity bill. I wish I would've had the foresight to put in night lights. I crept to the window and peered into the dark backyard.

I didn't see anything in or around the tree. There was something sitting on the concrete. It was small and wrapped in newspaper. I scanned the yard again, but I didn't see anyone walking away. Whoever left it had moved out fast. Was that who was in the tree?

"Maybe I should call the cops," I muttered under my breath. "Well, I might as well go see what the tree demon left me."

I counted all the ways this could end horribly but decided to go find out what was on my porch anyway. Grabbing the baseball bat we kept behind the upstairs bar, I headed toward the basement. There was no point in going out the front door and walking around the house. I might as well invite it directly into my room. As I reached the door, I found myself wondering, is this brave or bizarre? If anything, I'd get a new poem out of it.

Unlocking the door in the entryway; I took in a deep breath before hauling the door open to the night. It was quiet, with the stars still twinkling above. Now that I was closer to the package, it looked like a large canning jar. I looked to my left and right before walking out. The jar wasn't heavy, but it was full of something.

"Fuck it," I mumbled as I set the bat down, leaning it against my leg. "What have I got here?"

Unwrapping the jar, I saw it filled with moss and mushrooms. There wasn't a note or anything else. Why would anyone leave me a jar of moss and mushrooms? What kind of witchcraft was this? It didn't look like a bad thing, a jar full of plant life. Was Addi dating that Pagan boy again? That little botanist loved his plants and Green Man. Loved the latter so much it led to a role play that freaked Addi so much they ghosted the kid.

I snorted and pulled out my phone to take a picture of the jar. Addi wasn't going to be happy if that ex was hiding in our trees and leaving gifts on our doorstep. I took the picture and sent it to Addi with, '*I found this on the step. You banging the witch again?*' I didn't expect a response anytime soon. Those kids could be a handful at the center. Staff weren't allowed to have phones in patient care areas either.

Walking back inside with my Appalachia terrarium, I set it on an end table. Well, a stack of crates that served as a usable surface. A wave of sleepiness hit me after a long couple days of stress and substance use. Pulling off my shirt I headed to my bed. I hit the light switch and fell back into my blankets and pillows. I noticed a subtle glow. The jar was *shimmering*. Getting up to take a closer look, I realized that some of the fungus was bioluminescent.

The soft glow mesmerized me for what could have been minutes or hours. It was hypnotic. Something about it gave me comfort. In this dark, lonely room, to have a soft light was akin to having my back rubbed as I fell asleep. It'd been a long time since I'd had someone lay with me. It'd been a long time since I had felt this calm. Maybe the jar was magic. Too bad it wasn't for me.

CHAPTER 3

Coffee Shop Windows

GRAY

L eaning against the brick wall in the alley, I continued reliving the night before. I had scared Beloved. He senses me better than the other New People. While sitting in the branches, waiting for him to go to sleep, he knew I was there. I had made a gift for his nest like I had planned. Flying up and down the mountains, I spent the day finding tiny lighted fungi and perfect, soft mosses.

It took until the setting sun to find the right collections for his cave. The New People—well, all humans—do not see well in the dark and his room had no lights. Those sealed, dusty windows. The broken bulb in an overhanging fixture. I would fix that for Beloved.

I put the pretty trinkets in one of my many jars and wrapped them in some old papers that I had had discarded around my nest. It was going to be exquisite, except he *found* me.

I did not understand what he was saying to me. He had made the strangest of noises; I initially had thought him injured. Except no, Beloved had thought I was a clawed cave animal, the ones with long tails and equally long spite. The *humans* call them cats.

I am not a *fucking cat*. Those creatures are vile and taste like dried porcupines. The last time I came across one of them it had bitten me while I was trying to *give it pets*. My claws were retracted; I had had no intentions of using the beast as a meal. They are not edible looking. I did, however, eat that one.

I did not understand why Beloved would want to get one of those feral puffs out of a tree, but he tried last night. He is good. Beloved had heard my wings and darted to his house, slamming the door tight.

My heart ached. I did not mean to cause fear, but I could smell it coming from him where I perched. After a while, I swooped onto the back of the house to lay my present down. I landed a little harder than I had meant to, with my upper wing catching against the side of the house. The sound and shock reverberated through me. It stung enough that I shuddered as I took flight, going back to my resting place.

Beloved peered out of an upstairs window, eventually coming down to see what I had left. He gingerly walked outside, checking for threats before lifting the treasures from the ground. Greedily, he opened the jar, seeming genuinely pleased with the contents. He used his... hand box—the *phone camera,* the humans call it—and stole the jar's image. He must have been so excited that he posted it to his *socials.* I am still unsure of what those are, but they seem important to the young humans. After he went back inside, I waited. I waited until the moon had shifted toward the stars before seeing what he had done with my offering.

Something about my essence, the gift from the Well, allows me to get into any door I come across. Humans have desired essence, what they sometimes call *magic,* for eons. But that is the wish for *control* over others and our world, not balance. I do not abuse or overuse this power, although it comes in handy when one needs a new blanket.

I needed to see if Beloved was safe. After the noise and panic I caused, I wanted to ensure he slept well. I quietly moved toward the main area where his nest laid precariously on a floppy pad balanced on top of a lopsided metal frame. The Pooka was sitting in the corner, chewing on a can and watching Beloved sleep. The spiders I caught for Beloved's jar were given to the little goblin. They were a youngling and clearly underfed.

Lazily, they blinked up at me with their giant black eyes and quietly chirped. Pooka gestured to the can, an offer of a small snack.

Bowing my head with a hand over my heart, I extended the other with the palm facing down. It was one way to politely signal that I gave thanks but was also declining the kind proffering of their food. I would need to bring the youngling more spiders and maybe a chipmunk or two.

Beloved was sprawled across his blankets and pillows, deep in slumber. The jar gave off a soft glow. The light reminded me of the gold flecks that shone in Beloved's eyes. I wished I could tell him, but it was not time yet. Beloved was not ready for me. I had waited centuries for him, so I would wait a little longer. I had left the Pooka and Beloved in their home for the remainder of civil twilight.

I sighed to myself as I watched him through the front window. Instead of tending to the needs of the territory, I was slinking around in a garbage-filled alley that smelled like stomach contents and piss. I was unsure whose piss. Some of it smelled like it belonged to other Winged Folk. Most of it was the remnants of the young people who walked these streets.

I looked around again. Indrid had sworn to me that he was leaving the new people alone, but I trusted that bastard as much as I trusted a ravenous snake not to strike its prey. That's what *humans* were to Indrid—toys and prey. I felt my lip rise in a sneer. He had been too quiet recently, that never bode well for the new and the young people.

I glanced around some more. There were no signs of his *bullshit*, but that did not ease my concerns. When I return to my nest, I will seek him out. See what penance he has done this year.

A group of young humans on bicycles passed by discussing an upcoming *bar crawl*. They have bicycles, why crawl between drinking establishments? Crawl must mean another word, again. As much as I enjoy the young New People, it has been decades since I have walked this part of the territory.

I have been attempting to make an example for Indrid to follow. I actively avoided the New People, the *humans*, to show him that it was beneficial to not play with them. We did not need to scare them out of what we needed. We could simply slip in and out of their homes. It was rare we needed anything but a few blankets or new clothes when ours were threadbare.

Indrid, however, is a vain brute. He does not live in a simple nest; it is an abandoned cabin from when the New People first appeared in our mountains. In my futile attempts to show Indrid respectful distancing, I am now often confused by the young New... humans.

I rested my head on the cold brick. Beloved was in the beverage place across the street. He was jabbing his fingers angrily into his silver book. It was curious that the humans read books sideways now. Some of them read from small flat squares that were not phone cameras. Telephones were bizarre. They fit in pockets and were no longer attached to wires and cables. Humans kept moving forward in this world while I stayed here, being the Keeper.

Through the window, Beloved chugged that shit-colored drink that humans love. It makes them stay up later than the moon. There were plants in the valleys that did that for me. It also caused my skin to prickle. After a few days, the shadows inevitably started talking to me. Those shades were bound to prattle on and on, never shutting the fuck up until I found blissful sleep. Indrid had chewed so much it no longer had any spiritual value to it. He was such a wasteful bastard.

Beloved shifted in his seat as he stared at his glowing, silver book. So many of these humans had those books with apples on them. They are so fascinating, maybe Beloved would show me why this book is so popular. I have seen the older humans in the stiff jackets carrying them around, too. His face shifted to a scowl before he rubbed both hands down it, apparently trying to scrub away the foul mood. After a pause, he started to pack his things to leave.

I had taken to following him around the territory—no, the *campus*—on the days he strolled down here. Sometimes he stayed in the meeting places, but more often than not he was in the older buildings filled with *long* lectures and *too many* notes. That is what the young humans murmured as they walked across the *green*. I liked that name, except it was not very green during the winter months.

Beloved left the *café*, trudging up the hill to where he would turn left to go back to his nest for the day. He had too many meetings with humans younger than himself. I did not think he enjoyed that part of his day as much as he did when he talked about songs. I might have snuck into one of their great halls to listen to him talk through old songs, some I remember from moons of seasons past.

I stayed ten steps behind him as he briskly walked up the hill. Just as he was turning, someone called out loudly behind me. Along with an ability to not be seen, a secondary gift is to not be hit or run into. A body rushed past me, slowing to walk side-by-side with Beloved. He slowed down to take in the new human's face. This one did not seem as young as the others, closer to Beloved's age maybe. They carried a stack of books with a plastic bag hanging from one arm. The bag bulged with sharp corners of what appeared to have scholarly tomes poking out.

"Hey, Ezra!" They smiled at Beloved.

"Oh, hey Alex. Sorry, were you calling earlier? I just..." Beloved, no, *Ezra*, trailed off.

"Yeah, it's okay." Alex smiled at Ezra, and my skin shivered. I did not give in to the urge to growl or flare my wings. My claws pricked the insides of my hands as I made fists. "You seemed kinda out of it earlier. You okay?"

Ezra looked away, rubbing the back of his neck. "Yeah, it was a shitty Wednesday that bled into a hungover, weird Thursday."

"I wondered why you canceled office hours." Alex smiled again. "No judgment. We've all been there. Do you want to talk about it?"

"No," Ezra said quickly, then frowned. "I'm sorry. It's not that... I've talked about it before, like with a therapist. It's an old hurt." Ezra swallowed; I could see his throat move. "Uh, yesterday was the anniversary of my dad's death. You know, the great poet laureate?"

Alex was nodding, they shifted their body in a way that was probably meant to be comforting. It was not comforting to me. I wanted to toss this Alex into oncoming traffic. Alex set their plastic bag on the ground and continued to nod.

"And Wednesday's your weekly session with the word fascist... fuck, that had to be terrible. I'm so sorry, Ez." Alex leaned in, and, to my surprise, Ezra accepted the hug. Who was this human and where should I take their body?

"Thanks, Alex, you're a good friend." Ezra mumbled into Alex's shoulder. Beloved was crying. My Beloved was hurt and crying. I felt myself reach out but stopped short of allowing my claw to gently glide through a few strands of his hair.

"Dude, I wish I would've known sooner. I could've come over and at least spot checked your drinking. You look like you survived, though?" Alex looked Ezra over as he pulled away.

"Barely. At some point, I think I blacked out and fell on my face." Ezra chuckled. "Somehow, I managed to put myself to bed with minimal damage. There were glass shards from the moonshine bottle in my trash."

"Oh shit, you were drinking Mitch's paint thinner?" Alex squawked loudly.

Ezra blushed and chuckled. "We all fall for the trap at least once a degree, right?"

"Once? Oh, fuck. I must be ahead a few doctorates." Alex shifted and paused before reaching out to Ezra again, gently laying their hand on his arm. "Hey, let me know if you need anything. Okay? I don't want you to feel anymore alone than you have to."

Ezra nodded. "Yeah. Addi said the same thing. I needed some alone time, just sit with it, absolutely smashed out of my mind."

"Not just that, the whole..." Alex gestured vaguely around them, "Allen thing, too. Sometimes it's a good thing to parallel write. Or parallel drink. I can always be your man if you need a co-drinker." Alex smirked, looking up through his eyelashes at Ezra. That mother-fucker was flirting with Beloved.

Ezra smiled gently. "Thanks, Alex. Sorry to be abrupt, but I need to get home."

"Oh yeah, yeah. No problem. We'll catch up next week? Or if you're not busy, this weekend? We could go get a burrito and ponder our existence over our portfolios." Alex smelled like desperation. They were trying to court Ezra, here on the street.

Ezra blanched. "Uh, I think Addi planned on driving up to the city and asked me to come. They're getting a piercing somewhere that's going to cause them to not be able to sit straight. I didn't ask for details. Addi is... wild."

Alex laughed. "Then maybe next week?" They smelled sad. Good, go away. Beloved, *Ezra*, was mine.

Ezra said, "Let's catch up next week and see if the stars align in our favor."

The two broke apart with Ezra turning up the street to his home. I kept up with his pace, making sure I was two or three feet to his right. I knew he could sense me, and I did not want to cause him anymore distress. Beloved's parent was dead, the grief was not over the songs alone. I wonder if the songs were meant for the one who had passed through the veil. I internally sighed, grateful I had the foresight to pick up the scattered thoughts and put them back in place.

As we neared the cemetery, Ezra slowed. A stone angel sat at the front, behind the double doors of the gate. The keeper of the dead. He walked closer, peering beyond the wrought iron to the rows of graves. The dead had been collecting here for as long as this had been my home and territory.

There were some smaller varieties of folk and other peoples in the woods along the back. Most were harmless to the humans while others made it their life's mission to be obnoxious by inconveniencing their human neighbors. A pair of sprites enjoyed draining batteries. A tree trat ate any garden and bulb she found.

Ezra let out a long breath. The tension in his shoulders relaxed. He seemed so far away from this place, this moment in time. I edged closer, pulling my wings back as I leaned in. His scent was like fresh rain, *petrichor* is what I heard a human once call it. A mix of fresh rain and something like sunshine, lemons. It was lemons. I used to eat them before Indrid went on his terror spree and told the locals we were *little green men*. Fucking Indrid. I felt myself tense and focused on Beloved, my sad Ezra.

He was leaning against the top of the rails, arms hanging over to the other side. He leaned over a little, head bowed as if in prayer. I moved closer inch-by-inch until I was almost flush against his back. My arms wanted to wind around him, pulling him into my chest. I wanted to keep him warm. I wanted to ease his pain.

He abruptly stood, pushing against me, making solid contact with the front of my body. I could feel his back to my chest, his plump ass pushing into my groin. Every finger twitched and every thought I had screamed to not move. His scent was drowning me. I could not breathe anything but him. Beloved. He did not move away; he stayed pressed against me while his breathing slowed down.

I leaned in, drinking up his scent. I could feel myself becoming aroused at the proximity. Blood flooding to parts of me that had been silent for many years, waking up to the electric pulses coming from our contact. I opened my mouth, felt my tongue flick across my lips. I wanted to taste Beloved. He shifted and I pulled away quickly.

He looked over his shoulders, cheeks flushed in the late afternoon sun. He was still holding a bag in one hand, the knuckles turning white from gripping too tightly. He looked behind him again, through me, before quickly adjusting his pants. I smirked; he could feel me, too. I ached for him. Was he aching for me?

I followed him the rest of the way to his cave, ensuring he was safely tucked away before returning to my own. I flew harder than I had in decades, raw energy coursing through me. I made it a couple of steps into my cave before I quickly unlaced the front of my breeches. My top cock was straining, a string of precum attached to the fabric. With my right hand I encircled the base, giving myself one long stroke from root to the tip. I let out a low, guttural moan.

I took in a deep, calming breath, releasing my dick to walk to the sleeping corner of my nest. Slowly, I lowered myself onto the pillows and blankets I had collected over the years. Lifting my hips, I pushed the breeches down further until all of me was free of the fabric constraint. My right hand returned to my smaller cock, stroking again from base to head with the perfect amount of pressure. I ran my finger under the tip where the groove gave way to a slight tapper.

My left hand found my second, larger member, mimicking the motions. The two together looked more like rowing than jerking, and it felt wonderful. I kept smelling Beloved on me, his aroma had transferred to the fur on my chest. The scent would stay trapped until I got stuck in the rains again.

I stroked harder and faster, moaning as I imagined Beloved on his knees taking me in his mouth, in his firm ass. My hips involuntarily moved with the fantasy as I fucked both of my fists. I groaned out his name, *Ezra,* coming fast and hard, covering my hands, lap, and chest with a large amount of spend.

I sighed and laid down. I would clean myself later. Right now, I just wanted to feel the ecstasy of the sweet release. A simple touch with his scent drove me to near feral lust. What would happen when Beloved saw me, held my hand, or said my name? I would die from it. I would kill for it.

CHAPTER 4

The Professor's Treehouse

EZRA

D r. Richard Henderson lived on the outskirts of the city down a winding gravel path that led into the woods. He'd always made a point to invite promising undergraduates to his house at the end of the semester to celebrate a class well done. Every teaching assistant and grad student referred to his home as the "treehouse" because it was built with stilts on the side of a rocky hill. The wraparound deck had an amazing view of the tree-lined valley with a lazy creek trickling by on the property.

Rich's area of expertise was in Medieval Literature; however, he'd been an incredible mentor through my master's program. He was an old friend of my father's. They'd "roomed" together while in their doctorate program. While he never said it out loud, I always figured they'd been lovers. If they hadn't been, it was clear Rich had loved my father. They'd stayed friends and in contact over the years. He stood next to me at my father's funeral, and he was the second person I called when I got the acceptance letter for this program. The first, my dying dad.

I knocked on the door and waited for the eventual, "Come in, young scholar." It didn't matter that I was pushing 30. Rich was in his late-60s, and he'd told me at a certain age he'd decided everyone would always be young to him. That was a gift as much as it was a curse. There's probably some sense in that statement.

I stepped inside, the smell of garlic hitting me first. He was making spaghetti with homemade sauce. I walked into the kitchen to give my offer of help even though I knew he'd wave his hand and tell me to go sit down.

As I reached the kitchen, he was already standing in the doorway with a somewhat lost look on his face. He quickly put on a happy mask, but the sadness lingered in his eyes. The lines were deeper around his mouth. He looked tired. Last Wednesday had to have been hard for him, too. I didn't call or text. I left him on his own, which made me feel like shit. Rich had stepped into a paternal role when I had needed him, and I fucked off on a hard day. It felt like the wind had been knocked out of me as my eyes began to water.

"Rich... I, I'm sorry," I choked out. He quickly came to me, wrapping supportive arms around my shuddering frame.

"Shhh, kiddo. It's okay." He kissed the top of my head. "Don't be sorry. The way I miss him isn't the same for you."

As he held me, I sobbed into his shoulder, clinging on. I don't remember crying this hard since the phone call when I found out Dad was gone. I'd been stuck in a layover in the Denver airport. I hadn't made it home in time. If I would've asked Rich for the money sooner, I could've, but I was too young and too proud. The thought made me gasp for air; my whole body was trembling. Rich stroked my back and gently rocked our bodies together.

"Breathe, kiddo," he muttered in my ear. "Breathe with me, nice and slow."

I hadn't realized how hard I was struggling, gasping for air that I couldn't get enough of. I was hyperventilating. I was getting light-headed; rings of black grew around my watery vision. I swayed a little. Rich lowered us to the hardwood floor, pulling me into his lap. He continued to rock me like a child, trying to get my breathing to slow.

Eventually, the tears slowed, and I hiccupped against his chest. My face plastered to his neck with an embarrassingly large amount of tears sticking our skin together. I didn't want to move, I felt safe. I felt loved. I wish Dad was here with us. I wish I wasn't such a worthless piece of shit when it came to dealing with hard things. I wish I was a better writer, a better poet, and mostly, a better son.

"Whatever spiral you're in, stop." Rich spoke quietly as he stroked a hand through my hair. "I can hear you hating yourself; your father did the same thing."

"He had panic attacks at your house and sobbed on your floor?" I whispered, hoping he'd ignore the whine in my voice.

"On many occasions, yes; you inherited his anxiety." Rich sounded somewhat amused.

"You loved him," I blurted out before stopping myself.

"I loved him endlessly." I could feel Rich's smile against my forehead.

I pulled away, lifting my head to peer into his eyes. "Were... were you two together?"

Rich's lips quirked. "For seven years. We fought constantly about whose turn it was to make dinner. He was my greatest love. We knew once our programs were over, we had few options. I took a job in the northeast, and he stayed back here. Eventually married your mother. Had you and Chelsea."

"I..." I blinked up at him. I didn't know what to say. "Do you think he loved my mother?"

"Are you asking if he was strictly a homosexual like me, living a lie to survive?" Rich asked, no heat in his voice.

"I don't mean..." I sat up, my thoughts were jumbled. "I'm sorry. I'm sorry."

"Hey," he wrapped an arm around me, pulling him back to his chest, "your father never expressed any type of gender-based preferences to me. He fell in love with intelligent people. Your mother was both exceptionally gifted as an academic as well as gorgeous. Even I, as gay man, could appreciate her beauty. You look a lot like her."

I leaned into the hug I had needed for days. "He loved her," I said, more as a statement than a question.

"He loved her. I'll have to show you the letters he wrote about her." He paused. "Well, I'll show the less descriptive letters he wrote about her." Rich chuckled. "Your father had a knack for imagery."

"Jesus." I was giggling. "Was it about her breasts? After he died, we found a box of erotic poetry he wrote to her. Most of it was about how lovely her form was."

"I'm sorry you had to find that." He started to giggle with me. "There are some things about our parents we should never know."

"It made them more human, though. It made them..." I trailed off again. "Real."

"I suppose it would, regardless of how startling it may have been." He smiled again, kissing me on the top of my head. "Alright kiddo, my legs are going numb, and I need to finish up dinner."

I startled. "Sorry." I tried to get up abruptly, my shaky legs making it difficult.

Rich covered my mouth with two fingers. "No. Do not be sorry for this. Do not ever be sorry for this. For as long as I live, I want you to come to me. I want to be the one you wipe your tears and snot on. I want to have numb thighs and a sore ass from holding you while you grieve."

I felt my eyes sting a little as I nodded. "I'm going to go to the washroom."

"Okay, kid. Meet me in the kitchen." He lifted himself from the floor more gracefully than I had.

In the bathroom, I took inventory of how terrible I looked. My face was splotchy and puffy from crying. An addition to the dark circles and pallid skin from not taking care of myself for days, more like weeks. I needed to drink water and eat real food. I needed to go lay out on the green and get some sun. Rich was going to worry over me for the rest of the night. I wonder if he'd mind if I slept here. I didn't have the energy, emotionally, to go back to my off-campus house in town. I didn't want to be alone tonight.

When I walked into the kitchen, Rich was setting out bowls filled with steaming food. He had put out water instead of wine tonight. Goddamn him for reading my face so well. If I didn't take better care of myself, I'd continue to be a burden to this sweet man. He looked up and gestured for me to sit down as he headed back to grab the bread out of the oven. The house had a calm to it, one that I rarely felt anywhere else.

"Allen being an absolute fuck as usual?" he asked nonchalantly as he sat down.

"Isn't he your colleague?" I tried not to snicker.

"If he died tomorrow, no one would shed a tear or probably even attend his funeral. That fool has spent his career and most of his tenure alienating himself from everyone in the department." He frowned.

"So, it's not just me." I sounded far more timid than usual.

"What? Absolutely not. When I found out the Dean decided Allen was to be your primary on this," he growled, "we had a long discussion about poor decision-making skills."

I snorted. "What?"

"Allen hated your father," Rich sighed. "I shouldn't be saying this. The two of them had a long-standing feud. Your father was a better human and a better writer. Allen constantly got second or third place to your father. When I asked Everhart why he put you with Allen, he told me Allen had requested to be your chair."

"What the fuck?" I dropped my fork. "Why? He's been nothing but a night terror. He hates me. He loathes everything I do..." I gasped. "Rich, he wants me to fail at this."

"I've suspected as much." He leaned in. "You need to go to Dean Everhart and request a change immediately."

I cringed. "That's not a request taken lightly in our department."

"In this case, no one will blame you." He swallowed. "There are several professors who would gladly take you on. You're an incredible writer, Ez. Allen wants to crush you because it probably makes him feel like he's crushing John's legacy."

"I'm Dad's legacy?" I didn't realize I was holding my breath until Rich answered.

"You were John's everything, Ezra. He loved both of you so much. Your work is not remotely the same and he celebrated that. He wanted you to have your own voice, your own place in the literary world." Rich's voice was soothing as he reached out to clasp my hand. "Now eat up, you look like shit."

I choked on a laugh. "Yeah, well. I live in a basement with a diet primarily consisting of caffeine and breakfast bars."

"Jesus, Ez." Rich scowled as he took a bite of spaghetti.

"Is it alright if I sleep here tonight? I can..." Rich cut me off.

"Please do. It gets lonely up here. I'd like the company." He went back to eating as if that permission wasn't the lifeline I needed.

"Thanks," I mumbled into my garlic bread.

Rich nodded, continuing to eat. While he'd been attending to my emotional breakdown, I had ignored his grief completely. I guess I really was a kid sometimes. I was lucky to have someone who cared. I watched him a few more seconds before digging in with enthusiasm I hadn't had for food in weeks. Rich chuckled at me.

Later that night, he dimmed the lights as we sat in his living room that was wrapped in warm accent colors that so thoroughly complimented the rich, deep wood that made up the floors and walls. Everything about the treehouse was cabin like. Rich said the home was almost 100 years old by the time he remodeled it in the 1990s. The dark, worn leather sofas and a low, distressed wood coffee table added to the peace. He had started a fire since the nights got cooler, especially in the trees.

"How are you doing?" I asked.

He took in a deep breath. "I had a similar lapse in tranquility a few days ago. Today, though? I'm better; I read "Blue Bird." That one was always my favorite poem of his."

"I got black out drunk on moonshine, fell on my face, and still ended up in bed." I watched the flames lick the edges of the logs. "It was a very productive day. Allen also called me both a failure at my craft and an utter disappointment to my father's memory."

Rich stiffened. "Ezra, what were his exact words?" I could hear the anger simmering in his tone.

Closing my eyes, I repeated Allen's visceral, "'Mr. Williams, you have failed yet again at the basic construct of a poem.' Before I left, he told me something along the lines of, 'You're ruining the legacy of your father's work with this disappointment you call a portfolio.' I stopped listening after he said that. I've become proficient at dissociating after 30 or so minutes with him."

Rich and I sat there in silence for a few minutes before he leaned forward, looking me in the eye. "Why didn't you call me the minute you stepped out of his office?"

I shrugged, feeling small. "I don't want to be a bother. I don't want special attention."

"You're a doctoral student, Ezra. All of you get special attention when it comes to the department. You're the next generation of scholars, our future peers. We want you to succeed. That's hardly special attention; it's what you are paying for. It is why we're here," he huffed.

"Because you would've shown up at his office and beat the shit out of him," I said quickly.

"You're right. I would've," he snickered. "I have tenure. The worst that would happen is I'd have to take some unpaid leave but that's doubtful since we're understaffed. I'd more than likely have to get an evaluation and some counseling for *anger*."

Looking away, I muttered, "He intimidates me."

"I know. He feeds from that. He loves teaching undergrads because they give him unadulterated power." Rich's tone lowered. "I think he enjoys staring at young female students who are too afraid to report him."

"I've heard the rumors," I said quietly.

"We've all heard the rumors, but the university won't do anything unless it's formally reported. Either everyone's too frightened of him or he's smart enough to not get caught doing anything." Rich shook his head. "I'm having a meeting with Everhart on Monday."

"Rich, don't," I plead.

"No, Ezra. He's hurting you. I've had two reports last week from other students of his misconduct. It's not just you, kid. You, however, might have the most against him right now. The comments he's written on your drafts are borderline scandalous."

"Yeah, I..." sighing, I nodded. He was correct. If I'd enough to take him out, I wasn't only protecting myself. I had another tenured professor defending me, and apparently a whole department ready to support me. My silence emboldened Allen to continue to harm others. What was he going to do to someone who had less people on their side? "Okay," I conceded.

Rich nodded. "I'm sorry, Ez. This isn't your mess to clean up. It shouldn't be on the shoulders of any of our students. He finally made his mistake with you. I will support you, so will Emily and Sandra."

"Really?" Sounding surprised to my own ears.

"Oh yes, they bragged about having you every time you landed in one of their classes. Emily still preens that she had you as a teaching assistant last year."

I chuckled. "That's because she didn't have to grade the freshman comp papers."

"Our teaching assistants provide an invaluable service of not subjecting us to non-majors' ramblings about not liking English classed." Rich settled back into his seat.

We talked for hours, weaving in and out of old stories about Dad to musings of the last semester. We agreed that summer sessions were a breath of fresh air to the scholarly soul and looked forward to the bug-filled, muggy nights ahead. He put another log on the fire before pulling out blankets. He had a spare bedroom, but I always preferred sleeping out here, under the sky lights by the fireplace.

"Am I that predictable?" My lips quirked up a little.

He genuinely smiled. "You're that much of a romantic, I fear. Goodnight, sweet boy," Rich's voice filled with fondness as he leaned down, kissing me on the head for the dozenth time that night.

"Goodnight, Rich. Thank you." The weight of the weeks, the semester, and my crying session suddenly hit me like a tidal wave.

He nodded and left the room as I sunk into the soft leather of the couch. The flames danced and crackled as my eyelids got heavier. Above my head, there was a scratching sound on the roof. Probably a branch, but when I listened, I didn't hear any wind. Rolling over to look up, a shadow crossed the sky light. How's there a shadow? Unless it wasn't a shadow but an outline of something?

Sitting up, I couldn't look away for fear *it* would break through the thick pane, landing on top of me. Whatever it was shifted to the side. It was large, too large to be an animal. Something else twisted and shuddered on the shadowy being. It looked like a wing. A wing of a very large bird on the roof.

Motionless, I stared, too afraid to blink. My hand grasped for my phone; if I could record this, maybe Rich would know what it was in the morning.

The bird moved closer to the edge of the skylight frame, like it was peering down at me. Feeling my fingers wrap around the phone and pulling it closer, I double tapped the side to pull up camera mode. Carefully, I brought the phone to eye level, switching it to video as the creature slammed something against the roof and lifted off. The noise was terrifying, like a sledgehammer hitting the ceiling.

Rich moving quickly in his room, racing out to me. I sat there immobile, still holding my phone above my face. I could see Rich in my peripheral, staring at me in shock before following my line of sight to the glass.

"Ezra, what happened?" His tone was hushed.

"Can I sleep in your room..." My hands were shaking. "That's where the shotgun is, right?"

"Kiddo, what'd you see?" His voice sounded worried.

Shaking my head, voice quivering. "I don't... I don't know. It was big. It was watching me sleep, Rich."

The rest of the night was spent tucked into Rich's bed. He made sure the shotgun was loaded and next to his nightstand before pulling the blankets up over my shoulders. It was like being a small child, afraid of the nightmare creatures under the bed.

Rich didn't sleep that night. He didn't say why, but the look in his eyes told me he'd seen it, too. He knew he wasn't alone in the woods, and we definitely hadn't been alone tonight.

CHAPTER 5

Roads Made of Bricks

EZRA

The rain came down as more of a gentle fog than actual drops. Everything on the green glittered under the early morning light that was obscured by the cloud filled sky. Walking up the most cumbersome hill on campus, completely brick and blocked off to traffic, was a feat of skill.

The road had been closed due to several cars being totaled by the precarious nature of shifting brick streets. For people on foot, it was mostly a 'roll your ankle' problem if you tripped on an errant brick or fell into a hole where a brick used to be. The sidewalks were a terror, in their own state of disrepair.

I'd avoided confronting Allen about his behavior in the past, and certainly had no fucking desire to report it to Dr. Everhart. I didn't know if I was being spineless or simply spiteful. What Rich had told me last night, before the shadow demon appeared on the roof, got under my skin. Allen was jealous of a graduate student because his dad knew how to write and won a few awards.

Jesus Christ, how pathetic do you have to be to try to wreck a student's career because of an old feud with his daddy?

I supposed there were plenty of historical and literary references to that same level of trivial nonsense; it had a Globe Theatre vibe to it.

Maybe if it got dark enough with murder it would be more like Poe. I liked murder in my stories, it was easier than a lot of other traumas. Something in my brain had snapped. As much as I wanted to prove Allen wrong, I also wanted to destroy him completely. That's not the man I wanted to be or become, but goddamnit, it's the man Allen was turning me into. I knew I'd enough to get switched to a new chair, but I didn't have enough to end his reign of terror among the undergrads.

I was halfway up the hill heading toward the English building. It was one of the oldest structures on campus and the largest classroom building left. A truly impressive two-story brick hall built in the early 1900s. I loved being there, even when the roof leaked, and the basement started to smell like moldy socks. There was something peaceful about the rooms that looked out on the crooked streets. My favorite seasons here were summer and autumn. The colors were magnificent against the aging brick façade.

Not many students or staff were wandering around in the misty rain. I didn't blame them; it added a chill that I didn't need. Even with an umbrella and windbreaker coupled with a long-sleeved shirt underneath, I was shivering. This was the part of the spring to summer change that I could do without. I'd miss the chill when the buzzing of cicadas and humidity stuck to my skin, but for now, I was over the rainy Appalachian weather.

Climbing up the crumbling retaining wall, I made it to the cracked sidewalk. It's quicker to go between some of the smaller buildings to get to the front of the English Hall.

Approaching, I saw someone smoking by the doors. Not uncommon since no one had been allowed to smoke indoors for a couple of decades. It's a teaching assistant avoidance technique in not dealing with undergrads hunting for extra credit during our 15-minute breaks. I was known to smoke a clove or two when things were rough.

The person was slouched over, shoulders hunched up to their ears with their hood pulled up to protect them from the falling drizzle. I could see them furiously suck in as much smoke and fire as possible. Their left foot tapping as their whole body seemed to be keyed up for something, a fight maybe.

As I got closer to the doors, I shifted my umbrella to my other shoulder to not disturb the person on their clearly needed break. Over my water-laden footfalls, I could hear gentle sobs. I took a closer look to see that the person was more huddled in on them self than simply bent over to avoid the rain. I continued to walk. I was wet and cold. It's none of my business. I didn't make it to the second door before turning around to walk back outside.

Lifting my umbrella up high enough to shelter us both from the rain. I approached. The drizzle was coming lazily from every angle. How does rain float up? The person continued to shiver and smoke, rubbing the back of their damp hoodie sleeve over their face.

"Hey," I said gently, trying to avoid startling them.

Slowly they looked up, eyes rimmed with red and blinked. "Uh." Clearing their throat, they looked away.

"You okay?" Not wanting to push too hard. I didn't want this person to feel completely adrift and abandoned. I'd been there this week.

Shaking their head, they mumbled, "Bad day."

"You need to talk about it?" I was at a loss for words.

They shrugged. "It's not good. I probably should keep my fucking mouth shut."

"What's your name? I'm Ezra, by the way." Hoping they felt the warmth my tone was trying to convey.

"Ezra Williams?" The student looked up, surprised.

"Uh, yeah. Shit, am I your T.A., uh teaching assistant?" Suddenly feeling foolish, I shifted back.

"No, we had a writing course together last year." They smirked. "I didn't show up to half of the classes. I'm Nick." Nick rubbed the cigarette butt against the wet brick, tossing it in the garbage by the door.

"Want to go to my classroom for a bit? You don't have to talk but a warmer, drier change of scenery might be more comfortable." Pulling my umbrella away from both of us to close it, I reached for the door.

We walked into the building in silence. There were probably a few professors in their offices and random classrooms at this time of day, but there weren't any classes being held. Nick followed me down the stairs to the lower level where I'd been continuously working on a project for Rich. I was helping him and two of his prized T.As organize this anthology they'd been agonizing over. It looked good on my CV and was honestly more interesting than grading end of semester comp course papers. Grades were due by next week but fuck it, I was living chaos in the moment. I unlocked the door, being the first one in, and flicked the lights as I wandered to an empty desk.

"Have a seat anywhere. We'll be the only ones here for another hour or two." I gestured to the open space as Nick found a seat closer to the door, dropping their bag.

The student surveyed our surroundings. "What're you working on?"

"I'm assisting in piecing together an anthology for Dr. Henderson. He's helped me out enough times that I should probably pay it back in free labor. Some of it's interesting, not my area, though. You can take a look if you want." I turned away from them, going over the piles that'd been laid out for me to catalog.

"Can I ask you something?" Nick whispered.

Turning back around. "Sure."

"Wh... what kinds of things has Dr. Henderson done for you?" Nick seemed shy asking, a slight blush creeping up their cheeks.

"Oh, a lot actually. He... he and my father were old friends from grad school. He helped me with my writing style, wrote me a recommendation letter, and... have you heard of his treehouse?" Feeling my eyes crinkle at the cheerful memories.

Nick shook their head. "He has a treehouse?"

"Not a kid's treehouse. He has property up in the hills and has this old, remodeled cabin that's built partially into the hill with stilts. He likes having grad students up there to feed and banter with." Feeling lighter as I talked about it. "He's known for his 'theory parties.'"

Nick paled, eyes darting around the room. "I should go."

"Hey, what's wrong?" They looked genuinely frightened.

"Sorry, I'm bothering you."

"No, kid, you're not, but you look scared. Can I help you?" Crossing my arms, I attempted to look relaxed and calmer than I felt.

"You can't, I'm just... I'm overreacting." They gathered their things to leave.

"Doubtful; you don't feel safe. This is a normal reaction to that." I leaned back against an empty desk.

Nick shifted. "I'm not into guys." They paused. "Sorry, I'm not a homophobe. Fuck, a homophobe would say that. I'm a straight man. I should've led with that." Nick blew out a long breath he had been holding.

"Understood." I didn't like where this was leading us.

"Dr. Allen, he's weird." Nick looked at me like I could fill in the blanks.

"Weird how?" My stomach dropped. What the fuck had Allen been doing to undergrads?

"You have to see him every week, don't you?" Nick huffed, crossing his arms over his chest.

"Yes, and the adjective I'd use to describe him is *asshole*, not weird. What's he doing with you?" I softened my voice on the question. "And how'd you know I meet with him?"

"He mentioned you to me today. You're one of *his*." Nick frowned, running a hand through his hair. "And... he does these little things, like the way he looks at me. It's fucking predatory. He'll sit too close, sometimes leans a knee against mine."

I could feel my eyes get bigger. "Has he touched you?"

"Not like grabbing my ass or dick. But he gets too close. If I try to pull away, he gets agitated." Nick started hugging himself.

"Has he said anything..." not knowing how to finish that sentence without sounding livid.

"He told me he needs me to come to his house this weekend to discuss my final project." Nick's voice cracked at the end. "If I don't, I'll fail the course. He knows I'm on a scholarship. I don't have parents to help me out. It's just me."

"I'm so sorry." Taking a step forward, I dropped my hands to my sides.

"Yeah, me too." Nick looked up quickly. "Fuck, please don't tell anyone."

"You can't go there, not if you think he's planning on hurting you." My tone somehow still even.

"I can't lose my scholarship either." His eyes were filled with anguish. I didn't think this was the first time someone had hurt Nick for their own gain.

"Look, I'll figure something out." Pulling out my phone, I continue, "What's your number? I'll text you. I'm not going to let you go alone."

"Aren't you afraid he'll do something to you?" Nick hesitated.

"God, I hope he tries." Nick must've seen the rage in my eyes because he rattled off his digits. I texted him to make sure it worked. We sat there for 45 minutes talking about anything but school and exploitative professors.

He was young and in love with journalism. He wasn't sure what he was going to do after he graduated, probably move back to Columbus and find a job. He was gentle and kind, the type of student Allen liked to feed on.

AFTER SPENDING hours bantering with Rich and his acolytes, I headed to my favorite coffee shop to grade what would be the most abysmal papers of my career. This particular class had made it their mission to destroy any desire to be a teaching academic. Not really, but they'd been an excessively dramatic bunch. The first essay began with, 'While this project is worth ten percent of my final grade, I find I have zero fucks left to give and will use the remainder of my word count to describe in which the ways I hate watching Millennials on TikTok.'

Their arguments were valid and strong, earning them a B. They wouldn't know MLA style if it kicked them in the taint, and sadly, this paper did require students to show an understanding of MLA format. I'd given them a template to use. This student didn't bother to indent a goddamn line. At the end, they stated they were an engineering major, not in need of any qualifying writing skills. I'd taken a break after that one.

With a latte and in my usual spot by the front window, I took a moment to breathe. I enjoyed taking these tiny breaks, watching the world pass by while I wrap myself up in the beauty or pandemonium of words. I'd created many universes in this spot. On my pages, I'd seen the rise and fall of empires, seasons fade into centuries, and had muddled through enough of 'the greats' works to thoroughly understand perspective can be very static. This was my favorite place to write and read. My father had his last coffee with me here. In this seat, by the window.

Leaning back, I soaked in the last few days. Even after the visitor on the roof, that night at Rich's house was undoubtedly the best sleep I've had in ages. Maybe it was the feeling of security I got from being close to Rich. It probably had something to do with being starved for physical touch of any kind. I'd been having weird... sensations lately of ghostly hands breezing through my hair and specters leaning against my back.

Now, it felt like someone was waiting for me again. Glancing out the window to the front; no one was on the street. A dark alley littered with trash was between the taco shop and the bookstore. Closing my eyes, I doubted the dumpster was watching me.

The other day, I'd smelled something when I was at the cemetery. It was a mixture of smoke, pine, and fresh air. It reminded me of campfires from when I was younger and listening to spooky stories at night.

The difference though was Gothic tales rarely gave me throbbing erections. The sudden smell, the feel of something hard and warm pushing against me. For a second, I thought I'd felt the echo of another's arousal being pressed into the cleft of my ass.

I missed having a lover or a boyfriend. Hell, it'd been a while since I texted the fuck boy in the city. I wish I was going to Columbus this weekend; I could use obligation-less sex. I shifted in my chair to adjust the sudden fullness of my dick. I needed to stop thinking about fucking and start thinking about grading. *Ah, there's the boner killer.*

Digging out the laptop from my bag, I pulled up the last paper that needed grading. Thank all that was above and below that the professor had split the final papers in two. We did it alphabetically so no one would get stuck with too many TikTok-centered themes. I'm not sure if the method was of any help to either of us in the end. Halfway through the assignment, the door gusted open as cool air blew in.

My nose filled with the strong scent of pine and notes of smoke. My eyes flutter shut as I took in another deep breath. I became painfully aware that my dick was straining in my tight skinny jeans. These were the pair that accentuated every curve I had. It also made it obvious that I had a poorly timed hard on in the middle of the day at a coffee shop. Thankfully, it was empty except for staff, and they couldn't see much from their angle.

Shifting again, I attempted to subtly adjust what was quickly becoming more engorged. I am not a *small* man, and these jeans did not give any room for what I had. Pulling my computer over my lap, I looked around. The door had opened but no one was there. I looked outside again to see if there were any signs of branches moving from gusts, but the flags and banners along the street hung dead.

The two staff members weren't behind the counter. I knew them both from coming in over the years. They trusted me to sit in the shop alone while they either got high or blew one another in the backroom. I'd heard moaning from the kitchen when they both disappeared the last time I was here. I'd observed dilated pupils and red-rimmed eyes on several other occasions. It appeared they'd taken a break since I was the only one around.

The scent hit me again, this time stronger. My dick pulsed as I let out a soft groan. *What the fuck is wrong with me?* Taking in a slow, deep breath, an attempt to calm my racing heartbeat. Then I felt it, the gentle pressure along my right arm. Like fingertips stroking down to my hand. The pine and smoke scent filled my head, my lids growing heavier. The pressure on my arm increased and moved lower, stopping on the top of my hand.

My laptop had slid over, leaving my right hand resting on my inner thigh. My straining cock was below my palm and the invisible pressure. I squeezed myself gently and groaned. Whatever this was, I didn't want it to stop. Shifting again, I looked around for any witnesses to this haunting hand job. Something leaned into me. I felt a whisper of breath against my neck. A flick of something on my earlobe and I nearly came.

"Fuck... please," I murmured to myself.

My eyes opened wide. What was I doing? I grabbed my stuff and shoved it into my bag, quickly standing up and heading to the bathroom. It was a single toilet room, genderless and accommodating for anyone of any physical need. I didn't shut the door. Waiting, I stood in front of the mirror, hands clutching either side of the sink. Closing my eyes, I counted back from ten. I was losing my grip on reality. The smell returned as did the painful throbbing in my crotch.

After shutting and locking myself in the room I didn't feel or see anything, however; I didn't think I was alone. Whatever sex poltergeist following me was there. Turning the faucet on as high as I could without flooding the sink and floor with water, I unzipped my fly to pull out my cock. It was flushed, dark at the tip, with precum smeared everywhere inside my underwear.

Wrapping my left hand around myself, I frantically stroked and rubbed the head, tugging on my balls. The smell intensified. My dick swelled in my hand seconds before I came harder than I thought possible when one was alone in a public restroom. The torrent of come washed down the drain with the flow of the water. Biting my cheek hard, I cut off the shout about to leave my lips. After panting for a minute, I tucked myself away and washed my hands.

The scent still swirled around me; my cock started filling again. I needed to go home and get some sleep. I was hallucinating horny things because life had been incredibly stressful, grief is weird, and I needed to get laid.

Looking in the mirror again I noticed my appearance was better than it was a few days ago. I looked less tired. I was slightly less stressed. Picking my bag up off the floor, I headed out the door. I'd finish the paper later. It was just one paper. It could wait.

CHAPTER 6
Ghost on the Hill
EZRA

In a rush, I headed back home. Nothing seemed to be following me, but I had no idea what was really going on. Was this the shadow from last night? Was it the cat in the tree? Was it that otherworldly aroma that pushed me to frantic masturbation in a public bathroom? My thoughts whirled as I neared the top of the hill, coming into line of sight with the old cemetery gates.

I'd walked past the same rusted gates and weeping angel every morning and night on the way to and from campus. As a once rowdy undergrad and a perpetual grad student, I'd heard the litany of ghost stories freshman passed around in lecture halls.

I was beginning to wonder if my overworked mind had brought me to this point. A shell of an academic being hunted by some otherworldly creature, one bent on making me horny. Even now, as I stood on the precipice of my mental health and wellness, I didn't blame anyone for where my life was. I'd chosen this major, teaching, and grading shitty projects and papers. And instead of finishing that, I was spilling loads into sinks. *Jesus.*

I tried to rationalize mundane things like the fact that the university continued to make cuts to the department. They'd turned what was capped classrooms of 30, into hybrid courses of 100 students or more. There was a hiring freeze. Wages had stagnated. *Yes, keep thinking about class sizes and money that will make your dick go soft.* I needed to see a therapist again, but how? I couldn't afford private pay and the campus therapists were booked for two years out.

And I was alone. Why couldn't I make time to date? The only boys smiling at me had been freshmen. I *will not* date undergrads, especially those pretty, bright-eyed 18-year-olds. At this *advanced* Millennial age, there would be a chasm of knowledge, life experience, *and* needs in that kind of age gap relationship. Someone younger required more than I could give right now. I was afraid they wouldn't be able to provide anything to me in a relationship. I wasn't interested in another round of on campus fuck boys or after-bar romps in the dorms.

I shuddered thinking about dorm life, relieved that my boner was taking a break. *Jesus Christ.* I never could understand why anyone would agree to live in those communal nightmares of dirty feet and STIs. I'd purposefully avoided living in dorms by being a commuter student. It didn't help that I couldn't afford university accommodations. I barely managed for two years before moving into off-campus house my junior year, the same house I lived in now. *Yes, Ezra, keep thinking about unexciting shit and not about the dull ache in your pants.*

The house was still half a mile from where I was standing. This was the *haunted* graveyard campus kids avoided after dark. Addi was probably asleep. Hopefully asleep and not going to see me, a wicked mess, walk through the door. Closing my eyes, I contemplated continuing my academic career for what seemed like the hundredth time this week.

There'd been so many times I walked back this way, wishing I'd left my portfolio at home, not left with Allen to massacre in red ink. Yes, he always wanted fresh copies printed off so he could add his *corrections*. I should've expected no less with a focus on 20th Century American poetry. Some of the most brutal critiques came from that era, or so Allen told me.

Allen, always the sadist, enjoyed tearing holes into my work so that the tiny pieces left could be called, "uninspired postmodernist romanticism." I shuddered out of anger now, not fear. That was new. Chuckling, I added thoughts of Allen as another thing to make me less horny.

I reminded myself that I'd been published in numerous paid anthologies, those critics had never noted my prose to lack inspiration or depth. Allen was a certifiable asshole on a good day. Rich, after a particularly bad semester, had written a mantra on a Post-It note that I'd taped to the back of an old binder. *"I am intelligent enough to recognize that even cruel men have the ability to expand my writing abilities."* I, however, could've done without feeling like I wanted to puke, rage, and sob after weekly "check-ins." Not anymore, no more cowering to that bastard.

I hadn't been walking as fast as I should've been to get home. It was more of a meandering walk now. The initial spontaneous lust reaction was dissipating the farther I got from the café. Cool spring air coupled with my thinking of all the shit that stressed me out the most helped, too. It was getting darker later in the day, as the months headed toward solstice, but it'd gotten unsurprisingly overcast today.

The air was heavy, threatening spring rain. The same grayish sky matched the bark on the slowly blooming trees, the cracked pavement, and of course, the cemetery that stretched several blocks over rolling hills. I question to this day why I decided to live in the hillier part of town, on a campus that laid at the feet of Appalachian Mountains.

Reaching the top of the hill, I noticed the gates to the cemetery were slightly askew. Normally, a groundskeeper would've closed and locked them up tight by five p.m. This kept the eternally resting safe from ghost hunters that had nothing better to do than chatter at the dead or drink and fuck among the headstones. I'll never comprehend the appeal of having sex with so many... people watching.

Walking toward the gate, I noticed the chain hanging through the bars. Getting closer, I realized the gates weren't unlocked. They'd been forced opened. I lifted the padlock and chain, examining it in the dim light. The links looked as if they'd been pulled hard enough to bend the metal, breaking it where it was soldered. I felt a shudder travel down the base of my spine as I gazed into the darkening grounds. *What the fuck did this and why?*

Backing away, it felt as if something or someone was watching me from beyond the tree line that ran along the back of the property. Not predatory, that wasn't right; more like burning desire. The hunger from the coffee shop. The same energy from the day before. *What is that?*

No one was among the headstones. This graveyard was old enough that people would be visiting ancestors, not to mourn the recently deceased. It was a tourist stop. A nice piece of green space breaking up the noise of the surrounding neighborhoods. It was not a haunted place of horrors during the day, but something was out there beyond the farthest graves. *No, someone is waiting for me.*

Stepping back, I hear music faintly playing from one of the homes down the street. There were people all around. *I'm not alone.*

I kept telling myself that, yet that didn't stop the panic from creeping below my skin. It didn't stop the animal part of my brain from screaming, *RUN!* Dropping the busted lock and chain, I backed away toward the street. My mind continued to race with where I could go. The house was too far to sprint, let alone walk. I was better off jogging to the tattoo shop a block north to see Mitch. Mitch loved a good ghost story, he also openly carried.

"Hello." A voice carried on the wind that wasn't there.

Swinging quickly around, I saw no one on street. The voice had come from behind me.

"I am sorry, I did not mean to startle you." The voice came from behind my right shoulder this time. My heart thrashed against my ribs.

Turning around, I found myself gazing into the deepest rust-brown eyes. I swallowed audibly as I took in the stranger. They were tall, well over my six-foot-two. They wore what appeared to be a full-length hooded cloak that obscured most of their facial features. They stayed shrouded in darkness despite it not being late enough in the evening for anything to cast shadows that long.

I shifted my weight, the feeling of being *prey* overwhelming, but something about those eyes pinned me to that spot. I was trying to breathe and not hyperventilate.

"Hello," a voice whispered. The stranger had not moved since the start of this terrifying conversation. They stood between the gate doors. It occurred to me they must've been responsible for the break in. *How did they manage that?*

"Would you care to join me?" The cloaked figure gestured toward the winding path beyond the arches. The infamous weeping stone angel was in the center of the path, her arm raised to the skies in a plea to a God unseen. Maybe it was a plea to save me from whatever end I was about to meet.

"It's closed." I pointed to the posted sign. *Like that would work, good distraction, Ezra.*

The figure half-shrugged. "It does not seem closed to me." They reached out toward me, arm still covered in dark shadows.

"I, uh, don't think that's a good idea." I couldn't move my feet. I was frozen in place. Yet, a part of me felt captivated. Their eyes and lower face had become more visible within the hood.

"I will protect you from the ghosts." They leaned forward, revealing their face. What I saw was not human, but not a monster either. Those reddish-brown eyes were too large and bright, accentuated by a bluish-gray-tinted complexion. Their nose was narrow and flat. Instead of a distinct bridge, their cheeks slowly rose to a mound that delicately stretched down to their lips.

They had well-defined cheekbones and a strikingly pointed jawline, giving the appearance of a heart-shaped face. They had a wide mouth, with a slight split where a cupid's bow would've been on a human. Their upper lip had little definition from the rest of their face. The lower lip, however, was deliciously plump. I could see it glisten in the reflection of the streetlamp. *Why'd that turn me on?*

"Who are you?" I whispered.

"Who am I? Not *what*?" They paused, head cocked. Their mouth opened into what must've been their version of a wide smile, showing top and bottom rows of perfectly straight, sharp, white teeth. "I am Gray. I have been watching you, dear one. I have been listening to your songs. Please, walk with me." They turned and nodded to the beyond. "They will not listen, nor will they mind."

It slowly registered that Gray was talking about the dead. This creature knew me and wanted me to go on a stroll through the graveyard. I wasn't sure what was more terrifying, the almost seven-foot creature stalking me or the fact that I found the ethereal being attractive. I knew there was no running away from this situation. I could only hope what was about to happen didn't hurt for long.

Gray motioned for me to come closer. As soon as I was within reach, Gray took my hand in theirs. Their palm was warm and soft but with a firm solidness underneath. It didn't feel like skin to my touch, but it wasn't quiet fur either. Gray led us away from the street and lights, simply acting as a guide.

"I can see in the dim and the dark. I will not let you fall, dear one," Gray spoke quietly as we took in the view.

"Why've you been watching me?" My voice wavered.

"Please, dear one, do not fear me." Gray's voice was pained. "I would never let any harm come to such exquisiteness. Your songs. You speak them into the civil twilight. I have never felt such anguish and beauty."

I almost tripped on a dead branch. "Are you talking about my poems?"

"Yes, your songs. They are for me." Gray squeezed my hand to emphasize their possession of my poems, my *songs*.

"You like them?" I was baffled. Why'd this clearly not-human find any value in my work? Did the Fae not write their own ballads? Beings known for beauty and trickery. Some were the monsters of battle while others were healers of light. That's what Gray must be, some sort of ancient, winged folktale from Celtic traditions, looking for a human...

"Why would I not? I am not that old *human* that bothers you. The one whose tongue smells of rot." Gray made a sound like a tsking growl.

"Are you talking about Allen? He's a professor... his job is to tear me apart. Well, that's not true." I found myself chuckling at Gray. "That's not rot, the smell is stale coffee. Don't worry, he'll get what's coming to him."

"What is coming to him?" Gray made a humming sound. "I do not like his tongue. Your songs are perfection. One of so much rot does not deserve to feel."

"He's an asshole." I gasped as Gray pulled me toward them. We were standing at the back of the lot near the trees, hidden by mausoleums.

Leaning in, Gray purred, "May I show you something, dear one?"

Clearly Gray was tired of talking about Allen. I lifted my face to Gray's; those hypnotic eyes drew me in. "Yes, Gray. What do you want to show me?"

Gray pulled away, shrugging off their cloak. I didn't dare gasp as I drank the sight of them in. I didn't want Gray to think I was repulsed by what I saw. They were probably closer to six-foot-nine, not including the two protruding horns, one at each temple. Each one was thin and spiraled, curving back at least a foot long.

Gray's hair was a silver-tinted white that glowed in the dying light. Pointed tips of ears peeked out of the cascade of soft-looking, long hair that flowed over their chest and back. Gray's neck was slightly longer than a human's, curving down into broad shoulders.

The rest of the skin had the same bluish-gray tint as their face, blemish-free and taut over a muscular form. Tufts of the same silver-white hair appeared down their chest, trailing to their stomach dipping below the waistband of their pants. Gray's arms were longer than mine. Hands that looked humanoid, except Gray had extra joints with fingertips ending in claws. Gray's clothing was odd, their pants were made of animal hide, as if they belonged to another era.

Gray moved slightly, behind each shoulder two wings appeared, covered in a fuzz-like substance. Gray flexed their wings, making it apparent that there were claw-like appendages on the tip of each wing. Probably some type of grappling hook or maybe a weapon?

Gray opened their arms slightly. "What do you think, dear one?" Their voice apprehensive.

I hadn't noticed that I was breathing faster, my cock had started to harden as I stared at the stunning splendor before me. "You look like an angel."

Gray's head tilted. "Dear one, I do not look like an angel. They are made of stone and weep."

I found myself smiling, taking a step forward to reach out and touch them. Running my fingers down the path of silver-white down Gray's stomach I thought, *I should be scared.* This isn't one of my gay monster-fucking books filled with that 'instant mate omega alpha' shit. This is real life. I am a human, standing in a graveyard with a cryptid who's giving me a boner and the strangest *fuck me eyes* I've ever seen. There was more to this, though. I wasn't afraid of Gray, and my brain didn't understand why. I couldn't stop the cheesy words from falling out of my mouth. "You're my angel."

Gray moved too quickly for me to process, lifting me off the ground and pushing me gently against a large tree. Leaning in, they rubbed their face into my neck, smelling me. I absently ran my hands up and down their back, avoiding the moth-like wings. This was *who* was following me. This was the shadows, the smoke, the caress.

"It's been you the whole time?" I whispered.

"Yes. I was so afraid you would run from me, but in the stale-smelling place. The coffee home, you showed me you were not afraid."

"You were there when I..." my voice trailed off.

"Yes, sweet. It took all my will to not touch you." Their tongue swiped up my neck, flicking over my earlobe. My fingertips brushed over their wings.

"You're touching me now." My body still holding some tension.

Gray's hold relaxed. "If you do not want me to, I will stop. I would never do anything you do not want. I am sorry..." Their voice sounded strained.

"No, I'm just..." I didn't know how to respond to that. Gray wanted this to be consensual, but my mind was spinning with the fact that monsters were real and this one wanted to fuck me. They held me in silence before I continued, "Gray, don't stop."

They purred in my hair, kissing a trail down my face finding my lips. My fingers started on their shoulders, returning to play with the soft fuzz-like covered wings. The wings felt delicate, yet hard under my fingers. *This was unreal. Fuck, this is incredible.*

"You may touch them. Please, sweet, touch them." Gray breathed into my ear, rolling their hips into me.

Pulling myself up into their arms, I wrapped my legs tightly around Gray's waist. I began firmly rubbing my aching self against what was an equally aroused Gray. I matched their grinding motion as my fingers brushed along the edges of Gray's wings. They growled, thrusting themself into me, hard. I moaned lowly. Dampness was growing in my boxer briefs as the heat of desire flared. The building pressure in my balls caused me to groan again.

Gray's wet tongue pressed against my jawline, dragging down the front of my throat over my Adam's apple. Gray tore off my shirt over my head, tossing it out of sight. They continued their ministrations of my body, licking each nipple before sucking a tight bud between velvety soft lips. Gray set me back on my feet as they continued down the midline of my body with gentle kisses and licks. I was breathless, having a hard time keeping my eyes open.

"Gray." My voice strangled.

"Yes, *Beloved*?" Gray was kneeling before me, already in the act of unbuttoning my jeans.

"Wha... what are you going to do?" I was well on my way to being a wrecked mess by those kisses alone.

"I am showing you my appreciation for so many lullabies. I want you to feel as good as I felt. Let me, Beloved." Gray's eyes were darker from that angle, like a red wine or blood.

Wordlessly I nodded, licking my lips. Gray, not waiting a moment longer, pulled my straining cock from my tight skinny jeans. Gray looked pleased, tongue peeking out between the upper slit of their lip as it moved in and out slowly. My member twitched at that motion, tip leaking more precum.

Gray held my gaze as they moved forward, mouth open, showing a long, slender black tongue that'd been licking my body earlier. It was eight inches long, split in two, that went halfway down the muscle. Gray swiped at the head of my cock before spreading their tongue apart, wrapping both sides around the base of my shaft.

I gave a startled shout as Gray increased the pressure, never breaking eye contact as Gray took me to the back of their throat. I writhed at the sucking and swallowing around aching prick. The intensity of the sensations increasing along with my need to come down the back of Gray's throat. *Fuck*, I wanted to paint the inside of them white. Whining, I writhed as Gray pinned my hips against the tree, trapping my cock in their hot, wet mouth.

"Fff...fuck. Fuck, Gray," I panted and tried to thrust. There was no breaking the grip they had on me. Gray sucked harder, bobbing their head faster. Tingling built at the base of my spine, my balls tightening and pulling up. "Gray... I'm going to come."

My hands dug into Gray's hair, pulling harder than was polite. I wanted to keep that enchanting mouth in place for just another moment longer. The tugging on their hair only seemed to encourage them to suck with greater enthusiasm. Gray hallowed out their cheeks until I was moaning loudly, emptying into their mouth and down their throat. I shuddered and let out a soft whine in the shadows of the trees. My knees felt weak as I shook in the afterglow of my orgasm. Gray lifted me into their arms.

"Where are we going?" My words came out softly, spent.

"I will show you." Gray looked serene as they walked us into the trees.

CHAPTER 7

Weeping Angels

GRAY

Scooping Beloved up, I pulled him deeper into the wooded lot. I had not planned on losing control so quickly. The smell of his fresh cum earlier had spurned me on. I could not wait any longer to have my *picnic* with Beloved. I hoped he enjoyed this gift. It was only one of many I would give to him as we courted, as we mated, and as we spent the centuries together.

"Whe... where are we going, Gray?" Ezra panted, his heart beating wildly in his chest.

"I am sorry, Beloved, that was uncouth. I meant to have you back here, but you were so alluring and needy." I stopped, slowly lowering him to the ground. "You are so enchanting as you fall apart beneath my wings."

Ezra realized he was on a blanket surrounded by candles in globes, a small smile played at the corners of his lips. His pants were still halfway on, caught around at the knee. His taste lingered, filling my mouth with a salty sweetness. My greedy cocks wanted to know what he felt like.

Tenderly, I pulled each shoe off before removing Ezra's pants and setting them to the side. Ezra sat naked under the fading sun and candlelight staring at me, his *cryptid*.

Still wearing my breeches, I felt the front bulge and strain as I kneeled before him. Ezra was not the only one feeling needy, heedless to desire. He sat up straighter, biting his bottom lip as he gazed into my eyes. Those shining dark blue eyes flooded over me like a raging river. There were no words I could weave together that would eloquently describe this specter of lust and wonderment before me. My beautiful human.

"Do you enjoy what you are seeing, Beloved? Would you like more?" I stroked myself roughly through my breeches as his eyes followed the languid movement of my palm against my cocks. I wondered what he thought about how old-fashioned my clothes looked. I would need to find an *updated wardrobe* for Beloved.

Ezra sucked on his lower lip. Lust coursing through his blood, pumping directly into his firming dick. He cupped his balls and tugged gently as he stroked himself. I unbuttoned the front square of my breeches, giving him a glimpse of silver-white hair and the glistening tip of my upper member. Ezra gasped as I let the flap fall to unlace the rest.

My cocks stood proudly erect for him. The top one slightly shorter than the bottom, both having a good amount of length and girth. Humans seem concerned with those measurements. The tips were turning a dark blue, feeling swollen and heavier with every passing minute. I could not stop stroking my bottom cock; it leaked, slowly dripping to the ground. I groaned as I struggled to sit up on my knees, pushing my pants down to free *all* of me. I wanted Beloved to see every part of what made the Winged Folk fierce and mesmerizing. I wanted him to come alone at the thought of being impaled on me.

Behind my lower cock, the same silver hair continued, enveloping my two perfectly round balls. Ezra writhed on the blanket, sucking a finger into his mouth as he moaned at the reveal of me. He was painfully hard, precum dribbling down the underside of his flushed dick. Was he thinking of having one of my balls in his mouth, wondering what the feel of that soft fuzz would be like against his tongue? Was he imagining what my tongue would feel like snaking up his ass or down the slit into his cock?

I moved from my knees, dropping down to all fours so I was eye level with Ezra in his sitting position. I crawled toward my Beloved, running hands up the front of his thighs. He grunted as I pushed him flat on his back. Leaning down, I scented Ezra again, nuzzling his chest to neck. I could not stop myself from kissing and licking and tasting his warm skin.

He lacked any considerable amount of body hair. His skin was soft and smooth from chest to navel. He did have a thin line of rough hair from his belly button leading to a well-groomed curly dark patch around his proud dick. I would have to keep him warm in the winters. Ezra groaned as my tongue flickered at a nipple. I smelled his precum, noticing his twitching dick was leaving a trail of drops on his stomach. My cocks leaked steadily. Ezra lifted his hips up and ground against me in response to my kisses.

I let out a soft, inhuman sound. "Yes, Beloved," nuzzling into Ezra again, "Yes, Beloved."

"You have two cocks." Ezra kept up the roll and grind of his hips. "Am I going to take both?"

I let out the sound again, feeling more hot liquid leave me as it pooled onto his abdomen. "Is that what you want, Beloved? To mate me?" The request came out on a sigh.

Ezra raised his hips again, angling himself so one of my cocks ran down the seam of his ass and the other rubbed into the underside of his own member. Reaching down, I lined up his cock against mine and stroked both of us while I continued to kiss along the line of his jaw. My larger dick was heavy and rigid against the smooth, tight globes of his ass.

Cautiously, I retracted each claw as far as I could. Ezra jolted slightly as he felt the pressure of a fingertip with the hardness of my claw inside his tight heat. Tensing for a moment, he relaxed as my skilled digit opened him up. I added another and then another. Soon, he was moaning and squirming underneath my lips, my tongue, and my torturous strokes. I would not let him go far, never far away from me.

"Easy, Beloved, do not pull away too much. I do not want to cause you harm." My voice was husky. "I could never cause you harm." I rubbed my cheek against Ezra as a knuckle grazed his prostate, causing him to choke on a shout. As I pulled my fingers out, Ezra whimpered at the loss.

Running my hands over his body from shoulders to hips, I gently pulled him into my lap to settle us into a sitting position. Ezra's thighs were spread over my own opening him up perfectly for me. My slick cock heads pressed into him; his own aching dick trapped between our two bodies. Unlike humans, I do not need additional lubricant to make this pleasurable.

Reaching behind Ezra, I ran the back side of my claw from the top of his cleft to throbbing hole. He closed his eyes, letting out a hiss of pleasure. My lips were on his, heated tongue invading Ezra's mouth. He moaned as I deliberately pushed in the blunt head of my smaller cock, forcing open his entrance. Ezra cried out when the second cock head squeezed in seconds later.

"Beloved," I choked. "Beloved, tell me this is what you truly want. You want all of me. You need all of me. This is ours to keep."

His eyes met mine. "Please. Yes. I need all of you."

I plunged in with a hard thrust, lost in full body sensations, feeling every inch of his softness against my overheated skin. There were pinprick dents my claws left in his hips, his ass. The space between our pressed bodies was tight and hot. My cocks ached as I pushed into him, wanting to come but not wanting this to end. Ezra was enthralled, experiencing the feeling of mating with my kind. It was the steady, slow invasion of euphoria through his body; a pleasant tingling that would grow in intensity from my lower cock's cum.

Ezra breathed in deep as he took me completely, deeply. A few moments passed; the tingling turned to gentle vibrations. Pulling out unhurriedly, dragging the sensation over every inch of Ezra, I relished as he arched. Digging his fingers into my back, pushing deep into my tense muscles. Ezra gained traction and lifted himself off, slamming himself back down on my cocks with passionate force. The vibrations continued to intensify as he quickened his pace, riding me, groaning into my mouth. Our tongues ravaged each other's mouths and lips.

Pleading to Ezra, "Touch my wings, Beloved, please." My wings' erogenous spots were places for mates, and only mates, to touch.

Ezra's hands explored my back finding the base of my wings,

wrapping his fingers around the curves. He pressed his fingers in; my wings flared as I moaned, thrusting deeper into him. I was becoming lost in his body. Ezra continued rubbing the mate spots, my hips' movements becoming jerkier. A tightness was building in my balls as the mating vibrations fluttered through me.

Clutching desperately to Beloved, low-pitched sounds rumbled from deep in my throat. I breathed him in again, like it was my first and last breath. I had not hoped for this. I had planned to give him pleasure. I did not expect Ezra to ask to mate, to take all of me inside of him. I had desired for him to taste or feel what was meant for pleasure, but he took both into him.

"Beloved. My Beloved," I groaned as molten heat flooded out of me into him. His own release landed in hot ropes against his chest and stomach.

Laying us down on our sides, I smoothed the hair from Ezra's face. Leaning in, I gently kissed his temple. Dark blue eyes closed as he began to drift away in my arms.

"Shh, Beloved. Rest. I will take care of you," I murmured softly into the sleeping man's hair.

A slow panic began to build in my chest. We had not completed courtship, and there were so many gifts I had not given Beloved. How was he to know that I was serious in my affections toward him? How did he know I could provide for us into the winters of our years? There were so many things I needed to do to prepare for Beloved's arrival to our cave, our nest.

Wrapping my arms around him tighter, my hand hovered over his abdomen. Human males with this body type could not become pregnant. He would not be heavy with our children come the turning of the leaves. One less worry for the moment. There may be other changes Beloved was not prepared for; a part of him must know what he had asked of me. Did he know?

Lifting Ezra into my arms, I wrapped us in my essence. He would need to return to his empty nest with the Pooka for the evening. Perhaps he would think I was a dream. My precious one did not sleep well or often enough. He did not eat sufficiently either. Too often he smelled of sadness and lost dreams. My lips ghosted across Ezra's forehead.

As I walked back to his home, I continued to make a list of things I needed to accomplish to care for my Beloved. When we arrived, the Pooka was eating trash as usual. I chided myself for not thinking of having a new jar of spiders for the little one. Their big black eyes looked up at me adoringly. I would have to bring them back to the cave with us when Ezra was ready to come to my home. The Pooka would die here alone.

Ezra was tucked neatly under the sheets of his poorly decorated nest after I had cleaned and clothed him. I returned to the picnic site for our clothes and Ezra's book, the latter seemed more important than our pants. I ensured all items were packed away, propping it up in the same corner Beloved always left the bag. I scanned the room again before gently patting the Pooka on the head.

"Little one," I said in a hushed tone. "Ezra is now my mate. I need you to watch over him. Tell me if anything... changes, yes?"

The Pooka purred an agreement, my finger tenderly stroked their back. Pooka pressed into my hand. I gave in and scooped the youngling up. They had dropped their dinner of garbage to roll around in my hand. The tiny happy squeaks brought me joy.

"Youngling, I promise to bring more spiders when I visit later. I apologize for the oversight tonight. Do you forgive me?" Bringing the Pooka up to my face, they leaned in and churred against my cheek. "Thank you, that is more than I deserve."

Setting the Pooka down on the carpet; they took off under Ezra's nest pile and reappeared by his head. Pooka did three turns before snuggling in my mate's hair, quickly falling into slumber. I sighed, wishing I could join. I left the home latched tight with plans to return as soon as I had taken care of the turning of the stones.

CHAPTER 8

The Undergrad's Disillusion

EZRA

The incessant buzzing of my phone woke me up. Something soft and fuzzy was stuck to my cheek, mixed with saliva and whatever the hell else I was doing last night. *Gross.* I blindly waved my arm out in futile hopes that my fingers would connect with the tabletop. The warmth on my cheek vanished as I groaned.

What did I leave in my bed last night? The buzzing continued. Finally, I gave up the directionless thrashing for my phone, opening my eyes. What stared back at me was the cutest nightmare I'd ever seen.

Jumping up and backward, I slammed into the concrete wall behind me. A little creature stared up at me with large, round black eyes. The wee beast was about the size of two fists in the shaped of an elongated rabbit. They had long tilted ears attached to an oval-shaped head that melted into a thick neck. Their eyes were disproportionately large compared to the rest of their face that held a stubby snout filled with two rows of pointy little teeth.

The rest of the body was a comical fever dream. Limbs that looked awkwardly long with a plump body ending in a tail that would fit a skunk and not whatever this hallucination was. They squatted in my blankets in a way that was reminiscent of a squirrel perching on a branch. I blinked and then blinked again, thinking this was going to solve my early morning problems of seeing things that weren't really there.

The little one chirped, waving their seven-fingered hand at me. Each long digit had a cat like claw attached that looked sharp enough to pinch but not seriously hurt. When I didn't respond, they chirped again, louder, and stood to their full height on their hind legs. The longer I watched them, the more I wondered if this was a baby... something. The creature jumped into a somersault in midair. As I watched in abject horror or amusement, I wasn't sure, they used my shock as an opportunity to run up the front of my shirt.

Settling on my shoulder, the little one began chattering away in a language of squeaks and chirps I didn't speak or understand. My body had a soreness to it, the one felt deeply after an *eventful* night. Looking down at my hands; there was dirt under my nails. The tiny basement monster nibbled on my earlobe to get my attention before launching themself off to the floor. They raced across the carpet, disappearing under the crack of the door to the main section of the basement.

Slumping to my bed, I attempted to recall my day... my night. I had found Nick. I worked on the project with Rich. I went to the coffee shop... where I furiously masturbated for a ghost that was actually an invisible mothman who then fucked me in a graveyard. Clutching both sides of my head, I slid down, lying flat on my mattress. And now I'm seeing basement demons.

My phone buzzed again. I glared at the dim light as it sat on the table. I let go of a clump of hair I was dramatically pulling to see who was texting me this early in the morning. It was from Nick, asking me to call him before one p.m. It was five in the morning; he must not have gone to bed yet.

I heard a soft click and the push of my back door against the carpet. Someone was coming in my room. My breath caught in my throat, eyes searching for anything I could defend myself with. The room was dim, my nightlight mushroom jar casting more shadows than illumination. I saw the outline clearly enough though. It was them, *Gray*.

"Are you real?" I asked before stopping myself.

"Yes, Beloved." Gray moved closer, shifting weight from foot to foot, unsure of where to go in my room.

"You can come and sit here," I said, patting the bed. "I mean, it's not like you weren't just inside me..." I blushed, looking away. "Sorry."

Gray glided to my bed, lowering themself in a way that had us facing one another. Even sitting I had to look up into their eyes. We stayed in that warm silence for what felt like hours but was reasonably only minutes. Those rust-colored eyes were mournful looking. Their features weren't quiet human, but that didn't diminish the fact that Gray had the most beautiful face, full dark lips, those pointed ears that I wanted to run my fingers and tongue over. Gray leaned in a little more.

"How well can you see me?" they asked quietly.

"Perfectly well. Every tiny detail: you are breathtaking."

"Beloved..." they trailed off. "It is very dark in here. You can see me?"

"What? Yes, of course..." I stopped and looked around. Gray was correct; while I could see well, I realized there wasn't any light in here that'd allow me to make out fine details. When I looked away, things looked more like shadows until I focused and then...

"The Pooka called for me when you awoke. They told me you could *see* them." Gray reached out as if they wanted to touch me.

"Pooka?" The question came out sounding weak.

"Yes, they live down here with you." Gray attempted what was their version of a reassuring face.

"Why can I see..." I trailed off looking for the right words. "Why can I see so much now?"

"It sometimes happens between my people and yours," Gray paused, "humans."

"What happens?" The question came out barely above a whisper. Fear for what Gray was going tell me, filled me. How was life about to change, again?

"We..." They paused, taking a deep breath. "We are... there is no human word for it, but something like compatibles."

"Compatibles?" I asked, sounding more confused than concerned, which was also concerning.

"Yes, our scents are compatible, fueling our need to be matched. I meant to properly court you, but I lost myself to your smell of rain and fresh Earth. When you speak, I hear the whispers of the wind and the tumbling of cold-water creeks. I could not deny you or it. Our bodies fit well." Gray glanced down to my lips.

"Deny it? Gray," my voice barely audible, "what's 'it?'"

"When the Winged Folk court, they pleasure one another." Gray gave me a wolfish smile. "We pleasure one another when we do not court, too. We only use the cock meant for such things. The longer one is for mating; it is how we create new generations. You asked me for both, and your body greedily accepted, Beloved." A darker, almost bluish, tint flooded Gray's cheeks.

I blanched. "Gray, am I pregnant with your moth babies?"

They choked on what suspiciously sounded like a laugh. "No, you are a human male." Gray pointed to my crotch. "You cannot become heavy with my children with a cock."

"Okay, well that's..." I didn't know how to finish. Gray's face made me think they wouldn't have minded if I 'lay heavy' with their children. "Something else happened, though?"

"Yes. We are mates." Gray became very still as if waiting for me to panic.

Internally sighing, I showed more courage than I had. "Please don't be afraid to tell me what that means. I promise I won't scream or cry." They appraised my words, head titled to the side. "Okay, I will refrain from doing those things until you're done explaining."

"It is rare we complete a mating with a human, and each instance has been different. The last one was long before I lived, in the old world. The place across the water. There was a Winged Folk and a woman. She was of mixed descent. After they mated, she turned." He paused assessing my emotional state.

"How'd she turn?" I asked with more force than necessary.

"Completely." Gray's face twitched as if they'd thought better than smiling. "She looked like one of our kind. Her life was bound to her mate's, and they lived for a thousand years after that, or so the story goes."

"So, I'm going to grow horns and wings?" Anxiously, I held my breath. The numbness of disbelief was settling in. What's going to happen to my... what do I have?

"Probably not, unless you have Folk or essence in your blood." Gray studied my face before adding, "Which, you do have some essence."

My heart leaped into my throat. "I have essence?"

"The mundane human word is *magic*. It is more than something one can take; essence exists in everything around us. Some beings are of *it*, while other beings simply live in *it*. Most humans are in it, the magic of this world."

"So, I'm part magic and I can see in the dark and I'm going to do the best cosplay of Jeff Goldblum in the—" Gray's lips met mine, and my mind blanked out. "Hey, no fair. I listened, now it's time to panic."

"There is no need to panic, Beloved. We will not know the extent of your changes until something *happens*." Gray cringed. "It is expected for you to see through the veil now and have enhanced senses. Our essence is connected." Gray ran their claw along my jaw. "I am so very sorry that I did this to you."

A heavy sadness and warmth filled my chest. Was I feeling Gray's emotions? The longer I sat with those emotions, I realized I'd been feeling them since I woke up. Gray was in turmoil. While this wasn't an ideal way to finally get a partner, it certainly was an interesting way. I knew they weren't lying to me. I was experiencing their genuine care for me. I would for as long as I lived. This wasn't love, not after a single date—fucking in the woods does count as a date.

"I can feel you. What do you feel from me?"

They considered my question. "Curiosity." Gray's face scrunched up before they relaxed, scooping me into their lap. "I have seen your tears, but I did not know what caused them. I feel deep grief, exhaustion, and something else is blooming."

I couldn't help but snuggle into them. "Safe. Gray, I think I finally feel safe."

"Are you in danger?" A growl was rising up through their chest. Gray held me tighter. "I will not allow it."

Closing my eyes I reassured them, "No, I'm not in danger. I'm tired, though. Since we're mates, does that mean you'll stay in bed with me for a little while?'

Gray stiffened under my touch. They shuddered with a drawn out, relieved sigh. Their wings shifted as Gray pulled us back toward the wall, one arm wrapped around my waist and the other pulling blankets over us. Gray readjusted so their body wrapped around my own. I rested my forehead against their chest. A wing swept over me like a protective shield to the cool morning air. I realized now that the heat had been left off.

"I need to wake up in a few hours," I mumbled into the white fur that was now my pillow. "I promised Nick I'd help him with Allen."

"That is the spiteful man with *coffee* breath?" Gray's voice going deeper, a hint of anger.

"Yes. I think Allen is harming students, but I don't know how." Gray tensed under me.

"Allen is a danger to you?" This came out as a hiss.

"Not me," I said quickly, not wanting my mothman... moth person lover to go murder a professor. "He's more of an annoyance to me. There are stories that he takes advantage of younger students."

Gray remained rigid as they pressed their head to my ear. "Beloved, how does Allen *take advantage*?"

I paused. My mind was starting to spiral again. I was lying in a bed with a being from another world, discussing my daily stressors as if this was the absolute normal thing. This cryptid had been following me for I didn't know how long and then fucked me behind some trees in an old cemetery. Now we're just cuddling like it's a normal Saturday morning thing. What the actual fuck? Why was I not scared? I should've been scared.

"Beloved," Gray whispered before kissing the shell of my ear. "Beloved, I can feel your turmoil."

"I'm not scared of you…" Taking a deep breath. "I'm not scared of this." I tilted my head back to look up into their eyes. There was a deep sense of kindness. A spark of something else, more primal, too. How could I forget this enormous… person… isn't human? They're something I don't fully understand.

Gray shrugged slightly, kissing my temple. "Because we are compatibles who are now mates. Have you ever feared me?"

Thinking back to all the strange occurrences over the last few weeks. Was I frightened by the thought of someone like Gray, or was it more needing to flee the pain from *human* men? My anxiety and flight response were always higher after meeting with Allen. I got overwhelmed by constant student interactions where it wasn't fear that drove me home but the weariness of simply having to speak again.

Previous experiences taught me that large things in trees are either a stalker ex-boyfriend of Addi's or a bobcat. Every time I was worried or afraid, it wasn't because of Gray. When I knew they were there, I felt… relief.

"With you, no. The things that scare me, exhaust me, or outright terrorize me haven't been you." I burrowed into them, luxuriating in their all-encompassing warmth.

"Sleep, Beloved," they purred.

"I…" I pushed back against them as I felt my anxiety spike. "Gray, how does *this* work? How do we see one another? When I fall asleep, will you still be here? What do you do all day? How am I mated to a magical forest creature and still a grad student? Gray…" Gray placed a hand over my mouth to stifle the flow of rambling that would've continued.

"Our relationship will work the way we choose it to work. I cannot be here when you wake. There are things I must address as a *magical forest creature.*" They were teasing me now.

"You're making fun of me." I pouted a little while their eyes lit up with amusement.

"Not completely, sweet one. I am duty-bound to the hills here. I am more interested in holding you as you slumber than explaining to you what it is I do." A wing moved so Gray could pull me in closer.

"Uh, I feel like an asshole," I muttered quietly. "We slept together, and I barely knew your name. How do I refer to you, like uh, pronouns and what's... your race?" My cheeks heated up.

"Hmm, humans are often concerned with such things. I am one of the many forms of Winged Folk. Some have very specific names, often from humans and their different languages. My *modor* called us sciathán when we were little, but that is not the language of my people, the Winged Folk. We do not speak that out loud. More recently, my eldest sibling got us stuck with *mothman*." Gray scowled.

"Modor?" I asked, vaguely remembering that word from middle or old English.

"Mother." Gray leaned, rubbing the top of my head.

"Mothman, that was you?" I vaguely recalled the legends from the area.

"No, that was fucking Indrid," Gray replied tersely. "He does not have sense enough to leave the humans be. Since the English language is more prevalent in this area, I refer to myself as part of the Winged Folk, close enough to what Modor called us. As for pronouns," they shrugged, "I have never been too particularly fond of the human binary. It seems limiting to how I see myself and my role within this world. I appreciate the young humans that discuss on the green how they wish to, uh, 'enact gender neutrality language as a normative and push against harmful constructs of patriarchy and white supremacy.' I think that is what they said. Those who are closest to me use gender-neutral terms and pronouns when referring to myself or others they are not acquainted. I am not offended if called a he or she or any other pronoun variation that has become more common."

Raising an eyebrow, I asked, "Do you listen to undergrad students often on the green?"

"I like the white building that has all of the underground lecture rooms." Their gaze roamed my face. "It is my second favorite place after the halls that you voice your songs in."

"How long have you been watching me?" I settled in more, feeling my eyelids droop.

"Not long enough, my Beloved." They sighed. "Our time could

be until every star withers to blackness in the sky and it would not be long enough."

I began to fade along with Gray's idyllic way of speaking about *us*. They had moved from an archaic to more modern ways of speech in our brief conversations. Gray primarily used descriptors to explain an idea or a noun instead of using a single word. Perhaps the Winged Folk language was more descriptive, and that translated into the way Gray used English. Maybe Gray didn't know the word because it was something too new to them. I wasn't a linguistics major, but I'd recognized the unique way they spoke as something bigger than lack of knowledge.

My body became heavier as Gray's even breathing lulled me further into rest. My phone buzzed again, eyes shooting open. The room was still dark with Gray wrapped around me. I tried to move my arm up toward the table, but Gray got there first. They reached over, bringing the phone to my face. I tapped the screen to see Nick had texted again.

> Ezra, Allen told me to meet him at his place at 11 this morning instead of later. I can't go alone. I'm so sorry. You're probably asleep…

The message ended on what was probably a series of terrified thoughts.

I pulled the phone out of Gray's claws and typed.

> No worries. I'm gonna lay down for a couple of hours. Meet me at the Burrito Hut on Main at 10:30. I can drive us to dildo's house. He lives over by the ridge.

I saw a reply being typed.

> Thank you. I am so sorry.

The poor kid was frazzled. I remembered the look on his face in the classroom.

JAE DIXON

It will be my pleasure.

I turned on my alarm with Gray taking the phone, setting it gently back on the table. I didn't remember closing my eyes when my alarm woke me up to an empty bed. *Please don't be gone for too long.*

76

CHAPTER 9

The Historical Society

EZRA

"He said he didn't want to meet at his house and sent me this address." Nick showed me the e-mail Allen had sent him after Nick had revealed that I was driving.

"It's the historical society, but I don't even know if they're open today. Last I heard, budget cuts meant no weekend hours." I looked over at Nick as he chewed his thumb. Poor kid was on edge.

"That's what he sent me," he muttered, considering my words. His big brown eyes were shadowed with dark circles.

"I'll be fucking thrilled if he doesn't show up." I took in a deep breath; being an asshole about this wasn't going to help Nick. If I didn't support him in front of Allen, there would be another "meeting" alone at Allen's house or office. Nick didn't deserve that.

"What's at the historical society that he'd be interested in?" Nick asked me, probably believing I knew anything about the man who was supposed to help me succeed in my pursuit of knowledge.

Shrugging, I related what little gossip I'd heard from the department, "I've heard from Rich, uh Dr. Henderson, that they've recently had a lot of documents donated from the Simmons' estate."

"Simmons as in *the executioner*?" His eyes had gone round.

"Same estate, yeah. The English department chatter is the documents in the estate had death warrants hidden in there, but that's not the weird part." I paused; okay, maybe I was a slut for a good ghost story. "There's allegedly a collection of books of the *dark arts*." I used my *spooky* voice and waved my right hand, keeping the left firmly planted on the steering wheel.

"So... the historical society is now housing occult texts and the university wants them?" He was chuckling at my bullshit.

"Rich was only mildly interested because someone said there was a medieval text, but it's doubtful something that old would've survived in this climate without proper storage." I keenly watched the foot traffic as we drove through the main area of campus. Students had a bad habit of jumping in front of traffic for no good goddamn reason.

"Yeah, that's what the university's archivists would've said," he huffed.

"You think there's been some ancient wizard's grimoire in Appalachia for centuries and no one knew about it?" I raised an eyebrow, not looking directly at him as some sophomore lurched into the street. It's not even noon. *Jesus Christ.*

"This town is wild. You've heard about the haunted dorms where the student died. The way the city planner made this place look like a pentagram, punctuated with cemeteries. The old hospital and ridge view." Nick took in a deep breath as the old brick building that housed the historical society came into view as we crested the hill.

"You sound like one of those destination, 'discover this' channels on Halloween." I chuckled, trying to alleviate some of his growing anxiety. I lowered my voice dramatically. "Have you ever wondered what would happen if your college roommate was a terror? What if they were an actual sleep paralysis demon? Ladies and Gentlemen, what you are about to witness is real. My name is Ezra Williams and tonight we will explore Appalachia Unknown."

Nick barked out a laugh. "That was terrible; were you trying to do an impression?"

"I may've had crushes on both Frakes and Gates when I still had cable." I plastered on the goofiest smile as that answer sent him into a fit of uncontrollable laughter. It was infectious, I was giggling as I pulled into the rugged parking lot. Nick was wiping his eyes, choking on laughter. This was going to be the best moment of the morning, seeing him happy. It was good to see light in his eyes.

He froze. "Fuck, that's his car. Look at that douchebag's plate. P-R-F-P-R-O-F, that motherfucker has 'Perfect Professor' as his license plate." Nick continued to grimace as I howled like a hyena.

"We don't want to keep 'prf prof' waiting, do we?" I snickered as I released my seat belt, keys in hand. "Come on now, up and out. I don't want to hear him bitch about us being tardy on a Saturday morning."

"Do you really care?" he asked as he pushed the passenger side door open.

"I would've last week." I rested my weight against the open door, looking at Nick from across the roof. "I don't think I do anymore. My days being haunted by him are coming to a close."

"You really aren't afraid of him?" He frowned. That man had too much power over people, especially *young people*.

"No, he can do and try a lot of things. It'll be messy if he wants it to be." I frowned, knowing that he would fight this. "I've come to realize that I don't have to *win* this fight, but I most certainly will make sure he loses." There was a darkness in my tone that sounded foreign to my own ears.

Nick nodded. "I wish I could be that free. My next year depends on this grade. If he decides to give me an incomplete or fail me..." Nick trailed off.

"I know. I see you, though; you're not going to be alone in this."

Nick grunted as he shut the door, shoving both of his hands into hoodie pockets. He half-smiled, waiting for me to join him to walk in. The lot was mostly empty except for my vehicle, Allen's sedan, and a third older-looking hatchback. That must've belonged to the mystery staff member who was letting us in outside of business hours. I patted Nick on the back lightly as we approached.

It was dimly lit inside the front area of the society; I could see Allen's back and an older woman standing near the doors. They were talking about something that had the woman very animated. I vaguely remembered her from a tour a few years ago. She must be in her 80s or 90s.

Knocking gently on the glass, I noticed the closed sign hung proudly during the late Saturday morning. A reminder that there were better things to be done on a sunny, late spring morning. I should be home thinking about my giant moth lover, not slaying dragons for undergrads. I snorted out loud and Nick side eyed me. I smiled and nodded toward the specter of a failed English professor of years past.

Allen turned around, walking toward us. As he turned the lock, I could hear the metal slide through the shaft in the frame. The bottom of the door made a soft scratching sound as it pushed out toward us. The smell of musty old carpet rose in the seemingly draft-less room, stale air waiting. Everything about this moment felt wrong, dead. The hair on the back of my neck rose to the attention of what darkness crept beyond.

Allen's eyes bored into me, his smile just a shade too close to predatory for me. I gave him the same smile back. His posture stiffened as he moved away from the entrance so Nick and I could walk in. He didn't even glance at Nick, the student he was waiting for; he seemed mesmerized by me. *Good, you fucking nightmare. Come for me.*

I could feel heat in my blood, my fingers flexing like I was missing pieces of something. The lighting was dim inside, but I saw every fine line and wrinkle of the monster in front of me. Allen shifted again, as if he knew I suddenly was more than an idle threat in a dank room. I heard Nick and the woman chatting, a soft buzz in the background of my thoughts. I wanted to tear Allen apart. He smelled like rotting leaves, stale coffee, and the kind of black mud in creeks that reek of dead things when you step in it. Nick tapped my arm.

"Hey, Ez," Nick said awkwardly.

"What?" I looked over to see that he and the woman were staring at me. "Sorry, I didn't have enough coffee this morning. Kinda zoned out there." I smiled, lifting a hand in a subtle please don't shake it wave. "I'm Ezra Williams, ma'am."

"It's alright, I understand the need for coffee. I have a fresh pot brewing in the back if you don't mind store bought grounds." She seemed pleasant and genuine. "I'm Missy Jones, head volunteer of arrivals."

"I'd appreciate any caffeine after a long night, Ms. Jones." I tried to keep my tone pleasant when all I wanted to do was fist fight Allen who was standing silently behind me.

"Pleasure, I take it? You don't seem to write much these days." The motherfucker chuckled like he was funny.

"Oh, absolute pleasure. End of the semester and, of course, the anniversary of my father's passing..." I glanced at his face to see if he'd show any signs that he knew my father or cared about the death. "I needed to have something that was just for me this week."

"Oh, I'm sorry dear. And please, call me Missy." She patted my arm in the most grandmotherly gesture possible. "Let's go get you some coffee so I can scandalize you about today's project."

"Perfect, Nick and I weren't sure what *Dr.* Allen needed assistance with today." I smiled as she took my arm in hers and guided us to the back of the building, presumably the staff lounge.

"He didn't tell you?" She gave me the most flirtatiously wicked smile. "We're going to start sorting the Simmons' estate's *donations*."

"Holy fuck," Nick muttered, blushing when Missy turned to look at him.

She cackled. "Holy fuck indeed, young man. I've already started poking around in the boxes, and there are some incredible historical pieces. Things we shouldn't be housing in this little brick house. We asked the university if they were interested in our findings, and Dr. Allen was the only one able to come. I suppose you two were volun-told to help?"

Nick brightened up. "I'm a journalism major, ma'am. I wouldn't have to be *told* to see those kinds of secrets."

Allen huffed behind us. "I appreciate the enthusiasm, Nicholas. It will help that Ezra has decided to join our little sorting party, uninvited."

"Of course." I glanced over my shoulder. "Anywhere Nick goes, I go." I forced myself not to grimace at the man behind me but I'm not sure how successful I was when Missy gently nudged me to get my attention.

"Yes, it is lucky Ezra joined us and unfortunate you cannot stay for the afternoon." Missy pulled on my arm as we rounded a corner.

"Not staying?" I asked Allen.

"No. There were some issues with the grading system last night. It went down again; grades need to be in by Monday, but I have a trip tomorrow and won't be back for several weeks." He cleared his throat at the end. That was the most he's ever told me about his life.

"Oh, going anywhere fun?" Now I was just being a complete twat.

"As I wrote in the e-mail sent Thursday, out of state for a conference and some research." His tone was chastising, or it would have been, if anything in my tone or body language indicated that I cared.

"Oh, sorry, I was lost in grading comp papers since..." I gestured vaguely with my free arm. "I don't think I've checked emails since Wednesday. If I'm being honest, I'm afraid to see all the terror-stricken undergrad requests for summer sessions."

Nick's voice cut in, attempting to alleviate the growing tension between Allen and I, "You're doing summer sessions?"

"Yeah, Shakespeare. Both sessions." I shook my head. "Not my favorite, but the adjunct from the city is having back surgery and I offered to cover it. Of course, I'll continue my own work and Rich's project since his little helpers are on summer break."

Allen snorted at the mention of Rich as Nick enthusiastically told the room that Dr. Henderson was an incredible professor. Allen made a hissing between his teeth before telling us about our chores for the *summer*. I glanced at Nick, who was nodding. Allen expected us to come in every Saturday until the fall semester—or whenever the project was complete—to help Missy sort out the boxes from the estate.

The university had some interest in the legal documents and books. They'd need to be authenticated by *real* professionals, but we were a good enough start. This *motherfucker* knew I'd worked in special collections as an undergrad and had done an internship at a museum specifically with historical documents. This was all before I changed tracks in my MFA.

"Yeah, that'll be easy enough. I could even call some of my museum contacts for help." We were standing in front of the coffee maker; Missy had relinquished my arm so I could pour us each a cup.

"That," Allen emphasized the *t* at the end, "will not be necessary. Your job is to sort *under* Missy's direction."

"Missy, cream?" I asked, pleasantly ignoring Allen. I hadn't even bothered to turn to look at him when he spoke.

"Yes, dear. Thank you." Her shoulders held a slight tension. Allen and I needed to go to our own corners soon.

I handed her a cup. "Nick, coffee and cream?" He nodded, holding eye contact a bit too long. I gave him his cup, then pouring my own. It wasn't lost on anyone the level of petty I was being. "I'd make you a cup, professor, but you need to go *battle* grading papers."

"Correct, I expect detailed emails from both of you about your findings here. Mr. Williams, I also expect weekly updates on your portfolio as per my last e-mail." He turned to Missy. "Always a pleasure. We'll talk again soon." He had the slimiest of smiles on his face as he left the room.

We stood in silence, waiting to hear the front door click shut before letting out the collective breath we were holding. Missy had her back against the counter, sagging slightly while she clasped her hot cup. She stared off a few seconds before standing as straight as her back allowed, shaking her head slowly.

"He's such a bastard." She took a sip without adding anything more but she didn't need to because I started laughing.

"I'm sorry for my behavior." I cringed.

Nick shrugged. "For a second, I thought you were going to deck him when we first got in."

"I was thinking about it." I rolled my shoulders. "He gets to me more than I should let him."

Missy looked down into her cup. "I've known him for more years than I care to admit. He's always been this way, though. He's gotten colder, though. More obsessive about death."

I raised an eyebrow. "Do continue."

Missy smirked. "I probably shouldn't be talking to his students about him like this."

"Well, if it's any consolation, I won't be under his thumb for much longer and after today, Nick will be free." I glanced at Nick. "Wait, didn't he say the whole summer for you, too?"

Nick nodded. "Yeah, it was in the e-mail. He thinks I'm letting him be my mentor. He'll 'put in a good word' to my journalism program and this will help me expand my CV for grad school or some shit."

"Did you agree to that?" Missy asked.

"No, but I didn't explicitly tell him I wasn't interested. He still has to submit my grade." Nick shrugged, blowing on his coffee before taking a sip.

Missy frowned. "I'm well aware that students get roped into things for a variety of reasons, but this seems…" she looked between us, "malicious of him."

"Everything he does *is* malicious," I grumbled. "But it's okay. He's not here and I'm honestly kind of curious as to what you have to show us. Honestly, if he doesn't plan on joining, I'll keep coming back to help. There were some mentions of rare books that one of my mentors would be interested in if it's true. I can talk to the Dean for future support if you need it. We've a fresh batch of freshmen and teaching assistants in the fall that'd love to work on spooky projects."

Missy beamed at me. "And why would you do that?"

"Because the first thing you offered me was coffee, followed by calling Allen a bastard. How could I not help my new best friend out?" I was genuinely enchanted with her. "Besides, you clearly have some gossip on him that I will fondly remember when I'm typing up the bullshit reports he wants."

Missy laughed. "Alright, but don't tell anyone it came from me." She paused. "Well, I'm probably one of the few people who knows this about him. He'll figure it out, given enough time."

"So, it's just between us, then?" Nick smirked, gently nudging her with his shoulder. There was a twinkle of mischief in her bright gray eyes framed by smile lines and wisdom. She was beautiful; if there was such a thing as a fairy godmother, Missy was the embodiment of such a benevolent gossiping creature.

"Alright, boys, let's finish this sludge first and get to work. I don't want to waste your whole Saturday." She chugged the rest of the cup before placing it in the sink. I was amazed; the coffee was still hot enough that I was wondering how she didn't choke and sputter. Although, I have done many things to damage my gag reflex so maybe I'd have been okay. I smiled into my cup at that thought.

84

THE THREE OF us had been eagerly sorting through what were 40 boxes in various degrees of decay. The first dozen were full of business leftovers from the 1920s through the 1940s. Interesting to someone, but not what the university would deem important enough to archive. Missy had been slowing down. As late morning quickly turned to afternoon, she sighed loudly, getting my attention.

"Alright, I think that's more than enough. I knew there would be a lot of garbage in these boxes, but receipts from the town grocer from when I was born was not what I had in mind." She ran a hand through her pure white hair, looking exasperated.

I hid a smirk before I could be scolded. "Just one more box? Those over there toward the bottom are probably the most promising."

"And why's that?" Missy gave me a severe look, probably one she'd practiced on silly young men for decades.

"Because those boxes aren't moldy cardboard; they look more like storage crates. They were also the first ones loaded in here and would've been the last ones we got to if we followed an order to unpacking." I paused thoughtfully. "Who was spreading all the gossip about spell books and death warrants being in this cache? Unless someone saw something, those are oddly specific rumors."

Nick smiled brightly at me; it that hadn't dimmed since Allen had left us with Missy. "Maybe you're right or maybe it's more receipts. Either way, I'm in too deep to not play Tetris with a few centuries' worth of paperwork." He squinted at the larger containers in the corner. "Something about that one reminds me of Raiders of the Lost Ark. You know, your boyfriend's movie." Nick snorted at his own joke.

"Very funny, undergrad." I shook my head. Missy was quiet as she observed our playful banter.

"Ah, is it an attraction to Harrison Ford or archaeologists?" She smiled at me.

I grunted as I started lifting heavy boxes. "A little of both."

She giggled and walked over to supervise the heavy lifting. Nick joined me in reorganizing the cardboard boxes along the other wall so we could access the wooden crates. If anything, these had an air of mystery to them and held heavier objects. I understood wanting to process the paperwork first, but everyone needed a little adventure in their academic endeavors.

Missy had left the room for a moment, bringing back a crowbar that could have come from a movie set. There were five mid-sized crates in front of us of an undetermined age. Probably older than us, maybe younger than Missy. She handed Nick the crowbar and gestured to the crate closest to her.

"Since you have the youngest back, you can start," Missy said as she took a step back, allowing Nick to close in on his newest job. He did it with the efficiency of a man who probably spent some of his teen years breaking and entering into old farmhouses to take pictures or smoke pot. I'd have to ask him later what kind of delinquent he was in his small town. Nick lifted the lid, setting it upright against the box. Missy was the first to peer into the mystery itself.

"It's books, Ezra," she said in a solemn voice. "We need to get gloves and storage boxes before we start handling them. One looks like a photo album."

I walked over, grabbing the preservation materials while Missy pulled out a tablet to enter our findings. I put on the gloves, glancing over at her. She nodded for me to start unloading the contents. I gently lifted each volume, a hand on each side of the spine, before setting it down on the clean surface we had set up earlier. I placed the book on its back, noticing the intricacy of its leather cover and loose, sewn-in binding.

"That looks old," Nick whispered.

"It is, without further inspection I'd guess mid- to late-16th century." I crossed my arms without touching my clothes. The materials were high-quality. I could see part of the sewing and end band structure peeking through a missing section of leather on the spine. I ran my finger over the faded gold tooling and panel stamp.

"Ezra, open it up and see if this is our Necronomicon," Missy said impatiently.

"Did you make a Lovecraft reference, Missy?" Nick eyed our newest ally and friend.

"That dead racist? No." She straightened, pitching her voice low, and hissed, "Klaatu Verata..."

I barked out a surprise laugh. "Truly a classic. I knew I was falling in love with you for a good reason."

"Wait, you watch campy horror movies?" Nick was shocked.

Missy sighed. "I'm old, Nick, not a shut-in with no interests. Child, I've been watching sci-fi and horror movies probably longer than your parents have been alive. I was in the area hunting all the mothman gossip. I was there when the bridge went down, too."

I looked over. "Did you see them? The mothman?" I grimaced as I slipped a *them* instead of *it*. Would anyone notice?

Missy blinked. "We all saw something. It's true, though; he was trying to warn us about the bridge." She looked away.

Nick edged closer. "What do you mean *he* was trying to warn you?"

"Oh, one of the stories is that the mothman was a warning. Some folks got it into their heads that he caused the collapse. I don't believe it. He may have known what was about to cause it but couldn't stop it." She had a sad smile that didn't meet her eyes. "My late husband should have been on the bridge that day."

"That's luck," I said softly.

"He was all bad luck. The man was a bastard, just like his father was a bastard. He died a few weeks before in a mining accident that November. The bridge fell in December. I never remarried, just fucked wayward college professors and door-to-door salesmen after that." Missy beamed up at me. This woman was full of stories that I hoped to hear one day over a beer.

I snorted, looking back to the book, gently lifting its cover. There was a black and white photo of a white man, hung by the neck from an old oak tree. It was clear he'd died of asphyxiation; his neck didn't appear broken, which would have happened if he'd been executed properly.

"Jesus Christ," I muttered.

"What?" Nick moved toward me quickly, Missy by his side. "Oh, fuck... that's real."

"That's Simmons' work." Missy nodded to the photo. "I guess there's no questioning some of this is his."

I pulled the photograph out and flipped it around. In scrawled black ink, someone had written '1907' but nothing else. I slowly turned to the first printed page. I was taken aback by what I was holding, it was the strangest edition of a King James Bible. I have never seen one made from such high-quality materials but also be so plain. Under the title, the printing date was 1682 in London, but nothing else.

"This is all wrong." Missy had put on gloves and ran a finger along the cover.

"How is it wrong?" Nick asked, peering over our shoulders.

"The title page is, well, empty. I would have expected a Bible of this caliber to have more..." Nick cut me off.

"More jazz hands?" He waved his fingers at me as Missy chuffed at him in playful annoyance.

"Pull out your phone and do a Google image search for King James Bible in the 1600s." I continued to stare at the almost blank page in front of me. I could hear Nick loudly say, 'Oh,' behind me.

"This one totally lacks jazz anything," he cheerfully added as he put his phone away.

Missy turned the page and to our absolute horror there was another black and white photo. Missy hissed and shut the book quickly, but without the reverence deserving of a tome so old. She placed the book in the container along with the first photograph and sealed it tight. Nick and I stayed silent. Missy glanced back at the crate.

"I won't tell you to lie to him, but please don't tell him about this," she said quietly. "You know what that is, right?"

I nodded and felt Nick shift. "We won't say anything. What do you want to do?" I asked her.

"I think we've done enough digging today. I'm tired and I don't want to unlock any more horrors this close to bedtime," she sighed, "even if bedtime isn't for another eight hours."

"We could come back tomorrow. I don't mind, Missy." Nick was trying to be helpful; he really was a sweet guy.

She stared back at the crates as I shrugged. "I've got nothing tomorrow... after I submit a couple of grades."

"You didn't finish yesterday?" Nick sounded aghast.

I laughed. "You heard Dr. Allen. The system went down." I winked at him.

"If you two don't mind, could we start earlier?" she asked so sweetly. "I'll bring real coffee if you meet me at nine tomorrow."

Nick was bouncing like a happy puppy, and I agreed. Of course, I'd be there, coffee or not.

The rumors were true. We may have stumbled upon a treasure of Appalachia tradition.

CHAPTER 10
History Lessons
EZRA

Gray hadn't returned in weeks. Had I been dreaming? My heart ached the first few nights they didn't return. Now, I had a constant pulsing pain that burrowed deep in my chest. Pooka was still there, eating garbage and licking the ash trays Addi left on the porches. After a round with marijuana ash, Pooka would roll around on the floor like they were high. I considered stopping the tray licking, but they seemed genuinely thrilled with the little chore and Addi kept thanking me for tidying up.

Gray was real if Pooka was real, unless I was hallucinating the little goblin. Doubtful; I stopped picking up my trash weeks ago and my room had never looked cleaner. Apparently, Pooka knew to be discrete when eating the floor snacks while I was still unaware of them. Now they ate with reckless abandon. I started catching the little spiders I found in the windowsills and in the grass to add to their diet. Nothing too terrifying, just fuzzy little brown and black treats.

Spring had melted into muggy summer days and short star-filled nights. Nick and I religiously held service with Missy every weekend in the dimly lit back room of the historical society. After finding the first Bible, things seemed to only get more intense. Missy gave us an extraordinary education on Appalachia folklore, teaching us some of the old settler medicines and omens. I found myself googling late at night for some of the botany lessons she hinted at as we cataloged the more gruesome execution photographs.

Missy's family, the Mayes, had been Scotch-Irish settlers who landed in the region six decades before West Virginia was a federated state. She told us about the kitchen magic her great-grandma—Granny—would teach the little ones. She recited some psalms to us that were common to ward off a headache or bad luck. She described in detail how important the family Bible was. It listed births, deaths, and every anniversary worth remembering. She described the intricacy of instructions that'd been scribbled in the margins to remind the next generation of what to do in case of emergency.

Missy talked about how so much changed after the second world war, how the boys and men left and many never came home. Families packed up to make money in larger cities for the war effort leaving fields fallow and farms haunted. She said the men that hadn't been killed ended up staying away. As much as the mountains had held them, the loss kept them away. She was the only sibling to stay remotely close to where their family once thrived.

A deep anguish laid in her voice as she recounted what could only be heard as eulogies now. Her eyes told the truth. The longer I spent with Missy, the deeper I saw into that absolute grief and loss. She was someone I could go adrift with in the bottom of a moonshine bottle and not feel embarrassed. I think she recognized that in me as well. Nick was mostly enchanted by folktales that didn't seem to connect to a city boy.

But there was something about those romantically gothic accounts that took root in me. The words wound through me, snaking vines seeking a sun. I was spellbound when she spoke of her granny and grandma—Mawmaw. They were wise, take no shit, kind of people who were pragmatic to a fault but extraordinarily loving to every generation that came after them. They were buried in a family cemetery miles and miles away from here under a bunch of old red maple trees. A constant reminder of strength and endurance even in death.

I think Missy told us about her family and her youth to distract us from the tragic history we were slowly uncovering in each volume unearthed from the old crates. In part, she was passing on her family's history to us because her own children no longer cared. Mostly, Missy was giving us some frame of reference to how wrong what we were seeing was. The perversion of the Bibles was the most disturbing to her. They had been used in a similar way that most Appalachia families would have, but at some point, that was twisted. Missy blanched and struggled to articulate the horror of it.

The histories found written in the margins were mostly in German. After doing a quick ancestry search, Simmons was of German descent. We couldn't find anything about the family prior to their settling in Athens. Nick had a 200-level language requirement understanding of German, which was to say, a minimal understanding of German from almost three centuries ago. What he could translate was dark, sounding more like necromancy or alchemy than religious-tinted folklore.

Missy asked him to stop reading it and note on the tablet which book and page number the writings were scrawled on. She told us to "let the academics curse themselves."

"But I am an academic," I reminded her, glancing up from my volume.

"No, dear boy. You're so much more." She waved me off like the silly child I was and went back to documenting the family photographs we'd found wedged in some sonnets printed in 1842 France. She'd taken it upon herself to organize every 'death photo' as we called them.

Nick had started sorting the photos on our second weekend. He was in tears by lunch. He'd been at the back table lying them out one by one, meticulously following every protocol that'd been put into place for proper preservation when I heard the sound. At first, I thought he'd coughed, but he stood there, back to us, gently shaking. I walked over to find his eyes closed and face crumpled. Tears silently rolling down his face. I was shocked he hadn't said a word.

I looked down at the offending photograph, no, photographs. They were not the execution styled ones; these were images of people who'd clearly been murdered. He'd laid out nearly 50 without uttering a sound until he came to a collection of children. I wrapped my arms around him, pulling him to my chest. He sobbed, clinging to me. I stared at the warped little bodies in the pictures. The series looked as if they had all drowned or had been drowned. It was hard to tell, and I'd no desire to inspect them any further.

Missy hurried over to console Nick as much as inspect what he'd found. She grimaced at the children more than the adult victims before leaning against Nick. She rubbed circles on his back, telling him, "It's alright. The poor babes have been at peace for a long time now." He eventually quieted down, occasionally shuddering in my grip. I refused to let him go; something told me he needed me to stay close.

He sniffed, whispering to me, "My little sister..." as I hauled him away from the table. Missy quickly collected the set, placing them back in the shoe box.

The next weekend he didn't return to his table, nor did he ask about the photos. Missy had gone in alone and given them the proper care historical items deserved. She'd told me quietly one afternoon when Nick had gone to pick us up lunch that those photos were of a group of kids who had drowned in a flash flood.

Each weekend gave us a new mystery or impressive horror. No one had emailed Allen anything of relevance about the books or the photos. Nick and I emailed two different reports that essentially said the same boring things. We came up with a way of cataloging items that was useless without a key in case Allen asked for numbers. If anything, he'd think I'm useless and my previous experience was a trumped up nothing of an internship.

I'd held off on having a formal meeting with Dr. Everhart to remove Allen as my chair. However, there'd been an informal dinner discussing *changes* before fall quarter. I explained the project we'd been working on with the historical society and needing to see it completed. I was worried Allen would be vindictive enough to dump it all on Nick and Missy. Dr. Everhart agreed that it was the right thing to do but had no intention of releasing me from my regular duties any longer than the summer. I still taught Shakespeare. I put in the grades.

Nick and I arrived late, as usual, to the society's parking lot that

Saturday morning. I hadn't been feeling well all summer. To our horror, Missy's 90's Ford wasn't the only car parked on the gravel. The *perfect professor* was back in town, apparently, from his summer sabbatical. There was no e-mail; the last response we got from him said he would be back in late August. It was still early July.

    Motherfucker.

CHAPTER 11

Indrid's Mine

GRAY

Indrid had chained me to the wall. He had been rambling about "punishment of transgressors." He had not taken my lower wings, the hindwings, yet, but it was only a matter of time. That was his favorite way of releasing his anger, cutting my wings. It would be hard to land for a few months, an inconvenience, not a death sentence for our kind. It was dim in the old mine; this was one of many that had been abandoned but never properly sealed. This was not the same place he was held for over three decades. The one he escaped. The knowledge we did not speak. I buried that one.

He had kept me here for weeks, bringing food and water when necessary but rarely speaking more than a few words. I had tried to engage him, ask him what was wrong. Historically, he would simply jump from the trees or drag me out of my nest, rip off my wings, and fly away. Indrid was violent, but not to this extreme with me.

I knew he would be visiting soon, I waited patiently.

The mate bond was barely a faint buzzing between us. It had been weeks since I last held Beloved. In the first days after our bonding, there was the attraction that turned to lust. Then it was his range of human emotions. The most poignant one was worry. That worry, it chipped away at my resolve to show Indrid patience. I would return... but Ezra did not know that.

Something landed hard and entered the shaft. Indrid had not imprisoned me too deep, just far enough in where I would miss the sun. There was a crunching of gravel and old trash under feet. A scent of something smoky, probably more deer jerky. He did not sing or whistle. I needed to find out what was wrong. If *The Five* knew he was doing this, he risked being imprisoned again.

Looking up, I saw him in the faint light. He was not wearing his human glamour; that face always made me uncomfortable. His wings are larger than mine, presently they loomed over his head rubbing against the ceiling. Indrid's skin was slightly darker, his black hair shorter and wavier than mine. Instead of the same red tinted brown eyes common to the Winged Fold, his were a dark blue with gold. He stood taller than me, more like his sire.

He set down the water and strips of dried meat, so they were within my reach. I did not make a move to grab the items or him. His face was blank as he made no sounds. The only sound was our even breathing and steady heartbeats. The malice in his eyes ran centuries deep. I do not think I could help Indrid heal; that would be his journey.

Sighing as my human did with frequency, I asked, "Ind, why am I here?"

Frowning, he folded his arms across his chest in displeasure. "*Little bug*, why wouldn't you be here? You've broken our rules. The same rules I dismissed that sent me to the hills, or did *you* forget?"

"I have not done what you did. I am..." Pausing I realized he knew about Ezra. "He is my mate, Indrid. You know the rules are different."

"Bullshit!" Indrid hissed. "He's not your mate. We, *little bug*, don't get fucking mates. We get pain. We get hurt. We get to be alone."

I watched him seethe as he paced. I wanted him to talk; it appeared I was going to get a sermon. I had heard this before, Indrid believed our kind to be incapable of love. He never paid attention to the stories from the last world, the old world, of mating or compatibility with humans. He believed in fucking and fighting with occasional murder to satiate what the other two did not.

"You're a liar, *little bug*. What's wrong, did you need your dick sucked? Remember the last time I got my cocks wet?" He laughed at his own horrors. I did not believe he enjoyed that memory, the event that led to his punishment.

"I remember, brother. That is not what is happening." I leaned back, trying to look relaxed. "It is hard to describe. At first, I kept smelling this... rain that was not falling. Then I saw him. He was brighter than the others..." Indrid abruptly cut me off.

"A human with essence, yes, Gray, we've all seen them. Very pretty, their cunts taste good, too." The last part came out as a snarl.

Cringing at his words, I shook my head no. "Ind. It is more than that. We bonded."

Indrid snorted. "You started to bond. Keeping you here breaks whatever thin connection you made."

"That is why I am here? To break the bond with my mate?" I was startled by the cruelty of it. Indrid despised our kind. He was known for his ruthlessness. He has killed Winged Folk and humans alike but had never been found guilty enough to deserve the *final night, execution*. I would not let them sentence him to *that*. Instead, I asked to be bound by my honor to be his watcher.

"You," his voice was a low growl, "made me lose her. If you would've let them take my wings, I could've returned in time."

Frowning, I leaned in, "Indrid, there was no returning to your lover after what you did. You freed her. You freed her younglings." Indrid roared, I flinched, waiting for the blow.

"I. DID. NOTHING!" His screams filled the dark corners, white flashing teeth and claws came toward me. "HE DIED. I suffered the chain for years and he still died."

His lover's eldest son had walked into the veil after a car accident while away at college. I had been keeping track of her and the young boys while Indrid was punished for revealing us to humans and murdering one. Three years in the hill, the boy had tragically died, and the human lover with her younger boys left the mountains forever. I did not know where they went. I did not tell Indrid for 17 years. I deserved his anger.

"It was not your fault. There was nothing you could have done to change what happened." My attempts to soothe him fell short.

"You don't know that. Maybe she would've stayed if she knew I could keep the rest safe." He paced in agitation. "It doesn't matter. Humans don't live long. She's probably dead, the others old men now."

"Then why am I here?" My question came out softly, soothing his beast.

"Why are you here? Isn't it obvious, *little bug*? I want you to share my experience. Humans are fickle creatures. It won't be long until he decides you were a dream or better, you abandoned him. The bond has already faded to a trickle; he doesn't notice it. He won't stick around for long. There's no way you can find him when he leaves the mountains. Not without breaking your vows." Indrid's smile was all sharp edges, his eyes flared with the wrath he kept close to his heart.

"It was easier when you simply ripped my hindwings off, brother." Sitting up taller, no longer looking the part of the captive. Indrid shackled me in iron that was meant for our kind, to bind our essence. He was unaware that Keepers could access additional essence in the land. That flow eroded the bindings in the cuffs. It had taken several weeks, but soon I would snap them off to return to Beloved.

Indrid continued observing me. "Yes, I've been doing some *spring cleaning* and realized I should redecorate a bit." Indrid lunged with an old ax, pinning me face down to the ground. *How the fuck did I miss him holding an ax?* I internally chastised, reminding myself it would be easier to let him cut the wings off than fight. The sooner he did it, the sooner I would leave.

The first slice of my flesh was agonizing under the dulled blade. He gripped my left forewing, holding it taut as he hacked away at the base. He had found the dullest fucking blade on this side of the mountains. The space around us filled with my screams; he wanted me to be in agony. Again and again, he swung down through the thickest part of the wing root. Showered in my own blood, I shivered in my own anger. He dropped the ax, placing a foot between my should blades. With a loud grunt, he pulled the wing free leaving a bloody, mangled stump.

Tears ran down my face. I hissed, gasping for air. He had removed only one of my wings. He grabbed my shoulder, wrenching me up to grab the other forewing. The movement put enough strain on the cuffs, metal cracked and disintegrated. He paused in shock, before I heaved him across the narrow tunnel. He hit the wall with a sickening thump. His ax clattered to the ground in the fall next to me. Indrid did not move but that did not mean he was unconscious.

"Enough, brother." I winced, standing up, feeling blood flow down my back. "No more games. I hurt you. I know. I am sorry. I thought I was protecting you. I thought what I was doing was right. If you want to die, then do it, but do not ask me to help."

Indrid lay there as I assessed the damage to my being. The wing he had removed had been destroyed in his fury. The durable yet delicate membranes torn. The bones that made up the finer structure shattered. Even the hooked claw hung at an odd angle, looking like a finger bent the wrong way.

I would not be able to fly away. It would take a fortnight to regrow my forewing and only that quickly because of my connection to the Well. If I had not been The Keeper, it would have taken months to regenerate this kind of loss.

This is the damage killed Winged Folk, it made us prey instead of hunter. I dropped to the ground, grunting upon impact. The dried meat he had brought me was scattered in the dirt. I picked up a piece, gingerly chewing it. I was not only hungry, but I was weak with a now missing wing. Indrid stirred under my scrutiny. Pushing himself up into a sitting position, his face unnervingly blank.

Rivulets of blood came from his hairline near the temple. He did not blink, sitting in silence. The longer we were locked in this battle the more I believed he had completely lost his way. If that were true, then I was equally at fault for it. I knew he had always resented me; I looked too much like my sire and not enough like his sibling.

"Will you tell The Five?" His voice was like gravel.

"No. I will not play a part in your death wish." I took another large bite and chewed harder than necessary.

"It doesn't matter what I do? You won't end me?" He leaned back against the wall and closed his eyes.

I did not know what to say. I could feel a liquid burning sensation in the back of my eyes. Daggers of sorrow. Since mating with Ezra, I felt many things differently. Not because we folk cannot feel, but I had been closed off for too long. I was told for ages that I was pathetic and fragile. I had believed it. I had listened to my sire. I had allowed him to raise his claws against me, too. I felt my eyes brim with the unshed hurts, teetering to fall.

This is grief, I thought.

"I am not mad when a snake bites me or a bird shits on my shoulder. Why would I be angry with you?" A tear trailed down my cheek.

He snorted. "I'm bird shit, Gray?"

"No, but you are your nature. Same as me. You can pretend as much as you want that our territory is unimportant to you. I know you hunt the eastern borders. I know you have kept our cousins in line when they *visit*." Shrugging, I did not know what else to say.

"Ah, not bird shit. I'm full of shit then?" He huffed.

"We are all that is left of our modor's line," I whispered. The words hung heavily in the air like smoke. An issue not discussed, ever. We were both young, with millennia ahead of us, but in the end, he was my last direct blood kin as was I to him. Picking up another piece of jerky, I offered it to him. He nodded, and I tossed it to his open claws.

"I really fucked up that wing, it's not presentable to hang." He took a bite. "Too ugly."

With a huff, I slid down a little. "Ah, forgive me for not ripping along the seams better."

He lifted his lip in a semi-smile, showing a bit of fang. "You're an inconsiderate cunt, aren't you?"

Picking up the ax, I threw it at the wall next to his head. Despite the blood loss and lack of water, my strength forced the blunted edge deeply into jagged rock. He did not comment, continuing to eat his dried meat. Rolling my shoulders, another gush of warmth slid down my back. I would need somewhere to rest for a day or two. I would need him to not fight me until the wound closed.

102

"Are you going to kill me today, Indrid?" Knowing he would be honest in this.

"No." He took another bite.

"Tomorrow then, brother?" I titled my head, watching his face in the shadows.

"No, nor the day after, *little bug*." He took in a long breath. "If I kill you, then what will I do? The humans are not as interesting, they bleed out too quickly. How's that entertaining? I can torture you for weeks, yet you could still take my head if you wanted." Indrid gestured to the blade in the wall.

"I am glad my heartiness makes me useful to you, dear brother." I rubbed my shoulder, a deep ache now.

"Not useful, I like to prolong pain. You take it so well." His voice was brittle. "The last one died too quickly. I barely finished on his face in time."

Scowling at his words, the memory of that night was clear. It had been a horrific death, a worse clean up. We burned the body Indrid had brutally fucked and torn apart. The Winged Folk had whispered about it for decades. Some of them were eager to see bloodshed in such a way, worshipping Indrid's chaos. Others simply fascinated that he spilled his seed on the corpse in defiance. All had kept their distance upon his official release from his confinement in the cave, which was probably the most reasonable thing they could do.

The human who died was a monster, yes, but we were not his watcher. We could not dole out justice on humankind. That was our law. That was why we left to this new place centuries ago. This is why we had The Five. Indrid would continue to do as he pleased, and likely be left unpunished for most of it. It was all too common for humans to get *lost* in the woods to never be found. That was also very much our custom, our way with them.

"Brother." I waited until he gave me his attention. "You will vow on the blood that has been spilled, a blood shared, that you will not harm Ezra Williams in any way."

Indrid swayed his head from side-to-side, slowly whispering, "What will you do, *little bug*?"

"Vow it to me, Indrid. Vow it on our modor's wings and essence itself." My jaw clenched. I would kill him here.

"Will you kill me, *little bug*? The last of your blood kin..." his voice trailed off.

"Vow it, Indrid. Say the words." My anger was rising, blood flow slowing. Essence began to buzz around my clawed fingertips. "Say the fucking vow, Indrid."

"I want to taste his blood, *little bug*." He raised his hands, wings shifting behind him. "I want to know what his inside look like. Oh, to hear his moans, probably the same squeals when you stuff him. Ah, I would like to fuck his open throat." Indrid's face was a caricature of a wild smile. "I probably won't have time. I broke the bond. Don't you remember what that means, *little bug*? The stories of what happens to our *mates*?"

Wavering a little as I stood, I stalked toward him. He stayed firmly planted on the ground, grinning up at me like a skull. I caged him in with my arms. A single wing flared while the stump of the other ached. With fangs bared, eyes growing bloodier-looking with each passing moment, I towered over him. My talons grew to their full-length as I drug them down the stones, pieces flying free.

Indrid did not move as I drew in, now eye-to-eye. A single needle like claw slammed into his throat from the side. His body stiffened, choking out a spray of dark blood. I left it in there as more oozed out of the hole. He bared his fangs at me, making no move to fight what I was about to do. He would prefer things were forced on him, easier than making choices.

"Indrid of the Dark Waters, you are compelled by blood and stone to never harm the one called Ezra Williams, mate to Gray The Keeper of the Mist and Hills. With these words, you are bound." I felt the Well reach up and cover Indrid with faint gold before pulling away. He hissed as I removed my claw. He immediately spat a mouthful of blood in my face, forcing me away with clenched fists. Silently, he fled the tunnel after coercing me, once again, to make decisions for him.

Again, to be the villain in his stories. Again, I was left alone.

CHAPTER 12

Rebound

EZRA

Dinner with Rich wasn't going well. He looked unreasonably tired for summer session. This was usually his favorite time of year, mostly because it was his birthday, and he gave fuck all when it came to student attendance. His classes were filled with entrenched majors and grad students. They either all showed up or didn't bother. The ones that did come to class appeared haggard, working more than sleeping.

He'd made dinner, staying unusually quiet until he decided silence wasn't helping his mood. He informed me of his displeasure that I was working on Allen's project. He was irritated I'd used that as an excuse to not switch chairs until the fall. He was absolutely disgusted I hadn't worked on my portfolio in weeks. I hadn't added a line to anything, my heart just... couldn't. I hadn't told him about Gray, or the terrifying things we'd found in the estate collection. I didn't know how.

I kept my head down for most of the lecturing, accepting it as something I needed to hear. He was correct, partially. While Nick had passed the course, his scholarship was renewed, the newfound freedom from Allen changed him. He seemed more determined to catch the bastard in the act, by playing little lamb so we could snare the rabid, feral wolf. We agreed to continue to work every weekend with Missy. Missy had decided we were both her grandsons now, showering us with clearly needed attention.

"What is it that keeps you working there, Ezra? I don't understand." The sternness in his tone startled me. He hadn't used that voice since Dad died.

Attempting to act nonchalantly I told him. "It's interesting, I guess. You know I like avoiding what I should be doing by being helpful. Plus, Nick's become a good friend." *Nick's become my accomplice to catch the bastard.*

My mind wandered at that thought. I thought of hunting him, Allen. I could picture it, Allen racing through the woods bloody. Terrified. He'd stumble over branches or rocks. Making too much noise, easy to find him. I'd let him wear himself out a bit before I approached. I wanted him to have enough strength to fight back. I wanted him to experience the primal terror when he knew he'd lost.

I'd tear into him, fang and claw. His blood would feel hot and slippery running down my throat. My cock stiffened. I wanted to feast and fuck. I'd leave nothing discernible behind, just ribbons of flesh and entrails. Perhaps chunks of meat for the scavengers. Let his bones rot beneath the leaves, forgotten to the mountains.

"Are you and Nick seeing each other?" Rich's face was a mixture of curiosity and concern. "You don't date younger."

"What..." I glanced back to Rich from my plate, which I'd barely touched.

His question pulled me back to the conversation. Now I had to answer Rich with a painfully hard erection and the slight discomfort that I continued to fantasize about murdering my professor. Rich had caught me zoning out. He looked worried... and sad.

"Ez, sweetie." His face cracked into grief as he moved out of his chair to come to me. He cupped my face in his big, warm hands, searching my eyes. *Fuck*, he's concerned.

"I'm okay, Rich," I lied.

"You're not. You look like shit." He stopped, thinking about how to continue. "You're not eating, it looks like you haven't slept in weeks. You're not writing... Ezra, the last time this happened..." He didn't have to finish.

The last time this happened, I'd ended up in the emergency room, dehydrated with premature ventricular contractions. The hospital called a psych consult on me because I was *high risk*. I told them that was bullshit. Rich stepped in, promised to watch me for 72-hours so I wouldn't have to be transferred to Columbus for *further evaluation*. I'd agreed to grief and loss counseling through the campus health center. It'd helped to talk, I guess.

He wasn't wrong now. I knew I looked paler, lost some weight. I'd been staying awake all night in hopes Gray would return. That didn't mean I could sleep all day. Dark circles under my eyes attested to that bad habit. The first two weeks after my night with Gray, I vomited throughout the day. At first, I thought maybe I was pregnant. I took a few pregnancy tests to check. The results were negative, either that or human tests couldn't pick up magical moth babies.

My stomach still frequently hurt. I was eating far less than before. Pooka tried to feed me my own trash, a worried look on their little owl face. They curled up against my stomach and chest when I was having the worse of the spasms. Their warmth made it somewhat easier. My hair was duller looking. I didn't always shave, leaving patchy stubble on my jaw and cheeks. I looked more like a shade from myths than a living human.

Rich kneeled, making me feel wicked, he was getting on his bad knee. Rich put his hands on my shoulders pulling me in closer. His eyes looked glassy, tears forming. I didn't think I looked that bad, I mean I wasn't crying about it. I almost said the joke, but he broke the silence first.

"Honey, what's wrong?" He gently squeezed my shoulder as he brushed my shaggy hair from my face. Another thing I'd neglected. "You can tell me... or not. You can stay here, yeah? That helped before."

I started shaking my head no and then realized tears were falling. I didn't know why I was crying. I always crying around this man. He didn't deserve to have all this grief poured over him. He had his own life. His own sadness. He didn't need to collect mine once a week until I graduated and moved away.

Pulling me into his arms, my face was pressed against his neck.

"My stomach hurts all the time," I sniffed. "I don't know what's wrong. I can't eat."

He rubbed my back. "You're sick? How long?"

I stilled against him, tears trickling down my face. "I don't know. I don't sleep at night because it hurts. I threw up for a few weeks, that stopped. I thought it's getting better." *I miss Gray, my heart's broken.*

He kissed the side of my head. "Okay. It's okay, Ez. We'll get you into my PCP tomorrow to see what they think. I'll go with you, promise."

I hadn't moved from the safe, warm spot on his shoulder. I missed my dad so much right now. My eyes burned fresh. I choked on a sob. Again, poor Rich took care of me like the child he never had but would have been the perfect parent to. Like Missy, he filled in the pieces of love I was missing in my adult life.

As I pulled away to tell him how much I appreciated him, how much I loved him, searing white hot pain flared through my shoulder blade, lighting up my back. It was extreme agony tearing me to pieces. Gasping for air, I flailed my arms out, pushing Rich away. My stomach immediately cramped and tightened. I'd eaten just enough to cover the ground with more than bile.

I don't remember getting on the floor. I was on my hands and knees, retching as the unbearable, jagged tearing continued down my back. My vision blacked out as someone started screaming. My stomach was being gutted, slowly. I wanted to curl up into myself. Every muscle was contracting while I gasped for air. I choked every time I felt the stab in my shoulder.

It abruptly stopped, starting to recede. I panted, lying in my own vomit, tears and snot covered my face. Rich was on the phone, voice panicked, hovering over me. Afraid to touch. He was afraid his touch would hurt me. My vision blurred, my body lock up, then nothing.

"Ezra! Ezra, honey, open your eyes." Someone was calling out to me, my eyes too heavy to open. I wanted to sleep. Someone was holding me up on my side. Their hands pressed gently on my arm. "Ezra, please." There was another voice, it sounded smaller.

"No, he's not waking up," the closer voice sobbed. "Please, get here now. Please, I can't lose him, too." That voice was familiar. I tried opening my eyes, groaning instead.

"Ezra? Kiddo?" The voice was closer, but not louder.

My tongue was heavy and numb. "I... I..."

"Shhh, it's okay. I'm here. The ambulance is coming. You're going to be okay." The voice tight with panic.

Nothing made sense, and I was wet. "I... I'm..." Trying to catch my breath. "Wet."

"Oh, honey. It's okay." The voice a soothing tone. "It's okay, we'll get you cleaned up soon. Just rest."

I pressed my forehead on the cool flooring, letting out a soft moan. Everything hurt. A constant dull ache through every part of me. I thought I heard sirens. *Why are there sirens?* The voice told me he'd be back. "Don't move." I didn't. I heard voices and felt hands on me. Something tight around my bicep, something pinched my other arm. I thought I saw a flash of light.

I caught bits of what was being said.

"What drugs is he taking?"

"He's sick, how fucking dare you!"

"Looks like a seizure. Wet his pants. How long has he been sick? History of seizures? Are you two dating?"

"No, I'm his father."

"Medical history?"

The voice I recognized sounded angry. I wanted to tell him it's okay; I just needed a nap. I couldn't think of the right words, so I breathed out slowly again, letting the dark wrap around me.

EVERYTHING WAS NUMB. A dull ache sat in the back of my skull. My mouth tasted of cotton balls and old bile. My eyes were heavy. I heard someone murmuring near me. I cleared my throat; it felt like I'd swallowed sand mixed with shards of metal. The voices stopped. I felt something touch my hand. Its large warmth encompassing mine.

"Ezra," the voice sounded hesitant. "Kiddo, you there?"

I tried to clear my throat again, battling my eyelids to force open. When I defeated the leaden weight, my vision was blurry. Like someone had put Vaseline over my eyeballs. I tried to lift my arms, but they still felt numb and useless. I was blinking and squinting, staring up at the blurry face before me.

"Hey kiddo," a thumb gently stroked my face, pushing hair back, "there you are. Had me worried."

"Hmmm?" I didn't know what he was talking about, but the touch was grounding. I didn't want the warmth to leave, I was so cold.

"You're sick, kiddo. You had some sort of episode at the house. We're in the hospital." Another voice cut in. A second blurry figure appeared on the other side of me.

"Mr. Williams, do you remember what happened?" the new voice asked, higher pitched and grating. Suddenly, it felt like the sun was burning through my corneas, I screamed. My voice ragged. I tried to get away. *Fuck, it hurt so much.* The grating voice was calling for something. I felt two warm arms wrap around my biceps to settle me.

"Hey now," they said gently. "It's done. No more. Shhh, kiddo."

My face pressed into a warm chest. There was a lingering scent of aftershave mingling in with sweat. It was safe. I was safe. No more light. It's so hard to think.

I want to go home. I want Rich. Where's Rich? I tensed up, panic seeping into me.

"I... I... I..." Choking on fear I continued. "I need..." I tensed more.

"Honey, it's okay. What do you need?" The voice a soothing balm to my escalating fear. Other voices joined the room. I couldn't hear what was being said.

"I need, I need, I need..." I couldn't remember what I needed.

"Slowly, Ezra. Slow." The body holding me rocked a little, breathing evenly for me to follow.

"I need..." Acid hotness was in my eyes. I gasped, "I need Rich."

There was a stifled gasp. "Sweetie, I'm right here. I'm holding you." They squeezed me gently.

"Oh. Oh." I couldn't get out any more words as I leaned into Rich. "Oh."

"Are you in pain, Ez?" his voice soft.

"Hurt," I hissed, trying to straighten in bed. "Hurt... every."

The murmuring of voices continued talking about tests, high blood pressure, odd bruising, possible seizure, still waiting on tests, transfer, cancer. The last word echoed in my mind. *Cancer. Cancer. Cancer.* The thing that kept destroying my life was possibly eating me away.

More hands were on me, but I refused to let Rich go. Someone tilted my head enough to put something over my face. The air felt cold. I pressed my face back to his chest when they released me. I was shivering, more weight was placed on my legs. Then I started to feel light. I tried to open my eyes, say something. I couldn't, I was suddenly too tired. I felt myself being settled back, the warmth of Rich's body never completely leaving me.

I WAS DREAMING. I was floating in the woods, and it looked familiar but not. It was night, the moon full and vivid through trees. I felt—no, sensed—something moving slowly through the underbrush. They were dragging them self through the dirt, periodically hissing. Their gait was lumbering, a limp as they held their shoulder.

Whoever it was froze to look around then sniffed the air. I didn't have a body, I still shuddered at the sight. They knew I was watching them, following them. They were hurt. Who'd hurt them? Their shoulder felt like hot iron had been poured in it, like mine. Their back ached, like mine. Their stomach felt empty and cramped, like mine. The simmering anger bubbled under the surface, like mine.

They started moving faster, ignoring their pain, walking down a path I knew. That was the trail to Rich's house. The one the deer use the most. They moved faster than I could, faster than the deer did. I saw them hover near the porch, sniffing again. They leaped over the banister, landing at the door. With little force, the door was pushed open, frame cracking.

Somehow, I was able to follow them. They stood in the kitchen, littered with medical packaging, body fluids. The mess I made of Rich's kitchen. They wavered a little, before holding themself up by the counter. Their anger intensified. An icy rage that would consume everything it touched, spilling blood and ending life.

"Beloved," they whispered. They were talking to me. I couldn't answer. "I am sorry, Beloved, this is my fault." The rage dissipated into a chasm of sadness. "Beloved. I am sorry. I will find you. Please stay awake. Do not go into the deepest dark. This is my fault, but I can change it. You must stay awake. YOU. MUST. OPEN. YOUR. EYES!"

I gasped, my eyes flying open. There was a push of something. Like a small ball of heat, straight to my chest. I warmed a little as my vision cleared. Rich was in a chair next to me; he'd dozed off, but startled awake when I moved. He reached over to clasp my hands.

"Kiddo, you're awake. That's good." He studied my face, looking for something.

I looked away, searching the room for some clue as to where I was. There were medical machines beeping. I was lying in a hospital bed, hooked up to machines and tubes. IVs and wires going in me, on me, holding me together.

My head and back vaguely throbbed, part of me remembered that it'd been worse. There was a window facing toward the river, the sun lazily rising. I looked back at Rich.

"Wha... what happened?" My voice was torn up like when I thought it was a good idea to smoke cloves and drink whiskey all night.

"We were having dinner and you told me you had been sick. Then you collapsed in pain. It looked like a seizure, but so far, all the tests still have to be reviewed by a doctor. We're waiting on transport, but now the hospital in Columbus says they don't have a bed open." He sounded bitter.

"Oh, I feel better." That wasn't a complete lie.

"You're lucid," he sighed. "I'm kinda surprised; they've had you on a lot of meds for the pain and anxiety."

"Me," I tried to feign surprised. "Anxious? Never."

Rich huffed, "Right? When are grad students anxious?" His attempt at a smile was weak. A panic lurked in his eyes.

"I feel better, though." I said, an attempt at sounding positive. "Maybe I can just go home and follow up with a doctor tomorrow?"

"Ez..." The lines around his eyes and mouth had deepened since dinner. "It's really bad. You can't go home yet." He stroked my hand. "I'm not going to leave, okay? You'll never be alone in any of this. Don't worry about school, or work, or rent. I'll take care of everything until you feel better."

His guilt was shining through like the rays of the early morning sunshine currently peeking through the clouds outside. I mirrored that weak smile back. Something kept whispering that I needed to stay awake and go home. I'd be okay if I could get home, no, go back to Rich's house. I'd be okay there. We needed to leave the hospital.

"Why don't you try to sleep some more, hmmm, get rest?" He started rubbing my forehead like dad used to when I was sick as a kid. Mom did it before she died, too.

"I'm not really tired. I want to stay awake." I relaxed into his warmth. I felt so cold, and I realized there was something in my dick. "What's in my dick?"

Rich coughed a laugh. "A catheter."

A FEW HOURS LATER, a small team of doctors came in to discuss the findings of my imaging and blood work. Their grim faces were not the harbingers of good news that I wanted. I remember that look when I was with my dad at his diagnosis appointment. There was a pause before they told me *it* was terminal. I was going to die. They shut the door, so we'd have privacy. Rich squeezed my hand, a tremor from his hand to mine.

The attending nurse told me I was in end stage renal failure. They couldn't detect the cause but would need to start me on dialysis immediately. It explained the issues with my stomach and heart, and the bruising and seizure from last night. I would need more blood work and imaging to rule out cancer completely, but at this time that wasn't what they suspected. I would have to be put on a transplant list. If I declined dialysis, they would have a social worker discuss hospice options.

"Can I go home now?" I blurted before thinking better of it. Rich was a statue next to me.

"Ez..." he hissed, squeezing my hand harder than he probably had meant to. "Kiddo, I know this is a lot, but we have to *talk* about it. We need to make sure the cabin is safe for you while you recover." Going back to my apartment was clearly not a talking point.

"Mr. Williams, we would need to do dialysis today if that is the treatment plan. If you'd prefer to return home on hospice—" Rich stopped the doctor mid-sentence.

"No, that's *not* an option." He looked at me. "This isn't automatic death, Ez. We can still *do* something. It's not too late." Tears filled his eyes. He was going to break down with an audience.

I looked at the doctor. "No, I'm sorry. I... I'll do the dialysis, but I want to go home soon. I don't want to stay here. Whatever you gave me, I hurt less now. I'd feel better at home, with Rich." I added, "I got lucky enough to get a second dad who'll take care of me."

A tear trickled down his cheek. He leaned over, pulling me into a loose hug, mindful of my bruising and soreness. He kissed me on the crown of my head. "I'll always take care of you, sweetie, always."

They had me do a dialysis treatment, agreeing to discharge me to Rich with home health following up later. Rich was paying out of pocket some exorbitant fee, according to the social worker, to have someone there quickly and frequently. They took out the catheter, which hurt like a bitch, only to realize too late that I'd some type of bladder issues. I pissed on myself and the floor, not realizing it until my sock felt warm.

The doctor told me it happens with the disease process; I'd need a catheter on an ongoing basis. I kept nodding. My head felt fuzzy, my stomach ached after the treatment. I was exhausted and wanted to go home.

I needed to stay awake but couldn't remember why. We were discharged after dinner. Rich told me he was put on leave from the university and was filing paperwork to take a six-month sabbatical.

I needed to get home.

CHAPTER 13

The Wood

GRAY

E zra was watching me from the in between of worlds. He was sleeping in the veil, a place no human should be. Sometimes they find their way during death. Sometimes they walk there through their essence. Often, they get trapped.

Beloved was following me as I stumbled from mine entrance down the sloping hill. I vaguely knew the area as a place Indrid frequently haunted. There were few humans living out here; I never thought he bothered them.

As I stumbled in pain, I followed a worn trail. This was near the home where I had seen Ezra sleep. The older man there was a parent of some sort, not his sire but something akin. He was affectionate to Ezra. He fed him. Made sure he stayed warm. I sensed devotion there. I smelled traces of Indrid around the property. Fresher tracks now.

Ezra's presence lingered with me as I approached the deck. I smelled multiple living bodies in this area, recently here. There were harsh chemical smells, exhaust, and a tracking in of mud to the house. The door was locked as I slammed my weight into it, the wood frame splitting under my force. I had no intention of being careful, to stay concealed. I smelled Beloved inside.

The door swung open, and a stench of decay hit me. A sweetly sick smell combined with Ezra's scent. It was not mixed with, I realized; it *was* his scent. Changed again. He was dying.

I grabbed what essence I could, pushing my thoughts to him. His cooling energy danced at the tips of my claws. Even with death suffocating him, he was a bright source of energy.

"Beloved," I whispered, knowing he could not answer. "I am sorry, Beloved, this is my fault." A cascade of rage and sadness pulsed through me. I could not lose him, not like this. "Beloved. I am sorry. I will find you. Please stay awake. Do not go into the deepest dark. This is my fault. I can change it. You must stay awake. YOU. MUST. OPEN. YOUR. EYES!"

Graining in pain, my legs buckling under me. I grabbed onto the counter to hold myself up earlier—I nearly went down into the mess on the floor. His vomit and traces of urine. Garbage from whatever human intervention they attempted. It would not change his sickness. There was no cure, his body was dying.

Our bond had been more advanced than I thought. I had not completed it with him, his form could not handle the large amount of essence he was attracting. He was of it but not enough to counteract the rebound effect. A Keeper's direct line to the source at all times is too much for most mortal bodies. We had bonded and his body was being inundated. Our Elders warn us of this. Mating should not be rushed. I should have never left him.

Liquid fire of rage flowed up. Indrid knew it would kill him. He fucking knew Ezra would not survive a lapse in our mating. I would do more than silence Indrid with a binding. I would do more than take a fucking wing or an eye. Indrid would suffer my claw. I would not release him to death. I would never allow him peace.

Squeezing my hands so tightly, blood rained to the floor. Droplets trickled from both fists, adding to the vileness of the rebound's after-effects. I pulled my shoulders back. Closing my eyes, I looked for the tether between the source in the territory and myself. Between breaths, I severed it. That would be the only way to ensure Ezra did not get sicker before I found him.

I imagine this was one of Indrid's many possible plans. To either murder Ezra or cause me to relinquish my power.

He underestimated my abilities. He defied my position. He did not think I would bind him so cruelly for his doings. *Little bug,* I grumbled. I let him think he was in control. I submitted to the abuse over the years. Modor had asked me to protect him, knowing what his path would be. I made a promise, not an oath.

With the remaining essence I had, I cleared the home of filth, repairing the damaged door. That left me woozy. I did not have to worry about other Winged Folk finding me for now. I did not worry about predators while I stayed in the human's home. I shuffled to the back, finding a spare room. It looked less lived in than the other with the scents of others fainter here.

I sat down, the bed sinking under my weight. My skin rippled as I shifted. Thankfully I did not require essence to shift into familiar forms. I had played human enough in the past. I was wearing my breeches, stained with blackened blood. I had no shoes, no shirt. My hair hung limp around my shoulders, a dirty blond.

Unlike my brother, when I learned to shift, I wanted to look human, not human adjacent. I was considered beautiful, yes, in this form, but not in a disruptive way. I looked around the room. I imagined I looked frightful, like someone had been torturing me. I could not summon the energy to care or change it. I leaned back on the bed and sunk in further. It was an old, soft mattress. Sleep took me, I did not think I would sleep until they arrived home.

Voices came from outside. The one that alarmed me was Beloved's. It sounded ragged and exhausted. He must be in agony. I needed to bond us quickly, reverse whatever damage was done. We would both heal when I linked back to the Well. That was another thing Indrid did not understand. I no longer needed The Five to aid me in my connection. *I* summoned the mountains and the trees.

The front door opened; I heard shuffling. The older man, I could not remember his name, was telling Ezra to lay down in the living room. They were waiting for supplies of some kind. He said he would clean the kitchen while they waited and get something to drink. I sat up in the bed and waited.

Do I go out there and explain myself? Would Beloved recognize me? I did not want to shock the other human. I did enter his home without permission and slept there. That would be enough to distress the older man. Maybe he would shoot me with that rifle. I would not blame him after what I had done.

Standing up quietly, I entered the hall. I listened to their conversation. The older man was startled saying something about paramedics cleaning up for him. He sounded pleased there was not the filth of decay on his floor. I appreciate a clean human. Beloved needed to learn those skills.

"Ez, do you want some water? I know they said low sodium, but you could probably have some juice..." His voice trailed off.

Beloved cleared his throat. "Water is fine, Rich. Really."

I could not see Beloved where he sat, I knew the moment I moved into the light they would both respond to me. How they would react, I did not know. I could see *Rich* in the kitchen, his back toward the doorway. I breezed past, entering the larger area where Ezra was sitting, staring at the empty hearth. He looked and smelled like grave dirt.

"Beloved," I whispered.

He jolted, turning to see me standing there. He blinked a few times, not saying a word, taking in my form as I was. Did he miss my wings? My antlers? Perhaps the impressive height. Did he want two cocks instead of one? He frowned, rubbing a hand over his eyes.

"Why do you look like that?" his voice quiet, eyes locking with mine.

I heard a hiss, and something drop to the ground. Something wet and cold hit my feet. I swung around to see Rich, wide eyes quickly turning to anger. Before he could say a word, Ezra clapped his hands loudly.

"No, don't." Rich froze, askance written all over his face. Ezra pointed at me. "Rich, this is Gray. They're my mate."

Rich made a sound somewhere between a choke and a laugh. "No. I won't allow it, Ezra. He's why you're sick. He's killing you."

Lifting my hands up in a gesture of surrender. "Our incomplete bond is ending his life. I severed my line to the Well, but I need to complete the bond to heal us... both of us."

Rich sneered. "And what the fuck is wrong with you, moth demon?"

"Rich." Ezra took a breath then looked confused. "You know about the Winged Folk? How?"

Yes, Rich, how? I thought about Indrid's old tracks. I knew he had been wandering this valley for a few decades now. He would sometimes stay in this area for days, but I never heard any reports of a creature in the woods. No unexplained deaths or disappearances. Was he having some sort of relationship with this human? He had revealed himself yet again. *Fucking Indrid.*

"You have spoken with my brother, Indrid?" I asked blandly. Indrid played chess when the rest of us were still learning checkers. I sagged to the floor. The lack of essence was wearing on me.

Rich's look was surprised. "Indrid's your brother?"

I huffed in irritation. "Half-brother. We have different sires. He murdered his, I stopped mine from killing our modor and him. What has he told you of me? That I am evil? That I control him? That I have hurt him?"

"Something along those lines, yes." Rich crossed his arms over his chest. "And what's your story, then?"

"A long one, and maybe I will tell you if you would like to listen. I am more concerned about Beloved's welfare than whether or not you care for me." I stood back up, turning toward Beloved. "I am sorry, my love. I did not know how strong our bond had already become."

"You left me." His voice so quiet even with my hearing I almost missed it. "Why'd you leave me?" Tears welled in his eyes as his face crumpled.

My heart stopped as cold dread filled me. "No, love. I did not. Indrid, he... Fuck." What do I say that explains what happened but not upset the other human? He seems to have a fondness for that *asshole.* "Indrid and I have had our issues. He decided to imprison me, to keep us apart. He had hoped you would leave, and I would suffer for it."

"He wanted to kill Ezra?" Rich said behind me.

I shrugged. "He did not say that plainly, but I think he was watching Ezra. I think he saw the bond was brighter, something I was too slow to see myself."

"Your brother wants me dead?" Ezra was louder, angrier.

"Indrid wants chaos and pain. I do not think he personally wants Ezra Williams dead. He wants me to suffer." My gaze roamed over Ezra's body. "It is complicated, four centuries of complications..."

Ezra looked so much smaller than the last time I had held him. I leaped over the couch in a fluid motion that surprised Ezra and Rich. I needed to see him up close. Ezra was wearing sweats with a bag full of piss attached to his leg. I frowned, stopping myself from reaching for the bag. What was happening to his body? I crouched down on the floor and looked up into his face. Even in death, he looked beautiful. There was the swirling essence under his skin, darker from sickness but still vibrant enough. His body refused to succumb.

Ezra blushed. "I kept pissing on myself, so I have this fancy bag now."

I rested my hands on his thighs and kissed him deeply. He relaxed into the kiss and then into my arms as I wrapped myself around him. I nuzzled his throat, taking in his scent. I was wrong, death could not spoil this. It could not blemish him. I would balance us. I would give him my life if he needed it. My beautiful. My Beloved.

"Gray," Ezra murmured as I stroked his hair. "Why do you look like this?"

"I did not want to alarm Rich." I tried to mimic a smile at him over Ezra's shoulder.

"You thought a six-foot-five man in blood-stained breeches from another century, who clearly broke into his home, would be better than a giant moth?" He cocked his head, looking somewhat baffled.

"Yes..." I hesitated. "It was not better, was it?"

Ezra giggled. "No, Gray. It's somehow worse." He pulled me close to him again. "How do we fix the bond... wasn't it from..." He got quiet.

"Mating, yes. It would be quicker if we could, but I do not think your body would be receptive. I will have to tether myself to the source to reconnect to you. When I do that, I can restore your health faster, undo *this*." I cupped his face between clawed hands. "I am sorry, sweet one."

"I don't blame you." He paused. "Your brother's a dick, though."

I cringed. "Yes. I may not be much better after what I did to him in retaliation."

"Did you kill him?" Ezra hesitantly asked.

"No. Much worse for him. He cannot harm you for as long as you live. I, what the blood borns call, *cursed* him." I let my winged form shimmer back into place. Ezra gasped, running his finger down my cheekbone to my bottom lip. He leaned in and gently sucked on it. It took every ounce of will to stop the moan. When his eyes refocused, a look of shock erased the earlier calm.

"Gray, your wing is gone." Ezra sounded horrified.

"Yes, Indrid's work." I turned to Rich. "May we use the back room? I need to lay with him for some time." Scooping Beloved up in my arms, I began to walk around the couch.

"Yes..." Rich paused. "Home health is supposed to be coming up in an hour to deliver supplies and check on Ezra."

"Tell them I'm asleep and they can come back tomorrow." Ezra rubbed into my throat, scenting me. I was not sure if he was aware of what he had just done, scenting is not a human behavior. Rich nodded as I walked away.

I gently laid him on the bed first, settling beside him. He quickly nestled into my arms, facing me. I kissed his forehead, cheeks, and quickly on his lips. The abrupt connection would cause him pain, it would be quick, but the intensity of it is like shattering into fire. I stroked his back, watching him relax in my embrace. How I wanted this weeks ago, how we had had it briefly.

"This will be excruciating for a moment." I watched his face as I explained, "The process is difficult when reestablishing this kind of power. Because I am... because of my role in my world, I have a stronger link to the Well. That is why we mated so quickly, why you became so ill. The Well is a great, ancient power source. I flooded you with this primordial force. I will do my best to keep as much of the pain away as possible, but it will hurt."

He nodded. "I'm dying, Gray. Nothing hurts more than that."

I grimaced; living always hurts more than death. That is a lesson that comes with age, and he was still so very young, even for his kind. I reached out to the well, it greeted me like an old friend. I felt the tingle of reconnecting. I felt the soil, the air, the rivers, the trees, the bones in the hills, the ghosts along the ridge, the mountains so old they had forgotten their age. I felt connected to the other Folk; my awareness continued to expand until I was whole.

Using that awareness, I slowly pulled Ezra's essence back toward mine. His eyes were closed, he had gone pale with beads of sweat forming on his brow. His breath coming quicker. His body rigid in my hold. Slowly we joined, piece by piece. Each frayed thread spun back to a bright gold. He groaned louder this time, not in pain. He began to writhe against me, a hardness pressing into my thigh.

Our bond reconnected. I pushed in the force of the territory, healing every crack and blackened edge of his body. He groaned louder, arching in my arms. The healing was miraculous, I had never heard or seen such a thing occur. I felt my own wing bloom quickly. Every inch of beaten and cut flesh whole again. Ezra hissed.

"What, Beloved?" I kissed his sweaty brow.

"My dick, that fucking tube." I glanced down at the bag realizing it must be attached in him. I was stunned to see how it was... inserted into his softening cock.

"How do I help?" I raised my hand and felt for the device through my essence. I could see it clearly snaked down into him. With a gentle tug, the device was dissolved into the ether. The place where we throw things that disgust or anger us. Indrid may have a new home in the coming months.

Ezra gasped. "What did you do? If I piss everywhere because of it..."

I chuckled. "My love, you are whole again. If you need to piss, you should go to the toilet."

He grumbled at me before snuggling back in. "You said it would hurt but that didn't *all* hurt."

"Once the bond found itself again, it wanted to amplify. It is very euphoric, no?" I smiled into his hair.

"I want a blowjob." His words came out muffled.

I tipped his chin back. "You want me to suck your prick? Swallow you to the back of my throat? Lick up every drop of come you can give me?"

His pupils dilated and I felt his cock begin to harden again against my leg. A wave of lust vibrated through our bond and my own cocks perked up. I rolled us so he was lying flat on his back while under my body. My wings flared slightly behind me.

"Oh, you're healed, too." He reached up to touch them. I naturally moved into the embrace. He ran his fingers along the edges, finding the spots at the base of my wings. He rubbed, pressing in with the right amount of force. I rolled my throbbing cocks into his own. "Oh yeah, I remember how much you like that." His voice low, huskier.

We kissed, lazily exploring each other's mouth. Hands roamed, and clothes found their way to the floor. He came twice, once in my mouth and the second while frantically riding both of my cocks. The light within him was brighter than before. He had started to form direct connections to the Well itself, perhaps a side effect of mating a Keeper.

I realized he would experience other changes to his body, not the simple hearty and hale of a mate. I had hoped he could remain in his human life for some time longer, but now I doubted he had more than a few weeks. Maybe it was a blessing the humans thought he was dying. It would make it easier to disappear.

CHAPTER 14

Abandoned

EZRA

Since we had left the hospital on a Friday, we didn't have to worry about explaining to the dialysis people why I looked... healthy until Monday. The home health nurse came to visit, Rich being distracted her enough that she left me to *sleep*. Sleep was code for completing the bond on my lover's cocks, but hey, every guy needs some self-care after a stressful summer. I avoided the topic of Rich and Gray's brother, Indrid. That was a story for another day. Gray didn't mention it either.

I hadn't checked my phone since earlier in the week; that was well before I collapsed in Rich's kitchen, nearly dying. When I stepped out of the bedroom, I noticed Rich had left a fully charged phone with a bag of clothes by the door. There were 27 missed calls and 50 text messages from Nick. The last one he sent, the first one I saw, said it all. Allen was enraged we hid the books. That morning at the historical society he dismissed us as we crossed the threshold. Missy didn't look guilty, simply nodded to us as we left.

Nick's last text was around four p.m. on Friday telling me he was heading over to Allen's and hoped I was okay. *Fuck*. I'd left him all alone. Rich wouldn't have known or had time to call him to tell him I was in the hospital for three days, dying. I wasn't completely sure he'd called my sister to let her know I was sick. He probably did. I was delirious for most of the stay; I wasn't sure what had happened. I didn't see any texts or calls from her.

Gray was sitting on the bed, watching me swipe at my phone. I was concerned, seeing the clear escalation of Allen's behavior through Nick's messages made my skin crawl. Allen had made threats. He'd told Nick he was going to talk to the Dean, request expulsion for Nick's lack of academic integrity. All of it was bullshit. Allen would look like an asshole if he tried. Nick, the sweet and untested undergrad, hadn't had a clue what Allen's power limit was.

"What is wrong, Beloved? You have a look on your face like you want to skin an animal alive." Their voice soft and even.

"That's oddly specific, Gray, and unnervingly true." I showed them Nick's texts, wondering if they understood what any of it meant to me. I didn't think they were incapable of deciphering technology; I wasn't sure if they cared to.

"This one is frightened. What books?" They had a blank look, an inhuman one difficult to decipher.

"Nick's the student Allen was bothering, threatened to fail him if he didn't do extra work for free. When we got to the historical society for this *project*, Allen introduces us to one of the volunteers and then goes on about how he'll be gone most of the summer. We had to e-mail reports weekly reports of our *findings*. He'd abandoned us 15 minutes into it after looking at the crates from the estate, the dick." I paused. "There's this large collection from the Simmons' estate. The department was talking about how it had ancient magic texts and was haunted or some malarkey." Gray's eyebrows were raised. "What?"

"You said Simmons? Do you mean the Changeling?" they asked.

"A changeling, like a Fae cast-off child?" I was rusty on my European folk lore, although I was quickly realizing it wasn't purely stories to scare children to bed.

"Changelings were a trade of sorts, flesh for flesh. The humans made themselves to be victims, but usually the transaction was initiated by a blood born." Gray saw the next question in my eye and answered, "Witches. What you would call a witch called to the Folk for the babe. If a blood born was unable to conceive or had had a still-born babe, they would call for one of ours. They didn't just want a human child; they wanted one of power. They knew they were getting folk that were the least dangerous and often weaker in power. Simmons was from a particularly nasty boggart clan. They were cannibals and did not breed outside of their immediate kin. One of the first of the folk to come to the mountains since they had been banished from the old world."

"I'm sorry, what? Simmons was an inbred shape-shifting cannibal?" I stood there looking confused, or at least, lost in this conversation.

"A weak one. He never changed form, as far as I know. He did eat human flesh, though, with frequency. Because he was not completely under the watch of our kind we did not intervene." Gray looked away, shamed.

"So, not your problem? Let the humans deal with it." Anger bubbled up.

"He ate the flesh of the already deceased and no suspicion arose because of it. The Five let him be until... his death." Gray was still looking away from me.

"How'd he die? That's actually something no one figured out. Some records say he moved out of state and died; others make it seem like he disappeared." There was a birth record for him in one of the Bibles, but nothing that stated his death. There were a few documents that showed some things were moved to upstate New York, but nothing else. I moved closer to Gray.

"I ripped his head off and tossed it into a valley. Indrid took the body. I am not inclined to ask what was done with it." Gray stated, unfazed by what had been said.

"You killed him? Why?" It was in that moment I remembered Gray wasn't human. I may not understand why he murdered a changeling.

Gray waited a moment before answering. "You may already have that answer. In the things you found, what was there?" I recognized a good deflection when I saw one, but was Gray wrong?

"Spooky haunted shit," I sat in their lap. "Missy said a lot of it was connected to old Appalachian traditions. Things written in the margins of Bibles, apparently not odd, but the Bibles were from the 16th and 17th centuries. All unusual King James versions, at least, not as ornate as I would've expected, not that that's my expertise. It looked like there was a Geneva Bible too. In the early colonial days, that would've belonged to Puritans. It looks like the Simmons family came from the Boston area and changed their name when they got down here."

Gray listened patiently. "But there is more."

"Yeah, a lot of photos of... executions from Judge Simmons' days. The changeling?" Gray nodded, waiting for me to continue. "There were photos of people who died mysteriously, probably murder, but I don't know. There were, fuck, there were pictures of kids, too." A coldness filtered through the bond; Gray lifted my chin to study my features.

"This bothers you?" they asked.

"Dead kids? Yeah, Gray, that is bothersome." I leaned into his touch. "Wait, you said he ate the dead?"

"Yes, I imagine you saw his victims. Indrid sometimes keeps tokens from his kills as well." Gray made a shrugging gesture with their wings as if that were normal. It's normal for serial killers, again I reminded myself these weren't humans we were talking about.

"All the people executed were innocent?" My breath caught in my chest.

"The children probably were. The adults, maybe?" Gray shrugged. "I have tried to stay out of your world as much as I can. Simmons and I were about the same age. He had been in this territory longer." Gray hissed through sharp teeth. "I was born further north in a deep valley."

"You stopped him from killing more?" I asked quietly.

"No." Gray tilted their head, thinking of a way to explain the complexities of murder. "I ended his life because he was attempting to use essence in terrifying ways. He created a curse that still haunts Black Ridge. Those children did not die by his hands, but he was the one who orchestrated it. There were several humans who died because of their involvement; however, none of it looked supernatural at the time. The Changeling threatened the Folk in a way that had not been

seen in a millennium. That is how I became the Keeper of this territory. Taking the Changeling's life."

Gray's words settle before I asked, "So the ridge is haunted?"

Gray blinked slowly. "It is unfortunately more complicated than
what humans consider a haunting. It is not even a shade or an other-
world spirit. This is a true curse. I do not know if there a name for it.
No one in the territory or surrounding woods have known such a
thing to occur." Gray placed their hands on both of my arms, tugging
me toward them. "Promise me, Beloved, you will stay away from that
place."

"It scares you that much?" I asked, genuinely unsettled by their
plea.

"It is not fear that causes me to ask you to stay away, it is wisdom
that guides me to warn you. There is nothing that is known that can
reverse what is done. I cannot understand why the humans continue
to congregate in that place."

"It's the school's art studios and offices." I frowned. "No one likes
being there alone." I cringed then admitted, "I once broke into the
abandon building below the water tower. The only access points left
to the tunnels. Something..." My eyes get big as I realized what I had
seen.

Gray grimaced. "You saw him, then. Now that we are bonded you
cannot return. He will come for you, your light shines too brightly.
Even then, he could have taken you underground. He starves there."

I jumped up. "That... he could hurt someone?"

"Not a human, at least not a human unconnected to essence. Any
blood born would sense him and stay clear. The Folk have avoided
that area for decades. Even the animals have stopped going too close to
the tunnels." Gray waved a clawed hand at the air. "There is nothing
we can do. He is trapped to that land."

"That place is really damned? I thought that's just nonsense
stories for Halloween, but there's so much here." Gray sat on the bed
as I processed this. "This is what you do, right? Watch the supernatural and try to mitigate any damage to the mortal world? You help
keep the Folk hidden?"

"That is a very concise description. I do more odd tasks as

requested by The Five, our governing body, but mostly I watch." Gray made the vague wave again. Gray looked worn.

"Are you okay?" I had been standing over Gray, that had to make them nervous. I climbed back into their lap.

"No." They were looking at their claws. "Your life has been permanently changed because I could not stop myself from following your scent. When the Winged Folk intervene in a human's life, it is rearranged into chaos."

"Maybe I needed some chaos?" I half joked.

"Our chaos leads to death, even the most well intentioned of us eventually cause harm." Gray avoided my eyes, continuing to study their claws.

"I didn't die yet." I kissed Gray on their ear hoping they were wrong, that this was more dramatics. Perhaps they didn't trust me to be able to adapt to living in a cave with a giant moth Fae being.

They startled, finding my eyes. "If you die, Beloved, I will follow." They angled toward me for a gentle kiss, I opened to them, allowing that long tongue entry. We stayed in that embrace until I broke for air. We pulled away, panting. Gray's fangs showed between their full lips.

Why's that such a turn on?

GRAY REFUSED TO LEAVE ME. They said it was too dangerous with a new bonding. They'd made the error before; it would not happen again. I'd asked if Indrid was still a threat, to be told that as long as Indrid's heart beats, he will always be a problem. It was difficult to tell whether Gray truly hated their brother or not.

In some conversations, they'd made it seem like Indrid was a *normal* Winged Folk, to follow up in the next sentence that Indrid was a harbinger of death.

Gray had decided on a modern looking glamour to appear more like a college student. They were still beautiful, opting for light blond hair and dark brown eyes.

They were tall, towering over me by four inches. They copied the skinny jeans look paired with a faded band t-shirt and hoodie I favored. Aside from their stunningly good looks, they looked absolutely mundane in the late morning sun.

I'd tried to call Nick Friday night and again Saturday morning. I'd passed out after our changeling conversation. Gray assured me it was a part of the Well's effect on me. I was adjusting to being bonded to a powerful Folk. All of the descriptions Gray had given me, their people were some type of Fae-like beings, long lived as well. I guess it made sense mothman would be a type of Fae that traveled here from Europe with the colonists. Why not? Colonization brought a lot of baggage with it.

Their explanation also answered as to why some of the beings described weren't specific to the United Kingdom but appeared in tales from all over Europe. Gray had used words from French, German, and several Slavic languages when describing the Folk they oversaw. *The Keeper* was an exaggerated title; they didn't really *keep* as much as they observed the magical community in the territory designated by some ancient governing body. Gray rarely got involved unless the Folk committed a more heinous crime against the humans, or the Folk brought attention to the hills.

Gray explained why Indrid was on everyone's shit list. Apparently, Indrid was not only a practiced murderer, he was a brutal one. He left behind evidence and didn't care if humans found what he'd done. He'd also had non-mate-related relations with multiple humans over the centuries, something that risked their discovery.

Gray explained Indrid was one of three Folk who led an almost year-long campaign in West Virginia against humans, starting the whole "mothman" legend. The other two were distant cousins from a territory in New York who had gotten bored.

Gray had told me more, but I'd reached information overload long before my eyes decided to close themselves for me.

WE DECIDED to head over to the historical society to see if Nick happened to be there or if Missy knew what had happened. When we pulled into the parking lot, I saw Missy's old car in the handicap spot.

I parked next to her and took a deep breath before turning the engine off.

Gray raised an eyebrow at me. Their face was oddly comical now that it looked more human. They kind of exaggerated expressions and moved oddly at times. It was like they were trying to blend in and not look magical, failing miserably at it with every too smooth gesture turned jerky. Is that what they thought humans looked like when we moved? Gray was also trying to sound more modern; their use of contractions came out awkward. I couldn't help but chuckle out loud.

"Are you nervous, Beloved?" Gray asked in their slightly higher pitched *human* voice.

"About Missy? No. Never about her. I don't think Nick's going to be here. I know Missy's not going to tell us what we want to hear." I leaned my head back against the headrest, closing my eyes. They'd been throbbing since I woke up, a dull headache at the base of my skull. Considering I was a breath away from death a few days ago, a mild headache wasn't that much of a concern.

"Do you think Allen killed him?" Gray asked innocently.

"Jesus Christ, Gray!" I yelped. "Humans aren't that murderous."

Gray gave me a knowing look with a smirk. "Yes, humans are. Perhaps I desire a better reason to end Allen's life."

"Gray, you can't go and kill every asshole professor. I mean, I'm flattered, love, truly." I fluttered my eyelashes at them. Gray took the hint as an invitation to lean over and kissed my lips gently, caressing my face. I loved this feeling right here, being cherished.

Gray pulled back and rolled their shoulders. My mind sorted out what they had said again. Gray rarely threw out careless platitudes of half thought-out statements. They said a *better* reason for killing Allen meaning they had some sort of reason for offing my soon-to-be former chair. *What the fuck isn't this Folk telling me?*

"Gray, what do you mean *better* reason? What's your initial reason for wanting to take Allen officially off the census?" I had unlatched my seat belt, remaining seated in the car.

"Ah, well. I have reason to believe he's been dabbling in death magics by the ridge." Gray didn't elaborate, *bastard*.

"And that means death by moth?" I asked, cringing. I'm not sure what I was more dubious of, the fact that *professor perfect* was possibly practicing necromancy or that Gray had been planning on killing him.

"I've been watching the blood born for over a decade. He's smart enough to not leave any trails, but there've been bones found in the Blue Valley no one else has claimed. Many of us have felt pulses of death magic not connected to the cursed. He smells of *coffee* and death, Beloved." Gray's eyes were intense even without the red blooming beneath the deep brown.

"Wait, Allen's a witch who's been using necromancy for a decade?" I repeated, still not completely understanding what the fuck was just said to me. Annoyance gained traction, why couldn't Gray give me all the information I needed at once? Not these little snatches.

"Allen's a descendant of a blood born, weak in any power. The family was mostly archivists for other blood clans. He cannot access essence like other witches can. Indrid had told me he was in some sort of relationship with Nicolas Simmons until he died. I thought it was archiving. Nicolas, he was a *real witch*." I must have made a face because Gray chuckled.

"Allen is a witch?" I hissed with visions of him on a broom flying through tornadoes filled with red inked term papers while drinking the tears of undergrads.

"Yes, a weak one. Those tend to align with the more powerful, like the Simmons blood borns. Nicolas used to give Indrid boils on his ass for not keeping his end of a bargain." Gray beamed, finding the memory of his brother's unfortunate circumstances amusing.

"Another reason why Indrid is a troublemaker?" I snorted. "Trading with witches?"

"Hmm, not in this case. We have working relationships with those who are *of* essence. They know of us from their stories passed down through the generations; sometimes they call to us for practical things. Indrid is a proficient hunter and collector of dead things. Nicolas was a death singer. Indrid frequently brought Nicolas items for his work-ings, and when Indrid forgot Nicolas's power, he was gifted weeping ass boils for months." Gray snickered.

"Gray, what aren't you telling me about Allen and the whole

Simmons' estate?" Frustration flared. It was apparent Gray knew a lot about what was going on.

I needed to find Nick. I was worried. Why didn't Gray care that I was worried about my friend? I felt myself clenching my teeth. Gray looked beyond me through the driver's side window.

"Ezra, we're not alone." They nodded as I turned.

Missy was standing under the building's overhang, looking exhausted and worried. Her arms crossed holding herself, jaw set in a grimace. She was staring at Gray, not me.

I moved to leave the car when Gray took my elbow. I shook my head at him. Hesitantly, I opened the door and stepped out. Missy's voice boomed across the lot before the door shut.

"Where the fuck have you been?"

CHAPTER 15

Into The Stacks

EZRA

Missy was not happy to see me. If the nonverbals hadn't clued me in, the yelling from across the lot was a dead giveaway. Gray remained silent since getting out of the vehicle. Missy hadn't moved from the front steps. I could feel the anger vibrating from her small form. The gravel crunched under the weight of my many mistakes and regrets, although I worried what Missy was about to tell me would reach the top of that list.

"Ezra Williams, where in the fuck have you been, and it better have been on the devil's doorstep fighting for your sinner's soul. Child, it's a mess here." Her body was rigid, with lips pressed into a tight line. I never once associated the idea of *terror* when it came to Missy; how wrong I was.

"Well, more like death's door." I cringed. How much do I tell her? "I was in the hospital with a double kidney infection all week. Rich had my phone. I was delirious earlier this week." Missy's face fell at that, every line of anger dissipated as quickly as it had been summoned.

"Oh, Ezra, I'm so sorry. We knew something must have happened for you to disappear." She came down the two stairs and threw her arms around my waist.

I hugged her back just as fiercely. "Where's Nick?"

"I don't know. He called yesterday morning telling me Jim was still raging about those goddamned books."

"Jim?" I asked.

"Allen, James Allen." She pushed a few strands of white hair out of face before setting her eyes on Gray. "You look familiar, who are you?" Suspicion ran thick through her words.

"Uh, this is my boyfriend," I said too quickly. She looked at me sharply, leaning back to size me and my lies up.

"Your boyfriend? You go to the hospital and come out with a boyfriend?" Her hands were placed firmly on her hips. I knew I was in deeper shit than when I got out of the car.

"Um, we started seeing each other in the spring and just reconnected this last week." I gestured toward the building. "I was busy with school and our project. I just..." Gray was keeping their mouth shut and thank fuck for that small favor.

Missy sighed. "I'm sorry." She looked at Gray. "I'm sorry, dear. I'm usually not this frazzled. I'm sure you're a nice boy." She half-heartedly smiled at Gray.

"It is no trouble, ma'am." They inclined their head as if this were some period piece and Gray was secretly a courtier from someone's court. "It's a pleasure to meet you, I am Gray. I'm, uh, not a boy, though." I internally cringed at my own words. I shouldn't have said *boy*friend.

"Oh, apologies." She looked at me. "Forgive me, I'm sometimes a woman too much a product of my time. What pronouns should I use before I make a bigger fool of myself?"

"Again, no worries. There's nothing wrong with being called a man as much as there's nothing wrong with being called a woman. I'm neither as it stands, they and them seem to be a common enough for singular pronoun use in modern times." Gray smiled without the smile reaching their eyes. Something about the lip to teeth ratio was off. It was like they were trying to remember what a human looked like when smiling. The longer they stayed in this glamour, the more I felt like we were edging toward an *uncanny valley* kind of situation.

Something like recognition flickered across Missy's face. "Gray, it's a pleasure to meet you. Why don't we go inside and discuss our current problems?" She held that tight look as she took my arm in hers. "Come dear, help an old lady inside."

"Of course, Missy." I patted her arm entwined with mine as we headed to the front doors. Gray kept behind my right shoulder, not too close but close enough to protect me from all the evil that hung in the air.

Missy had already turned on the lights and opened the back hallway to where we'd been working. "Why don't you two head into the project room? I need to grab something out of my office." I nodded as she headed off to the left where the staff offices were located.

I reached back and took Gray's hand. The warmth from the night before filled their loving gaze. I couldn't help but smile at them. They brought my hand to their lips, grazing the back of my knuckles with a gentle kiss. As we entered the room, I saw what piles were missing immediately. The photograph series was still on the table, but every Bible was gone along with a collection of journals we'd unearthed the week before.

I heard Missy's steps come up from behind us, Gray grunted and moved quickly forward. They dropped my hand to turn quickly. I stepped back, seeing Missy with a double barrel shotgun pointed at Gray's face. She sneered at them, thrusting the muzzle closer before flicking it slightly to the right. Gray had both of their hands up, taking a half-step back before I finally found my voice.

"Missy, what the fuck are you doing?" I scream-whispered, if there was such a thing.

"You don't know what *they* are, Ezra? I know. I know well what this is. Who are you, then? Which one of you troublemaking winged bastards has graced my presence?" she snarled.

"As I said earlier, I am Gray." They paused. "I take it you've met one of my cousins?" Their eyebrows knitted together.

"That I did, until Indrid chased him off. Bastard was going after my car in the middle of the night." She didn't loosen her grip on the gun.

"Eamon hasn't been in this territory for decades. I saw to that long ago." Gray didn't move but also showed no fear of the gun. I wasn't so sure that would kill him; maybe piss him off, but not kill him.

"And Indrid? Did you take care of Indrid, too?" There was a waver in her voice, something like sadness.

"Wait, Missy, you really know Indrid?" I asked. She didn't take her eyes off Gray.

"Yes." She swallowed hard. "We were friends of a sort. He disappeared around the same time my husband did. We never got a proper goodbye."

For the first time, what looked like genuine emotion flashed across Gray's face, *regret*. Gray took in a deep breath, choosing their words wisely. "He didn't disappear, at least, he didn't purposefully leave you to silence."

She frowned, a quiver in her upper lip. "He's gone then? Dead?"

"That always seems to be the end goal for him. Death. No, Indrid of the Dark Waters is still a chaotic storm of our valleys and hills." Gray put their hands down, shoulders relaxing. "Your husband was a bastard, yes? He beat you and your children horrifically?"

Missy's cheeks flushed. She re-centered the gun to between Gray's eyes. "How dare you, *monster*." I was frozen in horror at Gray's words and Missy's reactions. I didn't know how to defuse the situation without someone getting hurt or shot.

"You weren't his only victims, so it seemed. Indrid had been following your husband to town, to the work camps, into the mines themselves. Apparently, *your* husband preyed on men at the work sites." Gray's eyes narrowed. "He'd pick the young and desperate, could offer them a little kindness or drink, and get them on their knees. That's when he'd really hurt them. Indrid watched him kill several *very young* men, dumping their bodies in the hills to look like an accident of the inexperienced."

Missy scoffed, looking away. It was enough of a distraction that Gray grabbed the shotgun away from her. She didn't fight them. Gray set the gun down on a table away from her, making no move to get closer to Missy. She wrapped an arm around her middle. Tears welled up as she fought to say something through her grief.

"He tried once with our boys." Her eyes closed, trying to will the tears back. "God, I caught him with our little ones. They were still asleep. I pulled him out of that room so fast and hit him. I've never been so angry. He beat me within an inch of my life. He would've killed me to keep the silence, but our oldest walked in from work and chased his pa out." She opened her eyes staring at Gray. "Indrid finished him off, yeah?"

Gray nodded. "Indrid laid him to ground."

"And his death, it was as horrible as his life?" Gray nodded again. Missy inhaled deeply. "Very good. That *man* deserved no less than the horrors of the other world itself. Why didn't Indrid come back?"

Gray took a small step forward. "He was punished for the execution among other things. He'd been entertaining too many humans at the time. Had caused a number of news articles to be published. He was sentenced to the caves for 50 years as penance."

Missy gasped but said no more. I didn't know who to go to; Missy to comfort her as she processed knowing for certain how her husband had died or Gray, who'd just been threatened by an almost 90-year-old woman. I approached Missy slowly, she turned to me as I opened my arms. I felt her body shiver in as I embraced her. She didn't cry.

"Missy, I'm sorry," I whispered.

"About what, Ezra?" She pulled back, wiping her face with a shaking hand. "You didn't force me to marry the bastard or get involved with an otherworldly being."

"It's still a lot." I paused at the 'get involved' part but left it alone. "I didn't ask if it was okay to bring Gray, either."

"Were you planning on telling me you're dating a mothman, then?" I saw the edge of her lips curve up.

"No. I guess not. Wait, how'd you know Gray is..." I trailed off.

"How did I know Gray is a giant moth being? They never smile right when they dress up as a human." Missy waved a hand at Gray. "I mean, this one is better with the outfit, and the beard is a nice college student touch."

"Ah, those were Ezra's suggestions. I am terrible at being human." Gray gave a slight bow. "I do apologize, Missy. I'd thought you and your youngest were gone from the mountains."

"You were watching me? Your people were watching us?" She

appeared far more relaxed than I would've been learning magical creatures were keeping tabs on me.

"Just me, no other. I did it for Indrid. He would howl all day and night unless I assured him that you were well." Gray tilted their head. "Until you moved after…"

"After Will died?" Gray nodded at her. "He was our light, and I suppose one of the few anchors to that place. The twins grew up, went to colleges on opposite sides of the country. One a writer, the other a pilot. I have seven grandchildren from those two." Missy looked thoughtful for a moment. "I returned to the family's heritage, though. Back to the root of things. Maybe I hoped to see one of your kind again before I died."

Gray took a step forward. "Ezra cares for you deeply. I can feel it in his spirit." Missy considered Gray's words. Gray clasped their hands around Missy's as they let the glamour drop. A look of awe crossed her face as she saw Gray in their true face. Gray leaned down so they were eye level. Missy reached out and traced her fingers along Gray's cheek bone down their jaw. Gray's wings gently fluttered behind them. I realized they were showing off for Missy and I couldn't help but smirk.

Gray moved forward, opening their hands and placing kisses on the backs of Missy's. She giggled like a teenage girl with their first crush and not the weather worn woman I'd come to know. It was sweet how easily and quiet literally Gray was able to disarm her. Their wings slowly edged around Gray and Missy, embracing them in the strangest hug ever had within the historical society walls.

Missy giggled again as Gray straightened and said, "I am sorry."

"You're sorry? I should be asking for forgiveness, pulling a shotgun on an ancient mountain God." She wiped at her eyes as she backed away.

Gray made a sound in the back of their throat as they pulled the glamour back around them. I could see gold threads appear in the air and weave into a web, latching onto their skin. "I am no God, ma'am. That is old world tales. We've never been Gods." There was a seriousness in their voice that made me wonder what the story was behind it.

Missy nodded. "Very well. Not a God and certainly not a monster, either. But we do have a problem."

"A different beast?" I added.

"The kind only human men seem to be the best at." She cringed. "I'm guessing Nick went over to Jim's last night. I tried calling both of them this morning, but neither's answering."

"What happened? After the initial explosion last week?" I thought about how Allen had raged at us for not letting him know about the books, the Bibles in particular were something of great value to him. He called me a variety of names, the things that he'd never had the gall to say to my face before. I remember Nick wincing at the words and sneers. I shrugged them off, I'd always known what he thought of me. It made no difference that he finally said it out loud.

"He called me that night, demanding I meet him back here to collect the items. I told him to fuck off." She smiled with all her teeth as I chuckled. "He didn't like that, so he took the chest beating route of threatening me. I told him under no uncertain terms was I going to release those books to him without a formal university request and society release. He hung up on me and went behind my back to the Executive Director who repeated the same thing. She got the request from the university, and he took off with the books on Thursday." Missy scowled.

"How'd Nick get roped in any further?" I sat down on one of the few folding chairs in the room as Missy joined me. Gray leaned against the counter, observing quietly.

"Jim kept blaming Nick for not telling him what we'd found." Missy held up a hand to stop me from interrupting. "I'm aware we had no inclination or actual responsibility to keep the old goat in the loop. He effectively waved his rights to knowing when he ran off for a summer vacation. He wasn't funding this little party; I don't know what entitles him to anything from it." She readjusted herself in the chair.

"Allen blustered away, freaking Nick out and getting Nick to go over and what? Apologize for not being a good little errand boy?" I wanted to spit every time I said Allen's name as if it were something profane. Then Gray's words came back to me, chilling me to my core. "Fuck, he's going to kill Nick, isn't he?" I turned in my chair toward Gray.

"I'm not doubting that, but it won't happen until tomorrow. Necromancy has never been a subject I was," Gray hesitated, "drawn to, but I remember it's connected to lunar phases. If he kills Nick now, whatever power he's trying to gain will be lessened or lost."

"You think he knows that?" I demanded, angry that Gray hadn't been as forthcoming with information. I chastised myself internally, of course they haven't. That wasn't their way or responsibility to humans.

"Yes," Missy said resolutely. "He has the books, well, most of them. I found one this morning, Nicolas Simmons' journal from about a decade ago. I've only gotten in a bit, it looks like Jim Allen was heavily tied to necromancy. Jim was sick, dying of something. Nicolas had been doing some sort of spell for years to lengthen Jim's life. He was still going to die according to Nicolas."

Missy walked over to where the photographs were being housed and picked up a battered-looking leather journal. It was the kind that one could put in new inserts as old ones were filled and locked away. My dad had given me one for the last birthday I had while he was alive.

I hissed, "Nicolas has been keeping that fucker alive for, what, two decades now?"

"Not possible." Gray stood, walking over to Missy. Gray had told me the night before that once a Winged Folk were revealed to a human, it was very difficult for any other Winged Folk to hide from that individual human. Whatever magic that kept them blind to us was cracked open like a wax seal on ancient, forbidden parchment.

Missy handed them the journal. Gray opened it, quickly flipping through the pages. They stayed silent as they sped read through about half of the journal before handing it back to Missy. Gray exhaled loudly. I could see it in their strange human face they were trying to measure out their words. Present us with something more palatable than what the conclusion really was. Gray was shit when it came to play acting people.

"Okay, you're killing us with the suspense, Gray. What's not possible?" I'd noticed Missy was remaining relatively quiet during all the revelations we'd had today. Maybe she was thinking about her dead bastard of a husband or maybe she was grieving everything she'd lost over 50 years ago. My heart twinged for her as my worry for Nick only increased.

Gray swallowed hard. "It's not possible because the death singer had paid the ultimate price for using necromancy. Necromancy is using death by force, often causing it, in order to harness it. Nicolas was a gifted death singer, there was always plenty of that type of energy here, especially this close to pockets of the Folk. Our valleys are ripe with it. It clings to us in ways that it cannot to beings that are in essence and not a part of it. The Well source that amplifies death songs."

"What was the price, Gray?" Missy was sitting on the edge of her seat, eyes wide and rounded.

"His mind. There's a slow decay of a blood born's mind when forcing too much death. It eats away at the organ. Humans have a word for it when it naturally occurs..." Gray looked off in their thoughts.

"Dementia," Missy supplied. "Nicolas Simmons was in a memory care unit for the last ten years due to having a form of dementia. I remember hearing about it when I first came back here." Missy gestured to the building. "Nicolas was a large dollar amount donor for us. When he went in, we got about half of what we used to. It was somewhere in his written estate maintenance that we were to continue to receive money for operating costs. He apparently wanted us to specifically have this collection and not the university directly."

"Why's that? Did he think Allen would get the books and continue?" I frowned. If that were the case that was bad planning on his part.

"No," Gray said softly. "I imagine that Nicolas thought Allen would be long dead by now. It's interesting that he's not. How his mind still functions is another matter. Perhaps it's his proximity to the curse that has altered the necromancy. Nothing seems to align well up near the ridge."

"What?" Missy looked astonished. I shook my head at her, trying to relay that this wasn't the best time or place to discuss curses Gray would be vague about. Yet another factor in the Simmons ever-spreading fuck ups. Missy seemed to accept that, Gray continued to not elaborate unless directly spoken to. They were kind of an ass about this.

"The original necromancy work was utilizing large game animals and cattle. Those would give Allen three to six months of time." Gray paced in front of us. I started to raise my hand as if to ask the teacher a question. Gray noticed and smirked. "It was in the journal. Now that Allen has the original texts, he can use the best ingredients possible, humans. It would give him years instead of months of life."

"Jesus." I felt my throat tighten. "Now we know how and why this started. We have an idea what he's going to do next. But how's he maintained this long without someone performing necromancy for him?"

Gray shrugged off my question. "Someone has. We just don't know who would be foolish enough to do such a thing for a creature like Allen. Any blood witch would feel the decay of him. A death singer would know it's futile and borderline dangerous at this point. The only beings I'd guess who'd be willing to assist him in this fool's errand would be another of the Folk." Gray seemed to ponder that.

"Indrid? Is Indrid capable of doing something like..." I didn't finish my sentence.

"Indrid likes causing death, he's no desire to try to harness it. Imagine a storm. It pours rain, swelling up creeks and rivers that floods the land. Wind whips through trees and breaks branches or trunks. Lightning fills the air striking near and far, burning and destroying. A storm creates chaos, but it doesn't try to imprison that ancient power to its will. It simply allows the energy to flow." Gray made a gesture with their hands that looked more like a bomb going off than being indicative of energy gently flowing out. I suppose that's a better visual for their brother.

Missy cleared her throat. "You mentioned a curse on the ridge. Jim moved up there about ten years ago. Is the curse feeding the necromancy? There's... a lot of death up there."

Gray blinked and nodded. "He could be feeding off the curse itself, which will be a problem when I kill him."

CHAPTER 16

The Last Journal

EZRA

G ray had not only decided we needed to lay Allen to rest, which oddly both Missy and I didn't question or argue with, but also decided to read the rest of the journal. I wanted to go get Nick now. Gray cautioned that we didn't know what state Allen was in or if he was truly alone up there. If there was another Folk or worse, the curse, acting in his favor we'd get ourselves killed trying to free Nick.

Missy and I were seated on either side of Gray as they turned to the first page of the journal. We'd decided to take notes as Gray read out loud. Missy with her canary yellow lined notepad and me with a Hello Kitty notebook. It had come with a glittery set of gel pens Addi got me for the holidays as a gag gift. They were one of my favorite things to pull out in front of undergrads. Gray cleared their throat and began to read from page one.

October 2007

Jim insists that I use my calling to help him. He's growing more desperate; this is the third time he's gotten a cancer diagnosis in a decade. I was able to soothe those

149

first two away, but it's like something else continues to eat away at him. Whatever it is attacks the bone marrow. He's aged so much in such little time. He refuses to go back to the doctors. He won't tell me what's wrong. He must know what it is and refuses to tell me.

I found some of the older texts from my ancestors. Translating has proved difficult as their handwriting was abominable coupled with crude spelling. According to The Changeling, there are necromancy techniques I can use to help extend Jim's life while masking the ailments themselves. I can continue to soothe the minor disease but...

Gray hummed to themself. "Nicolas didn't finish the last sentence. He knew Allen was dead, yet he continued to prolong his suffering. How cruel." Gray appeared to be talking to them self because they continued without any further commentary from us.

November 2007

We've been using smaller animals to experiment with the process. I've not noticed any impact on my own mind and wellness, yet I heed the warnings of my forebearers. It helps that we're so close to a Well and the Winged Folk supply me regularly with death song. Perhaps I shouldn't have cursed that one with ass boils so many times?

Gray gasped and outright cackled, startling both Missy and I. I'd never seen Gray laugh like that, it was one of the more human like things they'd done. Missy leaned back to give me a perplexed look. I covered my face with a hand, trying not to giggle, shaking my head. I knew that was a reference to Indrid and given the earlier revelation of his relationship with Missy, I didn't think she'd appreciate Gray's laughing.

Gray had set down the journal, flipping it to face downwards as they wiped at their eyes. They were still giggling when they finally got out, "Stupid fucking bastard has never known when to stop." Gray was wheezing in delight to see their brother's misdeeds so well rewarded by a now dead witch. I wondered if Missy would let us keep the journal so I could have that page sealed and displayed behind museum quality glass.

Missy cleared her throat. "That was about Indrid, wasn't it?"

Gray's eyes were filled with humor followed by a failed attempt at looking more somber for Missy. "Yes, he and the death singer traded for ten years or so. Very few blood born were permitted to enter the valley."

"Why's that?" I asked, curious.

"Because they risk their life every time they enter the depths of our territory. That's why so many human hikers and campers go missing every year. Not all the Folk want to trade or be disturbed. We also cannot risk the exposure, especially with the advent of..." They gestured to my pocket indicating my phone.

"Social media, video recording, any asshole with high resolution photography all in his pocket?" I quirked my lips into what I hoped looked winsome.

"Any asshole indeed." They picked the journal back over, cradling it in their left hand, continuing.

> *Regardless of my transgressions with the giant moth, he doesn't seem too put off by my reactions to his antics. If he were human and acted less homicidal, I would wonder if he were flirting. Their kind don't seem to have qualms about sex or gender influencing romantic partners. Perhaps, when Jim is gone, I'll see if the moth is interested in affaire de coeur. I'm so tired of dragging on the inevitable. It's not any fault of my own that Jim refuses to care for himself, admit that this is his end.*

Gray seemed more demur after reading the rest of the passage. It confirmed that Allen and Nicolas Simmons were lovers or romantically entangled at some point, but Nicolas was tired of their relationship. He also wanted to fuck a mothman; guess that was a common small-town occurrence? I opened my mouth to speak, Missy beating me to it.

"Nicolas didn't want to continue but did until he, what, magically lost cognitive functioning? He was aware of it, why did he continue? I don't get the sense he was deeply in love with Jim." She smirked at me. "What a shock. Yes, Ezra?"

I snorted and took the journal out of Gray's hand, flipping to the back. "This journal covers five years, sporadically." I looked at the date on the last page. "It ends on July 16 of 2012."

"That would be around the time Nicolas had to go into care. What does it say?" Missy had settled herself against Gray's shoulder. That was a 180 in behavior from shotgun to the face to cuddles around a witch's journal. I readjusted myself in the hard chair before reading Nicolas Simmons' last written words.

July 16, 2012

I warned him this would happen. The death songs are not enough to combat the disease progression. He has lesions on his back and stomach now. A large ulcer on the roof of his mouth. His hair's been falling out in clumps. I'm not sure how I have managed to sustain him this long. He says he's not in pain. I can smell the decay. He told me we need to stop playing games and sacrifice a human. He ranted about talking to an expert in Louisiana who told him about workings that would extend his life, pain free.

I told him we wouldn't be ending any more life. I was well aware of what he spoke of and the cost was too high. He needed to accept his death and I would help ease his transition. I could make sure it no longer hurt. He raged at me, throwing items around the room. Called me a murderer and a liar. I broke his heart. I broke his trust. I want him dead. He wasn't wrong on that account. I informed him that if he wanted to go to the expert in Louisiana to cure him, he had my blessing.

His eyes were bloodshot, his skin was waxen. He froze when I asked him to leave and then gave me a grin only fit for a rotting skull. I didn't know how to help him anymore. His mind was fading with the vestiges of our youth. All that malice and jealousy he kept pent up finally bubbling to the surface. I was about to ask him if he would reconsider the pain management, my mouth opened wide, when he threw it at me.

It felt like ash in my mouth. As I write this, I find my vision blurring. I'm forgetting words. My hands are shaking, a palsy I have never experienced before. I called my cousin in Pittsburgh, warned her what she might find at the estate. It seems that Jim is not the only one who will be dying soon. I only hope that both of us find some peace.

I closed the journal. "Allen killed him? Well, caused the cognitive decline with what?" We stayed quiet for a moment, digesting what had been read. Nicolas was always aware of what Allen needed to extend his life and didn't do it. Allen was desperate and felt, perhaps betrayed, that his lover wouldn't use vulgar methods, so Allen killed him? Cursed him?

We still didn't know who or what managed to keep Allen alive while he waited to get his hands on the texts. Why go to all this trouble himself if he had a necromancer in his corner? Too many questions and not enough time to sort it all out.

"Louisiana has an unusual amount of death singers and banshees." Gray picked the journal back up, tucking it inside their jacket pocket.

"Hey, wait, that..." Gray lifted their hand, effortlessly silencing Missy's objection.

"All of this needs to *disappear*, Missy. The Simmons' estate should have had the closest relatives collect these items a decade ago. Instead, ancient death songs are in the hands of an essence-connected human who potentially has portions of his brain rotting away." They paused. "Ah, yes, and they live next to one of the most volatile broken songs laid by Nicolas's ancestor." Gray scowled. "With each passing day, I find the more and more monstrous repercussions of allowing that Changeling to exist."

Missy looked lost at the statement and chose to overlook it by asking the most obvious question. "So, what do we do for Nick?"

Gray had sat down and held what they must've thought was a casual position in the metal folding chair. Missy had shifted her own position, facing us, she ran both hands through her hair. She looked adrift. After so many years and crisis, she was once again faced with saving a young man that she couldn't. I felt that twinge in my chest again. I didn't want to lose Nick, but none of this looked like it would end well.

Allen clearly was prepared, and we didn't know if he'd be alone. We couldn't just barge in, wings flared and guns blazing. He'd caused the demise of a prominent death singer from a powerful family. He'd managed to keep his failing health in check years longer than possible. Hell, I never once noticed Allen missing hair or having sores. He never missed office hours or classroom time. He was annoyingly always around.

"Nick may already be dead." Gray paused after I gasped but when neither of us commented they continued, "Regardless, I need to stop Allen. He's disrupted the territory enough that it calls for more than investigation. I will collect Indrid and perhaps another local death singer to aid me in Allen's capture."

"Indrid and you are on speaking terms?" I quirked an eyebrow at that comment.

"Indrid is not currently speaking at all." Gray flashed their teeth. "But he'll be invested in this death, I'd imagine. He would know where I can get the strongest death singer."

"And what happens to Allen when you, uh, detain him?" Missy probed, a dark look settled across her face. She already knew the answer.

Gray gave a half shrug. "I doubt I'll have to do much. If the death singer can cut the bond of the song, Allen will simply cease to live in this realm."

I lowered my head, folding my arms across my lap. "Do we want to know what that looks like?"

Gray shook their head no. "Some things are best left to the unknown, Beloved."

I smiled at that, *Beloved*. Then I noticed rain hitting the roof, softly.

CHAPTER 17

The Stars Sing To Us, Beloved

GRAY

After reading the journal and making several attempts to contact Nick with no avail, we agreed that Missy and Ezra would stay behind. It was not safe for them. The essence of necromancy was too unstable and equally unpredictable. I silently hoped that Allen would perform the song incorrectly and simply kill himself. Unfortunately, that would mean the young man would meet his demise as well. This was not the favorable outcome for Nick.

Ezra took me back to his tiny apartment that was huddled into the hill. I looked forward to checking in on the Pooka and laying with Beloved. I missed the warmth of his skin, the salty, smoky taste of it between my teeth. The soft kisses, tongue languidly searching for my own until that hot pressure turned into heated frantic desire. The press of his needy cock against my hip. I felt my own cocks stir at the thoughts. I need to get my mate into his nest with his legs over my shoulders.

The house was dimly lit as we slunk through the front door. Ezra had mentioned earlier that his roommate worked nights and would be asleep when we got there. To my surprise, this roommate was sitting in the kitchen awake and smelled of death, a death singer. They locked eyes with me. The hair on the back of my neck rose as I felt the Well's surge envelope the house itself. This one was powerful.

"Addi." Ezra shuddered as he sensed the uptick in energy. "This is..."

Addi stood up, chanting something under their breath. A binding spell. They knew what I was on sight. *Good for them*. I flexed my glamour, standing over Ezra with wings flared. *Addi* sneered and continued to chant. I flicked my wrist and their body locked up; words stuck in their mouth. I watched them wrestle for control as Ezra yelled for me to stop.

"This one is trying to bind me, Beloved," I hissed through clench teeth.

"Addi, don't hurt them. They're my mate." Ezra threw his hands up in an attempt to distract me. I was old enough to not need constant focus to hold a blood born, even an impressively powerful death singer, no *Necromancer, fuck*. I nodded at Addi and dropped my essence. They crashed to the floor with a grunt.

"Peace, Necromancer. I am not here to take what is not mine nor cause any discord or harm." I clasped my hands in front of me and bowed my head slightly, trying to placate Ezra's roommate. Conveniently, I have my death singer without needing my brother's help. This one must have held a strong shield to not be noticed.

"Yet you've been in my home, without invitation, on multiple occasions." Addi had not risen from the floor, yet somehow still gave the impression that they were looking down at me with the statement.

"If I had known a Necromancer resided here, I would have asked permission. You are powerful and well hidden." That was high praise from Winged Folk. I had hoped that was not lost on them.

They snorted. "The fuck I care about what one of you winged harpies think." They stood up, straightening out their clothes. I glared at the harpy comment which is what they wanted. Addi took a few steps back before deciding on sitting back at the table with their herbs. "You mated my friend. Why?"

"Ezra shines brightly. I know you can see he is of essence. His heart is a thing of exquisite beauty. His *songs* are as potent in their allure." I gazed at Ezra with every ounce of admiration I could summon. He had no idea how absolutely perfect he was. "We are of compatibility; our bond happened quickly and unexpectedly."

"And it nearly fucking killed him." Addi had gone back to sorting their herbs. They glanced up at Ezra. "Rich called and said you're going on dialysis." Ezra nodded but kept silent. "You know that's their fault, right? They find compatible humans or someone human adjacent and devour them whole."

I grunted. That was not wholly untrue of my kind. "The only thing I wish to devour of Ezra's is his cock." I heard Ezra choke while Addi paused, mid-motion, then began to laugh from their core.

"Good, he's not seen much action the last couple of years unless you count half-hearted hand jobs to substandard porn on his phone." Ezra objected as Addi continued to grin, rolling his herbs into tiny pieces of paper. "Why'd the bond snap like that?"

"My brother trapped me before we completed. It is my fault for not staying closer to Ezra. Indrid..." Addi cut in.

"Indrid? Fucking *smiles* is your brother?" Addi laughed again, this time sounding more forced with a vicious edge. "That fucking moth has gotten into some shady shit..."

"Gray," I supplied with a half bow. "Keeper of this territory." I let that knowledge sink in. This Necromancer would understand the significance of my title. I felt some glee as their eyes widened at my disclosure.

"You're the Keeper?" They snorted. "And you let fucking Indrid trap you?"

"He does not routinely keep me for so long and someone gave him songed iron manacles. It made it easier for him to rip pieces off me, quite distracting." I did not let emotion seep into my words. I could not think about his treachery in this moment.

"He's powerful?" I nodded at Addi. They continued, "But not as powerful as you. So, he got the upper hand and what happened? Is he finally dead?"

"I tongue bound him." Addi tilted their head at me in askance. I gestured my hand in a poking motion. "I ran a talon through his throat and bound him to a promise of causing no more harm to Ezra for as long as his light remains. Indrid will not utter another word unless released by my magic or death itself."

The Necromancer abandoned his herbs, biting their thumb nail between their front teeth. "Jesus, I'm not sure which one of you is more brutal."

I moved forward to wrap my arms around Ezra. I had not told him the specifics of what I had done to Indrid for interfering with our bond. Our ways allowed for a far greater punishment, I would settle for his silence for a century or two. Less if he behaved and stopped getting involved with humans. Ezra was stiff, slowly relaxing into my embrace. I leaned down to kiss his temple. My left wing lowered, brushing against his arm. My Beloved.

"You stabbed your brother in the throat." Ezra turned in my arms to face me. "Why do I think you let him off easy?"

"Because, Beloved, you know me well enough. Unlike Indrid, I rarely choose death as my means." I leaned forward to leave another gentle kiss on the tip of his nose. Something about this man was changing me. I could feel it through our bond. My mind and body were adjusting to my mate's needs. I also had been using *contractions* for his benefit and it was not so... bad.

"Well, I can't say I don't blame you. If I'd known Indrid made Ezra sick, I would've cut off his head or at least cursed his dick." The Necromancer was back to rolling his stock.

"Which one?" Ezra blurted before realizing what he had said.

"Which one?" Addison asked, "They have more than one dick? How did I not know that lore? Why haven't I seen a second one?" Addi looked up at me.

"We only share the whole of ourselves with our true mates, not quick fucks with humans." I rested my hands on Ezra's shoulders, smoothing out the wrinkled flannel he pulled off the floor that morning.

"Hey, I've never 'quick fucked' a Winged Folk in my life, that includes your dickhead brother. I do buy bones off him when I'm desperate. He's gotten me some interesting mushrooms. He probably thought they'd kill me and not make me hallucinate for a week... okay, I blew him when I was on the mushrooms, but it was a single dick."

Addi had their elbows on the table, their chin resting on their left palm as they appraised us. "What now?"

"I will spend time with Beloved in his nest for the afternoon. Then I must take care of the necromancy across the river. Hopefully, Ezra's friend won't be dead." I felt Ezra tense, pressing his face into my chest.

"Are you talking about the ridge?" Addi asked shocked.

"No, and you should stay clear from that accursed place as well." Addi nodded at my words. "Ezra's *professor* is being held together by a mismatch of death song and necromancy. Unsurprisingly related to the Changeling's family."

"Simmons?" Addi hadn't moved from the nonchalant position, but I saw the tension in their shoulders at the mention of the changeling.

I nodded. "Nicolas Simmons was the death singer. Allen..." Addi hissed and stood up, looking at Ezra.

"Your fucking chair is a wraith?!" Addi yelled that with more volume than I thought capable of a being so small.

"Not yet, he seems to still be mostly living but it is close. Nicolas sustained him, barely, until ten years ago. We do not know who or what has been helping since. Allen has all the Simmons' collection as well as a youthful student. He lives bordering to the ridge and I have no idea if or how that has impacted the necromancy." I pulled Ezra in tighter. "Ezra is to stay home while I tend to my... duties. If you are willing, it would be safer for the missing student if you came. Despite my current strife with Indrid, he will not turn down a good execution."

Addi nodded. "Do we know who's helping him? It's my understanding his line of Allens were mostly record keepers if they were even aware of their lineage. If he's half dead, how's he going to pull this off?"

"Yes, that is another unfortunate gap in our knowledge. It was referenced that he may have been receiving help from another death singer or Folk in Louisiana." I lifted my right wing in a half shrug.

"And that's as helpful as not." Addi walked toward me. "If I help you, risk my life and all, can you ensure all my supply needs will be met in the future? Indrid has always come through and now that he's magically muted it won't be as tiresome..." They hesitated, "there are some things I haven't exactly been able to find without my kinsfolk."

Ah, there it is. The reason we had a Necromancer in our territory is because they are unguarded. Banished from their own kin. That made them more dangerous, acting on their own with no oversight of an elder from their blood. It made them more useful to the territory because they would be dependent on the Folk for certain items or access to essence.

I held out my left arm, spreading my fingers open wide. I used a talon from my other hand, dragging it across my palm. A thin red line bloomed before Addison's eyes. They mimicked the gesture, using a pocketknife instead of my claw. A blood oath is a reckless thing if done in uncertainty. We both knew we would need as much as use the other in the coming seasons. They would be able to call me at will, and I would know what they were doing at all times.

With three simple words our wounds healed, leaving almost imperceptible white scars. I inclined my head as Addi rocked on their heels. It seemed we had come to an understanding. It also brought me comfort to know a powerful blood born cared about Beloved, even if they were cast out of their own kinship and a Necromancer. I wondered who they killed to earn that distinguished honor.

"Well, I'm going to get high. Wanna come, Ezra?" Addi gestured to their dried herbs. Ezra shook his head, staring at my healed hand.

"What was that?" he asked tentatively.

"Gray's way of tracking my magic so I don't create another cluster fuck ridge in his territory." Addi pulled out one their wrapped herbs, a *blunt* is what I heard the students on the green call it, and promptly lit it on fire. It smelled earthly and sour at the same time. I knew humans used it to get intoxicated. Ezra seemed to accept that explanation and tugged on my arm.

"It's been a long morning. I need a nap." Ezra continued to the kitchen to the back stairwell.

I heard Addi snort behind me. "Sure. You're going to take a nap with that giant wall of abs."

The moment I shut the door between Ezra's cave and the basement, Ezra's lips found my own. He pressed his body into me, there was a warmth on his skin I had never noticed before. He was feverish with lust and need. I could feel how hard he was already, pressing into my thigh. I kissed back, devouring his moans as they escaped his lips.

He started pulling off his clothes, tossing them on the floor as we shuffled back to his nest. My nose filled with the pungent scent of his arousal. Both of my cocks filled at the thought of plunging into him over and over again. For the rest of my days, I would have this body under mine, on top of me. Riding both cocks as he comes, painting stripes across my chest.

I felt his fingers work at the front of my breeches. I cursed silently wishing I had adopted more modern clothing. Something with a zipper and a single button, perhaps a *drawstring* like the one on Indrid's gray *sweatpants* he liked to wear in his cabin. *Fuck,* I do not want to think of Indrid, only my mate. Ezra had managed to strip himself to nothing and release my cocks but not free the rest of me. I chuckled at his impatient whine.

I kicked off my boots as I forced down the breeches. I was hard, leaking from both tips. Ezra pulled me down by my shoulders. I tucked my wings in tight. I could put them away, but I loved the way he clung to them as he climaxed. Ezra's pupils were blown wide. He panted as he straddled my hips. I wanted to take my time, kiss and lick every inch of him. Drown in his desire.

Ezra rebuked that idea and writhed on me as I sucked hard on his neck leaving a trail of wet, pink marks in my wake. He struggled to adjust his legs as his arms and hands groped at my back, my shoulders, the tender area of my wings. I groaned, a deep sound emanating from my chest, he rubbed circles into the spot. I nearly came from that motion alone. I bit him hard over his clavicle causing him to buck.

I took that bit of shock to grab both of his legs, pushing him to his back, exposing himself to me completely. He whined and tried to grind into his ass. His own hard length, flushed at the tip, precum dripping off to his abdomen. I spread him further and pushed down, neatly folding him in half. He growled at me as I dipped lower toward his cock and balls. I licked a sloppy line following the large vein to the crown, taking it into my mouth.

I took Ezra into the back of my throat, sucking hard enough that my cheeks hollowed. I looked up at him, his eyes hooded and mouth slack, an indication he was mindless with pleasure. Every bit of suction, every swallow of my throat, he groaned. I loved watching him lose himself to me, in me. I began to slowly move up and down his length, teasing the orgasm out of him as much as wanting to prolong this.

The musky scent of him filled my senses as much as his silky, salty flesh filled my mouth. I consumed him. His body. His mind. His essence. Then I would fill him with me. I continued my ministrations of his dick while I gently tugged and rubbed his balls. A finger stroking the skin between them and his precious tight hole. He pushed himself down on my hand as much as he tried to push up into my mouth. His mind at war with him what sensations he needed most.

He murmured my name like he was in prayer, softly and passionately. I would not make him chose which sensation to take precedence. I called upon my essence, creating a slickness around my fingers. I pressed in one, then two fingers. He rode my hand as I sucked his cock. I could feel him get harder in my mouth and his delicious heat begin to squeeze tighter around my digits.

I slowly pulled them out while applying pressure to the base of his dick. I was not ready for him to come yet. I wanted to watch it explode from him across our bodies. I wanted to watch him split himself open on me and ride me until he was breathless and completely senseless. I wanted to see him undone as if this were our last moments together. He tried to grab at me, begging me to keep going.

"Please, Gray," he whined.

I smiled at him as I laid down next to him, cupping his face, giving him gentle kisses across his lips and along his jawline. I scented him again. He smelled like summer rains, lightning about to strike. I was flat on my back now, Ezra clearly tired of my gentle worship. He quickly climbed on top of me, rocking himself against my rigid cocks. With a lascivious look he lifted himself off my hips and grabbed both of my cocks. To my delight he worked both into his puckered hole.

It took great patience to not thrust myself to the hilt. He held eye contact as he slowly dropped himself to a seated position. The moment I hit his prostate his head dropped back, dick twitching with more precum leaking out. He felt like he was on fire inside. I had covered my cocks in the same lubricant to ease in, but it felt like he was well prepped. He was so tight and hot and wet for me.

When flesh met flesh, he did not wait to adjust to the feeling of being filled, he simply rode me as fast and as heedless as he could. I felt the orgasm building quickly. This man, my mate, was just as good at wrecking me. I gripped onto his hips tighter, his moaning turning to wailing. His balls pulling up as his cock jerked, shooting ribbons of white across my chest, hitting my chin.

I lost it all in that vision of ecstasy. I felt both of my cocks spew heated spend into his quivering body. The intensity was overwhelmingly coupled with the contractions of his own orgasm. He continued to pump himself on me as he came again, spilling more come onto my stomach. I thrusted up into him, realizing a second round of orgasms were approaching. I came again, somehow harder, as Ezra rode me through it.

We were both panting as he collapsed against me. His come sticky and warm between us. I wrapped my arms around him as my wings were trapped underneath me. My cocks still painfully hard and in him. I wanted to flip him, pin him down and take him again but he was tired. I kissed his face and lips, humming happily as he smiled. Ezra's eyes were closed, a look of anxiety-free bliss across his face.

My *Beloved*. My *mate*.

The rain continued to pour.

CHAPTER 18

Bones of the Valley

GRAY

I sensed him before I heard the pounding on the brick wall. Indrid was outside the door to Beloved's home. I could not help the growl that tumbled out of me. Ezra was wrapped around me, head resting gently on my chest. His eyes flared open either from my tensing or growl, it did not matter what caused it. I was going to punch Indrid in the dick. I gently stroked Ezra's hair as he looked up quizzically at me. The pounding resumed with muffled flapping.

Indrid's pounding carried through walls too well. He was using some of his essence to make a point. I knew that *point* could be heard upstairs and in the neighbors' homes, too. He was flapping to harder, hitting the ground and walls. It never occurred to me that in sealing his voice he would somehow manage to make himself louder in other ways.

"Silence, you fucking cockalorum." Ezra snorted under me.

"Did you just call your brother a dick, but in a fancy way?" He was giggling as I moved him from my chest to the softest part of the nest. Pooka was snuggled on a small pillow that had been shoved against the wall.

"It means he thinks himself important. Did you not study your own language, Beloved?" I flashed my white, sharp teeth at him teasingly. He giggled again and threw a pillow at me.

"I didn't study outdated slang and insults of the English language, though Chaucer had some memorable vocabulary." The banging had ceased as Ezra looked at the doors nervously. "I should put some pants on before you let him in."

I tucked my wings tightly behind me as I stood from the bed. The room was unlit except for the muted light from the fungi and a trail of yellow peeking out under the closed bathroom door. Pooka was chattering behind me about the Winged Folk and their strange sleeping practices. Ezra held Pooka against his chest, stroking the little goblin's back.

"He will not hurt you," I said softly. "He cannot hurt you as long as you live in this form." I know the expression I made did not translate into a human smile. That was hard for my kind, our facial structures were different, and we relied heavily on the movement of our brows, ears, and wings to convey our emotions. Ezra seemed to understand my *smiles* and other bumbled, human nonverbal cues.

He nodded before looking serious. "Wait, what do you mean *this form*?"

"Ah, some of the beings of this world and others..." I could not think of the correct term, so attempted with lore-based examples. "They are similar to the story of the Phoenix. Or how humans say cats have nine lives?" I made it sound more like a question than an explanation. I sighed, knowing my way of explaining was inadequate. I would have to have his Necromancer explain our shared world better. These things I *knew* but did not always have the vocabulary to explain.

"What you did only includes this form as it is now? So, when I die, my energy changes form and releases him." I nearly choked when Ezra said *when he dies*. We are bound by essence now. He will live as long as I live. I will not lose him to darkness, we will walk into light together.

"Our life is woven together, Beloved." I rubbed my face, a fairly human gesture. "I will eventually have to release Indrid from the magical choke hold I have on him." Ezra flashed a brief smile at my attempts of using modern *slang*. "I am slightly younger than Indrid and it is unlikely he would find a mate to extend that life. I will not condemn him to eternal silence, as much as he deserves it. He does too much trade in our region and saves me the trouble of handling some of the less desirable tasks."

"He kills things for you." Ezra stated it bluntly. He was quick to pick up on Indrid's particular skill set.

"That he does." I turned to the door to let Indrid in. "Beloved, put your dick away or I will have to gouge out my brother's eyes for seeing something that is so precious to me." Ezra startled me by letting out a keening like cackle. "I need his eyesight for tonight."

Indrid must have hit the door because it shook violently along with the booming sound behind it. I waited until Ezra had tugged on a pair of loose, cotton bottoms and snuggled back into his nest with Pooka. When I open the door, I noticed Indrid was still a mess from our struggle in the cave.

Dried, flaking blood was around his neck where I had punctured him. The rain had not washed much away. There was blood still smeared around his mouth down his chin. That looked fresher, and for a moment I thought he had eaten something small. The blood smelled like him. The bruising was significant all over his body. I did not realize how hard he had slammed against the wall. I forgot my own strength at times, as did he. I rarely had to use it. I rarely chose to use it. His left wing hung at a slightly odd angle indicating some of the smaller bones must be fractured or dislocated.

"Are you coughing up blood, brother?" I pointed a claw toward his chin. He would have growled if I had not punctured his vocal cords. I could feel the rage vibrate off him in waves. He was not well enough to fight me and could not harm my mate. If I did not know he was so fond of gremlins I would have had the Pooka disappear. He swayed a little in the doorway. I stepped aside to let him in.

He limped across the threshold. When I saw his back, I realized why his wing was slightly off center. The primary joint to his back was dislocated and by the swelling around it, I guessed he still flew on it. Ezra's eyes were wide as he looked over Indrid in all his broken folly.

"Gray, did you do that to him?" He did not sound shocked or horrified, more aroused by it.

I sighed, again something more human than folk to do. "Yes, Beloved. Things got... heavy when I realized he had meant to *kill* you."

"Right, I forgot about that part." Ezra folded his arms across his chest, scowling at Indrid. "What the fuck did I do to you?"

Indrid blinked but gave Ezra no indication that he was listening to my mate's words. He was. I saw the tension rise in his back. The pain from his wing must be radiating to every part of him. Standing had to be almost unbearable, yet he stood as straight and tall as he could. Who was he trying to impress with this blustery show of utter damnable behavior?

"He hears you, Beloved, and is not happy. He is too arrogant and proud to let on how much pain he is in. He is insufferable on his best days." I watched his muscles twitch as I added insult to insult. He could not condemn me. He could not counter my words. That in itself was far more of a punishment than pain.

"Gray." Compassion filled Ezra's voice as my stomach turned. "Don't do that. He can't verbally defend himself and he looks... bad." Ezra winced and I knew what he was going to ask before he probably did. He was gentle and kind, of course he was going to ask it. "Can you heal some of this? He can't help us if his wing is broken."

Indrid made a snarl face at Ezra but did not move toward him. He did not flare his good wing either for the perceived insolence of my mate. That was curious, maybe Indrid did realize the horror of what he tried to do. No. That was not possible. Indrid did not care.

"His wing is dislocated, not broken." I stepped up behind him placing the heel of my hand between his wings and stretching the wing with my other. "And he took great offense to you saying that." I pushed and tugged roughly, setting the wing back in place. If Indrid had his voice he would have shrieked, instead he simply collapsed to his knees. I did not impede his fall.

"Gray! Jesus." Ezra jumped out of his nest, still clutching Pooka, who looked on curiously. Ezra set the gremlin down and reached for Indrid. I saw his claws extend as Ezra took his hands. Ezra noticed it, too. "I'm not going to hurt you. Stop acting like I'm the bad guy when you're the one who tried to kill me because I let your sibling rearrange my guts while simultaneously blowing out my back."

Indrid tilted his head at my mate, claws retracting. Some of the tension drained from his shoulders. He was finally seeing Ezra for what he was, perhaps. Indrid gently squeezed Ezra's hands and gave a subtle nod. Ezra helped him sit on our nest while he inspected Indrid's injuries.

"I guess Gray looked rough too right after." He gently lifted Indrid's chin up to look at the wounds on his neck. "I'm not going to ask him to lift whatever magic curse this is. What you did was shitty, and my understanding is that's kind of your norm. That doesn't mean I want you to be in pain and look like utter dogshit."

Indrid met Ezra's eyes. To Ezra that was most likely unreadable. There was too much Folk gestures happening. Indrid had lowered both his wing tips and ears. He kept his face in a neutral position with slight lifting of his eyebrows. Indrid would never ask for forgiveness out loud, he could never bring himself to say the words. His body language was screaming it now.

Ezra caught some of it because he reached out to brush some of Indrid's matted hair from his face. "What's wrong, Indrid? You suddenly look so... sad." Ezra shifted and placed his hand on top of Indrid's. Indrid froze, in shock. Ezra was showing him more kindness than our own people did. Perhaps this is why he chose humans over Folk more and more often. They were kind to him. Ezra looked at me for help or perhaps an explanation.

"He may be feeling a bit amiss for causing you harm." I half-shrugged. "Indrid likes gremlins and some humans. I think he is realizing you are the type of human he would like."

Indrid looked up at me, his ears dropped more. I was right, he did not mean to hurt this precious human. I would help heal him, but I would not lift the binding, for now. It did not matter how bad Indrid felt, he could go fuck himself if he believed a drooping set of ears and wings would be enough to be forgiven. At least not today.

I moved close enough to lay my hands on his shoulders. If I accessed the well for him. I could feed him enough essence so he could heal himself. I did not think he would allow me to heal him directly.

His ears perked up as he felt the flow, more powerful than what he could pull. His eyes closed; wings lowered in a more relaxed position. He leaned into my touch, pulling from me. I would be concerned if I were any younger or a less practiced folk. Indrid could absorb my life force from me doing this.

Eventually he was healed, slight marks left where I had stabbed his throat. Indrid sat up to pull a small satchel out from under his left wing. He smiled maliciously as he showed me a grinning Folk skull. It was slightly larger than a human's but not as delicate in the front to be one of our cousins. Even if he had a voice, I doubt he would tell me who it was. I wonder where the rest of them lay.

"He doesn't know what's happening, does he?" Ezra asked.

I shook my head. "It really does not matter now." Indrid was fixed on Ezra now. He was breathing in Ezra's mild disgust as if it were fresh air. I nudged him with my foot. "Who is it?" He smiled again showing both sets of fangs before shrugging and waving his other hand.

"He doesn't know, does he?" Ezra asked.

"Well, he does not kill everything he trades." Indrid nodded at that. "But he kills enough of them. That's a Folk skull, something smaller than us, though."

"Who else is out there?" Ezra licked his lips as he watched Indrid toss the skull between his hands.

"Many." I grabbed the skull before Indrid could continue in his macabre juggling routine. I had heard the Necromancer move about when Indrid was pounding on the house. They were sitting in the basement, listening to us. They were probably curious as to why two Winged Folk were in their basement or they recognized Indrid's presence and were wondering if they were going to have a problem.

"Addi, come in. Indrid brought you something." Indrid shifted quickly in an attempt to grab the skull, but I moved toward the door as Addi opened it, looking confused. They knew Indrid did not give gifts. Indrid was on his feet behind me, ready to tear the skull away when he stopped short and stared at Addi. Another human he liked?

"Hello, Indrid." Addi gave a curt nod. "I don't remember inviting you into my home. Ah, yes, wait. Your sibling's mate bond with my roommate gives you access?" The Necromancer waited for a catty response and got none.

Indrid pointed to his throat then gestured to the skull with a bow. He was making the skull a gift to the Necromancer, probably to save face. I did not think he cared enough to break into a blood born's home on a regular basis. It was never worth the hassle or the potential curse when we did. Addi's smile was more predatory as they took it from my hand.

"Thank you, Indrid. Your sibling did a wonderful binding curse there." They examined the bones. "What species of Folk is this? Something quite large and powerful, I can feel it infused in the bones."

I suddenly realized why Indrid had been avoiding answering. "Indrid, where did you get a banshee skull?"

Addi nearly dropped it before catching themself. "You killed a fucking banshee. What in the hells is wrong with you?!"

Indrid shook his head and put out both of his hands. He made a gesture of having something in one and setting it in the other, before repeating it the opposite direction. He had traded for the banshee skull which was mildly better. They were a Folk with strict death customs. If Indrid got the skull it either meant a relative desecrated one of their kin for profit or this one had been condemned. The bones though were usually smashed and dumped in large bodies of water.

"Was this one a condemned?" I asked as Indrid nodded. "Do you know why? And do not pantomime it, just write it down. You have been muted, not made illiterate."

Addi giggled as Ezra searched his bag for paper and a pen. Indrid settled back down, this time on Ezra's lone couch and began to write quickly. I silently hoped that he would write it in English so I did not have to translate it for Ezra and the Necromancer, although Addi may know enough to understand. When Indrid was done, he handed the pad to Addi.

It's why I'm here and an ongoing problem for your mate. This banshee went by the name Baysea and has been living in the pond near the Blue Valley. They come from the Loch line in Louisiana.

Addi stopped reading and asked Indrid, "Isn't that where you were getting all of those bones from, the valley?" Indrid nodded and gestured for Addi to continue.

They've been helping kill random humans for a while now. I didn't notice them right away and I didn't understand why a banshee would be up here. I assumed the godsdamned Folk was banished and since my trade was up. Fuck it.

Addi stopped and glared. "You're a piece of work, aren't you?" Indrid nodded in agreement, pointing at the notebook.

The poor beast was rotting or at least looked like they were rotting. I've never heard or seen that before, but those people are so insular maybe this was some type of magical leprosy? I saw it wander around the forest for a while. It stopped eating months ago. Clearly didn't bathe or even clean the shit and piss from their body. Their mind was rotted out. They died last month near the mushrooms. I was afraid that would ruin them, so I stripped the bones with magic and burned the flesh. I didn't sense any curse or magic on it, nothing that would spread past their death.

Ezra was the first to speak. "Indrid, how many years did you notice an increase in your... trade?" Indrid held up ten digits. Ten years this banshee has been killing humans and in doing so slowly rotting away.

"Oh fuck," Addi cursed loudly. "A banshee has been doing necromancy next to a broken curse for a fucking wraith?" Indrid seemed startled at that concise appraisal of how grim our problem looked now.

"Well, that is one less answer we need to search for. It appeared any loose ends had unraveled themselves." I looked back to the skull I was holding as Addi read on. "Also, it is luck we have their skull."

"It'll make unraveling the necromancy easier, much easier." Addi handed the notebook back to Indrid. He set it down on the couch, clearly done talking to us. "I won't need to go with you. I can stay here with Ezra and show him how to deconstruct dirty spells. Allen will either be dead by the time you get there or close to it."

"Then I can go." Ezra stood up. "Nick is still there, Gray. He's going to be terrified."

Addi grabbed Ezra's arm, shaking his head no. "It's still not safe. Allen's been at this a long time, long enough to sacrifice everyone who has ever helped him. We don't know what barriers or traps he's put up around the house. These two will be able to sense them without triggering them, especially Gray. They'll know if anyone is alive in the house if they can't get around them." Addi did not believe Nick was still alive, neither did I.

Ezra's pained look made my heart stutter. "Gray, please bring him back."

"Beloved, I will do everything I can, I promise." Ezra came into my open arms, nuzzling into my neck. His words were muffled but I understood them as I felt wetness collect on my chest.

"You don't think he's coming back, do you?" His voice was strained.

I hugged him tightly. "I do not know for sure, my love. We will bring him back, regardless. We will take care of him. He will not be left alone." Ezra stiffened before leaning his weight into me and crying. I kissed the top of his hair, humming gently while Indrid stared at the wall and Addi looked away.

"How soon can you break the necromancy?" Addi extended their hand for the skull. "Now. In most circumstances I would be worried about the integrity of the spell as it relates to the beings involved but since most are dead or should be." They shrugged. "I'll snap it hard enough to rip his leeching soul out."

"That wouldn't hurt Nick?" Ezra's eyes were red and a little puffy. My poor mate.

"Nah. He might be severely traumatized by what happens to

Allen if they're in the same room, but he wouldn't be hurt by it. Any other ward or trap should disintegrate with Allen." The Necromancer's eyes had a faint glow to them. They were calculating all the ways they could destroy what the banshee had done. They looked... hungry.

"When you say disintegrate, you mean what?" Ezra asked hesitantly.

"Ezra, I know you love Harrison Ford, did you ever see *The Last Crusade*? You know the part where they drink from the *wrong* grail?" A smirk appeared on both Indrid and Addi's mouths. Ezra blanched. "Something like that. Oh, watch where you step when you get in there, moths."

Lightning blazed across the sky, filling the tiny windows as thunder clapped outside. The rain pounded down. Ezra visibly shivered. I could feel how oppressive the air had become. It would be a good night to pull from the well. Indrid was watching the Necromancer intently as they stroked the front of the skull with their long, pale fingers.

A small smile turned up the edges of Addi's mouth, their eyes continued with a soft violet glow. The Necromancer should be pleased.

CHAPTER 19

The Flood

EZRA

They left in silence, Gray swallowed in pensiveness and Indrid in his curse. Addi told me the spell would be simple enough and over before I realized it was started. I had to leave my phone along with theirs on the kitchen table. They drug me up to their room, I rarely stepped into without explicit direction. I'd never really seen the inside before. They must've had some sort of charm on it for me to miss all the magical elements.

They glanced over their shoulder at me as I stared at the floor. "Seeing it all for the first time?"

"Yeah," I swallowed. "I guess. It's always been this way?"

"It has, but your eyes have been closed to magic even though you do contain some essence in you." They began prepping the skull among other objects. I didn't bother to pay attention since I'd no desire to learn witchcraft or spell work or whatever it was called.

"That's what Gray said, too." I sat on the only empty chair in the space.

They looked up. "Do you understand any of it?" There was no malice or scorn in their voice. It was all Addi in their curiosity. But I really didn't know Addi. A blood born who apparently practiced magic in their bedroom all the years we lived together, and I hadn't a clue. Did they see Pooka, too?

"No, I don't, but I'm not sure if Gray knows how to explain it. Sometimes they struggle with what words to use, like they are thinking in too many eras or too many languages." I grimaced at my own poor explanation of Gray. It wasn't fair, maybe they were choosing to not explain this world to me.

"That's the most succinct way of describing the Folk that I've ever heard." Addi nodded as they stood, seemingly done with their set up. "The older they are the harder it is to communicate with them. It's not even a language barrier, they understand the definition of the words but seem at a loss when it comes to meaning. Body language and facial affect are another barrier, depending on the Folk. They live in insular territories or "colonies," as some of them still call it. Sometimes they are diverse within their own supernatural neighborhoods, but they avoid humans to the point it becomes a detriment."

"You know a lot about them." I was staring at them like they were a stranger, it was hard to see them as my trusted friend. Then again, I was fucking mothman and hadn't uttered a word about it.

"I'm still Addison, Ezra." They frowned. "I'm still the same person that got too drunk on Halloween sophomore year and puked off the balcony on the sorority girls." I snorted as they smiled. "I'm still the person who cuddled on the couch with you after *every* breakup both of us had. I took all of those horrible classes with you so you wouldn't be alone even though I fucking hate Brit lit. You've seen my balls get pierced. We're still the same best friends, Ez. You always knew I was a little eccentric, now you know *how* eccentric."

I rubbed my face, suddenly feeling too weary for this conversation. "I know, Addi. Everything is so..."

"Bright?" they offered.

I looked around the room, and they were right. My vision now always seemed crisper, and things seemed brighter. I rarely saw shadows as shadows anymore. It was an odd thought but also a calming one. I never liked the dark, not complete dark at least. I cringed a little thinking about photography class when we had to go in the *dark,* dark room to roll film. I always paid someone to do it for me.

"What was that?" they asked.

"What?" I came back to the present. My mind focused completely on a room that shined in ways it shouldn't with a banshee's skull as a centerpiece.

"That little shiver there after I said bright?" They looked concerned.

"Oh," I sagged. "I was thinking how you're right; everything is so bright and that it really isn't so bad. Then I thought about photography class and that horrible little closet." I grimaced. "I like being in the light, Addi."

They watched me for a second before turning and saying, "Well, I suppose you picked the right Winged Folk. Gray was chosen for their light. Okay, let's get going. Time to undo all the nastiness that lives in that wretch."

"Do I need to do anything?" I continued to perch on the edge of the seat.

"Nah, just hang out and let me do my magic." They gave me a wicked smile. Addi sat next to their pile of things with the skull and did nothing that was observable. I wondered if they were waiting for something, then it felt like the room had dropped ten degrees. Every candle suddenly lit; flames danced in air flow that didn't seem to exist. There were symbols and words all over the room that shown dimly. I could feel something get pulled closer to us. It felt like sunshine and fire mixed with cool breezes and the scent of fresh air.

The skull began to turn from an off white to a dingy yellow, then brown and black. The skull itself looked like it was in a time lapse of rotting. Chunk by chunk it caved in on itself until it was a pile of dark colored sludge. The room flared to a blinding light that violently expanded before collapsing in on itself where the skull had been. I was left breathless, physically and emotionally.

My heart rate sped up before it started skipping beats. I'd had PVCs in the past, they hurt, but were nothing like this. I gasped, clutching my chest. Addi was wavering where they still sat on the floor. I saw blood on their hands and by their knees. I tried to take another ragged breath in as my heart pounded against my ribs. Everything was starting to hurt now. Something had gone wrong.

I tried to say Addi's name, but I could only choke. I dropped to the floor, struggling for air. I didn't know if Addi could breathe. The edges of my vision were starting to go dark. I realized everything in the room was blazing with blinding colors. My stomach roiled, it felt like glass was inside me. I had felt this before. Something was wrong with my bond.

I heard Addi make a hissing sound before feeling their hands on my shoulders. They were trying to get me back up. I was too unsteady and collapsed. Addi rolled me to my back; there was blood smeared all around their face and down the front of them. Their eyes were a deep black from iris to sclera. I tried to lift my arms to protect myself from whatever this was.

Addi laid their hands on my head and chest, mumbling words I did not understand. The pain increased and I felt myself arch off the floor. I couldn't scream. I gasped for air. I felt something soft rub against my cheek. I turned my head and there sat Pooka looking frightened, eyes wide. I wanted to ask for help, tears streaming down my face.

"Pooka, tell Gray the necromancy was a trap. Ezra needs him now." Addi was barely holding themself up by one arm as bloody tears rolled down their face. More oozed from their nose and mouth. "Ez," they choked out, "I'm so sorry. Please forgive me." They collapsed next to me as I felt every part of my body tense. Heat ripped through my body. I let out a scream, my vision blacking out.

I came to, rolling over to find Addi curled on their side. They were still taking shallow breaths. It felt like every nerve I had was on fire. I couldn't stand, but I knew I needed to get us help. Pooka was no longer in the room. I fumbled around my pockets for my phone before remembering it was in the kitchen. I crawled, more on my belly than on my keens. I hissed in pain with each inch of floor I covered.

The table seemed 40 feet tall from when I lay. I struggled to sit up long enough to grab my phone. I pulled up Rich's contact first. He knew about this. He could help. I hit dial before I could change my mind. He answered on the second ring.

"Ezra?" His voice heavy with anticipation. I had told him about Allen and the necromancy before Gray had left.

"Help..." My breath rattled. "Something. Wrong." I dropped to the floor, managing to keep the phone in my hand.

"Ezra! Ezra!" Rich was panicking. I kept doing this to him. "Where are you? I'm coming to you. Kiddo, where are you?"

"H... home." I closed my eyes. Tears filled them and I hoped that they weren't bloody. A new wave of agony tore through me. I wasn't sure if I screamed or simply wanted to. I must've closed my eyes because everything suddenly got darker.

I listened to the rain as it pounded down on the roof and then there was silence.

CHAPTER 20

Broken Promises

GRAY

We left Beloved and the Necromancer safely tucked away from the rain and danger. Indrid kept up with me in flight, almost completely healed. He seemed keen on homicide, setting aside our fight from earlier. Perhaps he was only annoyed he was unable to insult me. He was calm with Ezra, meaning he sensed our mate bond which would have that effect on him. Perhaps I could release the binding after this since he was less likely to harm my love.

It was a quick trip to the houses beyond the ridge. There were few in the area set on large lots with dense forest in between them. I doubted the neighbors would hear him scream. That is probably why he picked that spot. It was a perfect place to brutally take a life force for your own gain. I grimaced at the thought of what we were going to encounter. Addi did not try to soften the expectation of what was to come of this particular song work. There would be very little of Allen left.

As we approached the house, I felt unstable barriers and the unmistakable presence of death, both old and new. Indrid nudged my elbow, pointing to an uneven section of land near a swollen creek. The rain had not dissipated, coming down in a heavy torrent from above.

There were places the ground had sunk. Unmarked graves. Indrid held up ten digits followed by two. He suspected at least 12 bodies to be there. That was in addition to what the banshee had been dumping in the valley.

My body was tense. The situation worsened every moment. Allen had been killing more than we realized. The necromancy was highly unstable to require multiple human deaths a year. Perhaps the ridge was absorbing a large amount as well, tomorrow's disconcerting problem. Tonight, we would recover Nick and end Allen's life.

I had told Indrid the best recourse would be to burn the home with Allen's remains in it. The surrounding land was saturated with enough rain that the fire would not spread with any ease. We needed to destroy the body and anything in the home that has absorbed that volume of death. It was too risky to leave any items whole; they could fall into the hands of an inexperienced blood born or worse, a human with enough essence to unleash a plague of rot. It would not be the first time that has happened in their history.

Indrid pointed to the house and showed me two digits again. I nodded. I heard two heartbeats as well. We would not know who was inside until we entered. There was no point in glamouring ourselves. Allen was familiar with the Folk, and Nick was in too deep. If he could not hold our secrets, I would have to... think of something. Nick was Beloved's friend. Indrid would rip off his head if I did not take care of the situation.

Each barrier fell easily under my touch. Thin veils crumbling under my claws, far easier than they should. They were old blood born wards; things that had not been maintained for some time. We carefully approached the deck that surrounded the home. It was dark enough outside that we blended in with the shadows. I could see dim light deep from within the house. A lamp here and there on, throwing a soft yellowish orange pool of light beyond the windows.

Indrid raised his chin, subtly gesturing toward the door as he took a step in front of me. I kept myself from chuckling. If this had been anyone else, I would have seen it as a gesture of good will and protection. Knowing my brother, he simply wanted to gut whoever popped up first. I subtly laid my right hand on his shoulder to halt his movement. He glared back at me.

"Do not kill the young human. If he is alive, we are to keep him in that state. If he is dead, we recover what we can and return him to his people. Understood?" My voice was firm. Indrid nodded, pulling away from me.

The closer we got to the house, the more charged the air felt. The stench of rot was unbearable. Indrid had always been the one to deal with the blood and gore. I had never heard him complain about his odd jobs or duties to the territory. I was startled to see the look of disgust as he silently snarled at the rancid tinged air. He looked back at me, shaking his head, eyes wide. Concern played in his features about what was to be uncovered.

He pushed the door, cracking the wood frame. I heard metal snap as he continued to push against it with his shoulder and bulk. We were assailed by a blast of putrid hot air as we crossed the threshold. I had to swallow twice before moving forward. Indrid's wings shuddered as if pushing away any lingering aroma. We both heard the heartbeats coming from below, probably from the basement.

Before he could reach the top of the stairs to below, a tidal wave of energy force crashed over us. Indrid and I were flung backward, slamming into the wall and door behind us. Every wall creaked under the force as glass shattered outward from the house. Whatever the Necromancer had done, it had rebounded. Rebounded harder than it should. There was no surviving that. There was only one sluggish heartbeat below.

I struggled to my feet, Indrid knocking pieces of plaster off his body, making a menacing face at the chunk of wood in his hand. His eyes flicked up to mine, shaking his head. I headed for the stairs and whatever was left of Allen and Nick. The explosion of essence would have killed anyone too close. We were fortunate to be on a second level when it happened. I bounded down to the lower level, stopping abruptly enough Indrid stumbled into my back and wings.

Allen stood in his circle, wavering like a dying flame. His skin looked wet, like it was wax pulling away from muscle and bone. Sections of his chest and arms were missing, showing rotten muscle and blackened bones. His face was partially intact. An eye was gone, leaving a darkened, infected looking reddish-brown tunnel. Strips of skin were missing from his right cheek, yellow rotting teeth shown through.

Behind him were the remnants of a fresh death. I could see it was human and, by the size, male. The magic had stripped the body so that only bloody pulp hung in strings from bone. The victim had been strapped to the wall, perched above a worktable. No, *he,* was chained there while Allen stole his youth and his life after terrorizing him for months. We would not be able to recover Nick. *I am so sorry young one, I failed you. I could not keep my promise.*

Allen's remaining eye locked on us. He tried to take a step back, and his leg snapped under his weight with a sickening crack. He collapsed to the floor, a low wailing growl rumbling from his chest. I watched as flesh continued to fall off in small pieces. His skin continued to boil under the weight of the essence sliding off his form. Rivulets of dark blood with blobs of fat followed. Allen was melting faster than a tallow candle.

Indrid pressed his chest to my shoulder, intently watching as Allen's body rotted quickly while he still lived. Sounds gurgled out of him as various bodily fluids slowly oozed out, progressing to gushes from his abdomen and chest. He attempted to lift his arm, flesh falling from his fingertips revealing more darkened bone. He tried to say something, but when he opened his mouth, his jaw dislocated and hung at an angle.

Allen collapsed in the pile of wretched filth as his body finally succumbed. I could still hear his heart beating. He was alive, probably no longer able to feel the quickened decay of his body but fully aware of his death. The absolute horror of it must be agonizing. Neither I nor Indrid made a move to end it prematurely for him. I abhor unnecessary suffering of any being. I also detest injustice and the theft of someone's light. Allen had taken too much in his time.

The beat slowed, as the magic of the place settled. Despite the putrid pool of remains, the smells began to fade some. I could hear the rain pour outside; the creek raged along the property, trying to consume everything in its path.

Something tugged in my mind and then on my bond, a sharp pain in my chest. I doubled over and groaned. Indrid grabbed my arm. I tried to take a breath as my lungs began to feel leaden. I wobbled, Indrid quickly wrapping an arm around my waist.

"Indrid," I choked. "Something is wrong with the bond. I need..." My legs collapsed under me. Indrid scooped me up and then we were back in the air in the rain. I squeezed my eyes closed. *Beloved, what has happened?*

CHAPTER 21

Eyes Closed

EZRA

Everything felt numb and swollen. My mouth was dry like I had been sucking on cotton swabs for hours. My eyelids were heavy. I tried to move but I felt glued to the ground... or was it wood flooring? Sounds were muffled. I thought I heard someone talking. I thought I heard sirens or was it music, no singing. Someone is singing. Something brushed against my forehead. Soft. Pooka is soft.

Now something firmer is pulling on me, digging into my arms. Hands and fingers, probably. Someone is trying to pull me up. I don't remember drinking that much. I don't remember drinking. I don't remember how I got here. I'm home, but I don't know. I wish they'd stop shaking me. I'm tired. My head is throbbing. I need to stop drinking that terrible moonshine.

"Ezra!" a voice kept calling to me. They sound panicked. Did I fall and hit my head?

"How long has he been this way?" a different voice asked. Someone touched me. "Kiddo, can you open your eyes for me?"

"I don't know," I heard the second voice gasp.

"Why are you covered in blood?" the first voice asked. "Honey, I need you to look at me." The voice sounded kinder that time, worried.

"I..." the second voice trailed off. I felt hands on me again.

"You're one of them?" The question sounded angry, hateful. "Ezra, sweetie. I'm here now. It'll be okay." They were pleading.

"Folk?" The second voice huffed. "No, I'm human, or at least mostly human." They paused, and I felt the tugging again. "Ezra, sit the fuck up."

"Be fucking careful," the first voice snarled. "He nearly died the last time the magic went wrong. What's happening to him?" they hissed with barely contained fury.

"A significantly nasty spell rebounded on us. It shouldn't have fucking happened. That piece of shit was out of his league." The second voice cut in; they sounded like they'd been chewing glass.

"What piece of shit?" The first voice came out low rumble, a warning of the storm to come.

"The corpse, formally known as Dr. Allen." I could hear the sneer in the second voice. *Wait, Allen's dead?* I could feel waves of liquid hot rage coming from that person, the second voice. "If the rebound didn't finish him, the moths did. Ezra, up now. We're okay. Sit up."

I felt more pressure on me, and suddenly I was being lifted up onto something. Hands on my face, steadying my head. My body felt like half-melted Jell-O, wobbly and sliding out of position. I felt the warmth of someone behind me and heard a gentle heartbeat next to my head. This was nice. This felt safe.

I wanted to open my mouth and tell them thank you. I was exhausted. So tired. I think I'd felt this tired before, but I couldn't remember right now. I just needed to sleep for a bit.

Eyes closed. It felt like I could sleep forever. Just sleep.

CHAPTER 22

Faded Light

GRAY

The greater the distance from the slaughterhouse and the ridge, the clearer my head became. I could sense the angry pulsating of the Well. The vibrations stirred every sleeping thing that lived within the hills and mound. I reached for our bond; it ached and throbbed like a festering wound. I could no longer sense Ezra in any meaningful way.

It was like hearing the static on the radio or the thunderous pounding of rain in a summer storm. Indrid and I were both soaked from flying back to Beloved. I shuddered from the chill, surprised when Indrid nudged me with his head.

He landed as gently as he could while carrying me, he still healing from our fight only days ago. Indrid set me to my feet, both of us nearly slipping on the sodden grass of the backyard. I could hear three heartbeats in the home but was too disoriented to get a better sense of who was inside. Indrid raced up the side of the house to the front. I followed, barely a step behind.

Inside, we found Rich cradling Ezra against his chest. Ezra was pale looking blue gray, not too dissimilar from my own tone. Humans, even tethered ones, should not be that color. The Necromancer was equally pale and covered in their own blood. Rich glared at Indrid before turning the heated stare on me. He blamed us for Ezra's illness, not completely unreasonable.

Rich misunderstood the cause; bonds are not meant to destroy. They are an act of love. It was not our tied essence that was doing this, it was decades and centuries of abominations laid in those hills. If anyone was to blame, it would be the Simmons' and their long history of power-hungry brutality. I could not blame Indrid this time for the misery that laid at my feet.

"Fix it," Rich hissed at us. Tears wetting his face. He gently rocked with Ezra in his arms. Beloved's breaths were raspy sounding, his heartbeat becoming more erratic. I stared at the shredded golden thread that linked us. Our bond had been almost completely severed. Ezra's light was in tatters.

Indrid did not move as I fell to my knees beside Ezra and Rich. The Necromancer had their arms wrapped around them; bloody tear tracks down their face. They could see the broken bond, the fading light, too. That was the gift they had to endure tonight. Indrid felt it, tasted it in the air. He always knew when death was present. Rich pulled Ezra away from me, trying to shelter him from any more harm.

"I told you to fucking fix it. Stop crying and do something." He sobbed. I touched my face, not realizing it had become wet. "You're powerful. You're supposed to be his mate!" Rich wailed, a sound that landed somewhere between sorrow and rage.

I reached out, running the back of my claw down Ezra's face. I could not even begin to explain what happened. This was wrong. Everything in *his* house was wrong. We went in not knowing enough, and it would cost us everything in return. Another death. Another pile of bones for Indrid to sell off. Hot tears burned slick trails down my face. My vision blurred Ezra's soft features.

"Indrid," I whispered. "Help me. Please." I looked back at him. His wings were pulled back tight, he had lowered his ears. He was waiting for it all to come crashing down on me. Why did he not look happier about it?

"Addi?" My voice broke. I pulled Ezra's hand into mine, pressing it against my chest.

"Keeper," the Necromancer rasped. "My powers have been almost completely stripped. That shouldn't be possible." They coughed, and I smelled fresh blood. Indrid stepped toward them, immediately helping them sit. Was this one to die, too?

Rich was murmuring things into Ezra's hair. Telling him how he was *so gentle* and *so sweet*. That he would always be loved. That his father is proud of the man Ezra had become. Ezra let out tiny moans in between worsening, shivering. Rich attempted to reposition himself, causing Ezra to cry out in pain. Rich whimpered, cradling Ezra closer as the tremors took over his weakening body.

"It's okay, honey. I'm here. I've got you." Rich's voice tremulous as he spoke. "I've got you, kiddo."

I swallowed hard, my throat constricting on the scream I wanted to let out. I leaned forward on my knees, my wings stretched out behind me butting up against a table. I pulled at the Well, demanding it to feed me what I needed. I felt the spark of life force swell up to meet my fingertips, a jagged stinging erupted across the pads and palm of my hand. I hissed, physically pulling my left arm back toward me. Addi let out a small sound of surprise.

I attempted to raise the Well to me again, feeling the same sharp pricks of rejection again. My hand trembled. The Well no longer recognized me. I dropped my head and my wings. The only sounds left in the room were the falling rain and soft, slow pants coming from Ezra. Our essence had been shattered, not simply on an individual level, but at the source itself.

"I can't feel the Well, keeper," Addi whispered.

"I know." I closed my eyes. I had enough power stored to send out a call to the Elders. They would be the ones to repair the damage or simply cap this place and move us on. I did not think I would be leaving my grave. "Let me hold him, please." I was not used to begging, not like this.

I was startled when Rich shifted enough so I could ease Ezra out of his arms. He had been unconscious this whole time. I longed to see those startling eyes, the ones I found myself sinking into. The way they shifted in the light from a dark blue to stormy gray, a dark ring reminiscent of an ocean we crossed long ago. I ran my fingers through his hair; he was so young not a thread of silver or white yet.

I adjusted us so I could press my forehead to his, taking in his smell of rain and lightning. I wanted to drown in it. Fill my lungs until there was no room left that it backed into my heart, silencing it. His skin was clammy and cool to the touch. I nuzzled him, praying he was too far gone to feel pain from my caresses. His weight in my lap was the only thing grounding me, making this moment real.

I wrapped my wings around us, creating a tiny cave where all I could be is with him. Ezra's rattling breaths filled the space between us. I reached out one last time as he inhaled. I felt something snap inside of me. A surge of raw essence filled every bone, every muscle, every fiber, every pore of my body. I could not breathe or scream. I could not move. My vision whited out before going black.

When the sounds of the room and the world outside started to come back to me, I was slumped over on Ezra's still form. The Necromancer was coughing, as was Indrid. The Well was singing loudly to me, screaming for me to be one with it again. My skin sizzled with energy; muscles twitched with the newfound life. Ezra's color had returned to the fair pink. His lips faintly parted as his breath returned.

My bones ached, the weight of him on me was almost unbearable, but I needed to see his eyes. I needed to hear his voice. He stirred, shifting his weight from one side to the other, an attempt to roll. I caught him before he hit the floor, pulling him into a seated position. I felt Rich on my shoulder, but my wing kept him back. He seemed to understand or have enough sense to not interfere. Perhaps it was the sharp tip at eye level that indicated the need for space.

"Beloved," I breathed into his ear. I gently shook him, an attempt to break this sleep. "Beloved, it is done now. I need you to open your eyes."

I kissed his temple as he grumbled something incoherently. A warm chuckle became muffled in his hair. His eyes opened, slits at first, as he tilted his head toward me. I kissed him again on the forehead.

"Hello, my love." He lazily blinked at me a few times before giving me a tired smile.

"Mmm." Ezra cleared his throat. "I was asleep?"

"For a moment." My voice caught in my throat. "But you are back now, yes?"

Ezra nuzzled my neck, kissing my throat gently. "I love you." He abruptly stopped. "Hmm."

"What is it, sweetness?" I asked quietly, afraid that if I spoke too loud, whatever dream this was would end.

"I can't feel..." his voice faded off. I looked down, his bright eyes now dull and faded. The pink hue that had filled the apples of his cheeks quickly returned to a sickly pallor. A small huff left his chest as he sunk into my arms. There was no beat, no air, no life. Everything in the room collapsed in on me. In that moment, there was nothing left but the two of us sitting in a void of endless sorrow.

I can't feel.

CHAPTER 23

Graveside

GRAY

We sat in the kitchen for hours. I could not let him go. If I stopped holding him, he would get cold. His muscles would harden. His skin would turn waxen and yellow. As long as I held him, my essence kept his body from decaying. I would sit here and hold him until the stars themselves came to consume us. As long as it meant his body would not be turned to dust. My wings wrapped around us would keep us safe as the world around us burned to nothing.

It was Indrid who finally took Ezra, my Beloved, from me. I did not fight him. He did not speak, despite the binding leaving him as Beloved's last breath fell from his lips. Indrid would be free to sing in the mountains, joyous rounds of my failures and loss. I sat alone in that spot for minutes or days, it did not matter. Addi roused me, attempting to pull me into a hug. I startled like a wounded animal and fled from their home.

I took to wing until I could no longer hold myself in the sky. I do not remember much of the time that passed after. Indrid and an Elder found me near the mound where the sentinel stood. I had been wishing for it to open and take me to the beyond. I had no need for this form anymore. I had no use for living. They drug me back to my cave. I fought only a little, before the Elder backhanded me into a trunk, pieces of bark crumbling into my eyes.

Cold fury began to trickle in as the Elder droned on about how I must make use of my grief. I am responsible for the territory and a damaged Well. He had pointed to the decayed sentinel I now pressed against. The Elders would give me a week to clear my mind of the human, but there was damage done from the necromancy. I was needed whole.

Indrid stayed with me. He hated caves, or at least living in them for long periods of time. It felt like a nice enough tomb. A place for my body's internment. He continued to maintain silence. I watched him as he dug through my food stores, finding my water low. He studied me, probably wondering if I would rip my own throat out if he left me alone.

"I know you can speak," I growled.

He looked at me. "Did you want me to?"

I huffed in irritation. "Brother, that has never stopped you before."

"Hmm. Yes." He paused, considering what to say. "Perhaps I've learned something in the past few weeks. That's always what you want from me, isn't it? To learn. To *grow* from my past decisions."

I wanted a fight, and I knew he would give it to me. I wanted to rip flesh and break bones. I snarled at him. I wanted to taste blood, mine or his, it did not matter. My claws extended; I lifted my wings. I wanted to hear wails of agony, pleas to stop. I wanted to ground something, anyone, into nothing. An offer to what is ancient in exchange for Beloved. I would bleed the world to have him back.

Indrid raised his hands in front of him, gesturing me to stop. His wings held behind him, looking rigid and tense. His ears and eyes alert, waiting for me to strike. We held those poses until my muscles ached and I was too thirsty to care about drinking his blood when I would rather have water. When I relaxed and dropped to the hard ground, he began to move again.

"It has only been two days, brother," he murmured softly as he filled two cups. It had only been two days? It had already felt like an eternity. The sun had fallen without him and dared rise again and then again? I held my head in my hands.

My mind was filled with every thought and none at the same time. A cacophony of angry sounds, Rich screaming, Addi crying. Something I could not recognize until I started making it again. Now.

Indrid came to me, kneeling next to me with a cup. He pulled me against him and hummed a song I had not heard in centuries. It was the one Modor sang when I was too little to understand the storms would not steal us away. I hummed with him, swaying in his embrace. Something about his warmth and the vibration from his chest was more soothing than I could have ever imagined.

"Now, little bug." He nuzzled the side of my head. "You must rest some. When you have had some water, food, and sleep, we will go see where he lays." I stilled. "You must say our words over his bones. Leave a gift for the ancients so they know to let him pass."

"You do not believe that," I whispered into his chest.

"It does not matter what I believe, little bug. What matters is that this is done for your mate." He squeezed me tightly before laying a gentle kiss on the top of my head. "Go to sleep. We'll visit with the moon and the stars in the sky."

I crawled into my nest and closed my eyes. I did not bother with blankets or pillows. I curled on my side. No more moans or tears left me. I was weary, body and mind. I did not believe the sweet silence of sleep would take me.

And then it was dark.

CHAPTER 24

Song

Dark.
It.Is. Dark.
The world is wrapped tightly around me.
Cool.

Like the frost on curved stones.
Like the chilled wind dancing in the branches.

Knock.
Knock.

Pound. A pound of flesh. A pound of bone.

All that is left of me. I can't see.

I can't feel.

Slam. Pull. Dig. Dig. Dig.

I can't see. I can't feel. I. Can't.

BREATHE.

Let me...

Out.

Epilogue of Spiders

INDRID

T he human's body had been dead three days now. The Necromancer, Addison, promised me that the mundane wouldn't wreck the body with chemicals. They assured me Ezra would be buried intact, without the mishandling of his blood or organs. I was very clear that one that has been tethered to Winged Folk cannot be subjected to such a heinous act. Richard had nodded along; he'd keep doctors from performing an autopsy and request the body not be embalmed. It helped that Ezra had been gravely ill, it would look like heart failure and nothing more. It also helped that I'd fucked both the Necromancer and Richard; they were listening to me. Why not use that to my advantage?

I'd visited Addison before I was forced to go out and dig Gray out of whatever hole they were sobbing in. I knew the funeral was this afternoon and that Ezra had been placed in the newer section of the Angel's yard. I hadn't mentioned this to Addison, but that was the first place Gray blew Ezra. I hoped Gray enjoyed that bit once we got there. They'd probably fall to their knees and keen like a dying coyote again. I've never heard such a terrible sound in my life.

Gray was starting to stir on their mound of rags. I'd never under-stand why they stayed in this damp, moldy place when they could easily take over a home in the woods. The Elders wouldn't give a shit if they did it. It might further *Dresden's* long-term goals. I sighed, thinking about the nice little murder hut I'd burned down after the Well snapped back into place.

Gray had taken off, leaving the humans to clean up their mess in Addison's kitchen. I'd excused myself to finish the night's earlier activities. Briefly, I'd considered taking the bones, then the putrid smell of decayed essence reached me in the yard. Fuck did that place stink of every hell created by man. It was strong enough humans would notice. I needed to move quickly. How does one explain puddle man in the basement? I burned it all quickly; the rain had slowed so it didn't douse my flames that danced under a shrouded moon.

I spent the next two days watching the humans scatter around, offering my sincerest condolences to my lovers. Richard was less amorous with me than he'd been in the past. He stayed withdrawn while I sat in his little treehouse. Flipping through books of old pictures and sorting out handwritten poems. Tears a constant shimmer in his eye. I asked him if he needed anything, and he dismissed me with a wave of his hand. Other humans, mundane, came to him and stayed.

Addison, however, could not stop themself from riding my *cocks* until their balls were empty and asshole was a swollen puckered mess of my spend. The revival of the Well had had a different effect on their body. Their powers hummed in ways I had never seen before. While Ezra's simply flared and collapsed on itself, Addison's had tripled in strength. My little death singer, no Necromancer, was going to be a handful.

I wondered how deep they would let me sink my cock into their throat when I showed them I had Allen's book collection. Gray believed I only take and trade in flesh or bone, when the reality is I'd been running an underground market for anything *magic* related since my official release from the mines. The hills were full of artifacts that had no business in anyone's hands, especially mine. That's how I met my favorite little death singing outcast.

As much as I wanted to think about my little blood born mewling under me, Gray was now awake and scowling at nothing in particular.

I imagine waking up to find oneself alive and in good health while your soul crumbles will do that to you. I went back to my tender care of the broken *little bug*. They are utterly incapable of doing anything for themself. Thankfully, they have remembered how to hold their dicks to piss; I do have limits.

I wiped the dirt and sweat from Gray's face. There were chunks of debris tangled in their hair, a small section had matted with mud. I internally sighed. They needed a bath. After a few rounds of prodding and pleading, reminders of how to properly honor the dead, Gray acquiesced. Once they were rinsed of whatever squirrel shit they'd been caked in from wallowing on the forest floor, we took to wing.

It was a warm evening late in the summer. The moon was waxing its way back into darkness, returning to something fresh and new. The days were still relatively long, so I had waited until the sun bowed beneath the horizon. I wasn't worried about being observed by passing humans, but I did worry that the dying animal sounds that my sibling would indubitably make would bring unwanted attention. At least at night the locals would think it's a cat in heat and not a centuries old cryptid crying about a lost lover.

We walked past ancient graves and crypts. There was still a faint smell of sex. I vaguely wondered if that was little bug's adventure or some other college student with a line struck through a bucket list item. As we approached Ezra's grave, I hung back. I didn't relish in Gray's pain. I wasn't opposed to them being knocked down a peg or ripping off their wings when they became too arrogant, but this particular display was pathetic.

They didn't notice when I moved away from being their shadow. They had the items of the final night rest, a ritual passed down for generations so long that no one remembered why we did this or for what God. I crept behind a larger mausoleum, silently jumping to the roof. From here I could see the freshly turned Earth of the grave. Gray stood, hunched over, frozen in their loss. Not an echo of a sound or the breath of the wind rustled through the cemetery.

Eventually, Gray began to move about, setting our ancestors' words and pieces around his *Beloved*. They seemed lost in the final rites, not noticing the slight stir from below. Six feet of dirt would make any internal light dim, but even I heard the knocking from over here. *Poor little bug. Your human's dead, but this night is far from being over.* I sat on the edge of the roof, swinging my legs as Gray continued to be oblivious.

Dirt shifted again. Gray paused that time. Did they hear it? Did they feel it? Or were they finally aware that the faint tether that had remained wrapped around their heart for days was now tugging from below? I rested my chin in my hands, suppressing a giggle. Gray dropped to their knees, frantically scrabbling at the Earth with their hands. So much for the bath I made them take.

Ah, there it is. A clawed, moon white hand shot up from the ground. Gray yelled in surprise as they wildly pushed the dirt aside. Another hand appeared, grasping for anything solid to pull him free from his grave.

Gray tugged at both arms until a head and body appeared, the two forms collapsing on the ground. I could hear the ragged breaths and panting from below. Then it was absolute silence as one lover gazed at their heart, transformed. A tiny spider crawled across my leg; I flicked it away with a sharp claw.

Ezra's human body had died...

So, the Well gave him wings.

End.

THE LOVERS

Thank You

Thank you for reading Gray and Ezra's story. The next book focuses on Indrid's love of chaos and the Necromancer who will happily give it to him. Turn the page if you'd like to read more about *why* Indrid was imprisoned for decades, Missy's first meeting with the Folk, and the prologue to Book Two, *Cold*.

About the Author

Jae Dixon (They/Them) is a Queer, Trans Indie Author hailing from "back East" if asked. Jae grew up in and around Appalachia culture in the 1990s & 2000s. They have a BSS in English Creative Writing & Gender Studies, a Masters in something else, and dropped out of their Doctorate program to write about Mothman & Beloved.

Jae presently lives in Ohio when not traveling for their full-time job. They are a partner, a parent, and a dog lover. Seriously, Jae has too many dogs but there's really no such thing. Jae enjoys drinking Scotch, hiking the Rockies, going to live shows (music), being punk as fuck, reading adult fantasy books, and everything related to spooky & horror.

- For Jae's newsletter, updates and more info about their works, you can visit **NecromancyPublishing.com**
- Join Jae's FB group at **Jae's Winged Song**
- Jae's **Cursed Instagram**: @Rainbow.Necromancy
- Necromancy Publishing **TikTok**: @Rainbow.Necromancy
- Want to ALPHA, BETA, or ARC read for Jae? Sign up **HERE**! *https://www.cognitoforms.com/JaeDixon/ ALPHABETAARCReader*

Author's Note

CONTENT

This short comes from the world of Appalachia Cryptids. This story takes place in southeastern Ohio in the fall of 1967 before the novel *Song*. It can be read as a stand-alone horror piece or along with *Song*.

HISTORICAL/LORE MENTIONS

This story is completely fiction. If any of the characters resemble someone from real life... well, I imagine they are a very interesting person, but it is coincidental. This is *loosely* based on the legends of mothman as well as other folklore from Europe and European-centered cryptids of the colonies.

If you have read anything about the legend of mothman, you will pick up on some of the references, such as "Indrid Cold," the factory, and the mention of the Silver Bridge Collapse.

The Silver Bridge collapse was a horrific tragedy. Forty-six people drowned in the Ohio River that day. There is legend and lore around why it collapsed, such as mothman being the harbinger of it. This short story uses the idea that an *unknown terror* is at fault and not a fatal structural design.

AUTHOR'S NOTE

I grew up in Appalachia and went to college in the foothills of Appalachia. While I am not *from* there, almost half of my life was spent with people who were. Between my experiences growing up, stories from friends, and additional research, I added some elements from that area to this story and others. Do not take this as anything more than a piece of fiction.

WARNINGS

Mention of Sexual Assault Within Marriage, Domestic Violence, Child Abuse, Language, Consensual Sexual Situation, Homicide, Violence During Sexual Situation, Joy of Murder, Blood & Gore

The Fall

AN APPALACHIAN CRYPTID TALE

INDRID

Why did you give them your name? It is all over their papers." Gray was furious; I could see the light begin to shine in their eyes. Not as bloody as their sire's, but red enough to remind me we were half-siblings.

I shrugged, unbothered by their anger. "Little bug, it was only my first name that was true. We don't have surnames like the mortals."

"You are not a god, Indrid. You were born, and you will die like the *New People*," Gray hissed at me, their impressively large wingspan flaring as the sun set behind them in the distance. The fall leaves were bathed in the reds and oranges of the sky; it was glorious, like fire or bloodshed.

"I believe they call themselves humans, Gray." I turned my back on them. They could attack me, but it was unlikely. I was the only one that ever seemed to upset the *gentle* Gray, and even then, their patience with me seemed endless. I tried, with frequency, to rattle them, especially since they'd taken the mantle of *The Keeper*. It was only fair. I needed to give them something to do.

"They are watching you, Indrid," Gray growled before I cut them off.

"When have *The Five* ever intervened with us, hmm? When have they given a fuck about me... or even you, Gray? I remember a youngling that once needed their aid." I looked at them over my left shoulder. They were now standing in the doorway with their wings lowered but still not tucked in enough to enter. Gray had never approved of my taking over this relic of time, a *settler's* cabin.

"It has been centuries, Indrid. I do not bear ill will to our Elders for what was done or not done. It does not change the outcome." Their voice grew softer. It always did when I brought up our dead sires. I'd killed mine when I was barely a season past two decades. Gray killed theirs almost as young. Not all the Winged Folk who'd come to this continent had good intentions for their own kind; humans, it seemed, fared worse. The abuse of our own young and numerous killings of young bearers led to The Five being elected. Our sires were fine examples of the contemptuous arrogance our people had brought from the old world.

"True, but that does not mean I cannot be petty about it." I smiled, showing the sharpest of my teeth. Gray had a way of seeing through me.

"Ind, please. The humans are..." they paused, "are not truly aware of us. It is better that way."

"They have their stories, little one. The old world remembers us for what we were, what we still are." I ruffled my wings.

"Yes, stories they tell their younglings as fantasy." Gray walked across the floorboards. "Please, Ind. Leave them be for now. No more hallucinations of, uh, *aliens* and no more men smiling on the roadside."

"Not all of it has been me," I said quietly. "Eamon was chasing them over by the old factory and then took to the air to dance about it. You call me arrogant; he thinks the town and territory are his."

"Eamon has been dealt with." Gray moved closer.

"Did you kill him, little brother?" I turned, eyes wide with glee.

"No, not all matters are dealt with in death sentences." Gray frowned.

"Ah, yes, I forgot, you are better than me." I mirrored their frown.

"I am not better, Ind. As you remind me so frequently, I do not lust for life in the ways that you do." Gray glanced at the pinned wings that hung above the mantle before looking back at me.

"Oh, do you want them back, *little bug*?" I grinned widely as I stepped toward the fireplace. I'd ripped that set off Gray's back seven summers ago when the last pair had started to disintegrate. It would be another fifty years before I would need to replace them, but if Gray continued to push the matter, I'd add two more to my wall tonight. I never took their flight wings, simply the ones that made it easier to land.

They shook their head, "No brother, keep my wings. They clearly bring you comfort when I am not able to be near." There was no malice in their voice, no anger in their eyes.

I snarled, "What makes you think I want you near?" Gray had gotten too close; I took the opportunity to slam the back of my fist into their jaw. They stumbled back before quickly recovering, pulling their wings tight to their body. *Ah, yes, you know the mood I am in leads to me ripping you to pieces.* I sneered as they took another step back, hands raised with a look of askance crossing their features. *Finally.*

"Enough, Indrid of the Dark Cold Waters. I will not request you to cease your meddling again." They stood tall; they were no longer playing the little sibling but now approached me as *The Keeper*. I took a step forward; they pulled their wings above their head, flashing razor-sharp talons hidden within the soft scales. I froze. Gray could hurt me if they wanted. They took their new position seriously; perhaps we were done for the day.

I waved my hand and turned away, grabbing the matches and kindling to start a fire. "Good night, *little bug*."

As I leaned down, Gray's gaze bore into my back. I suppressed the urge to shudder. They were powerful, more powerful than either of our sires had been. It was a waste, in the end. I could've used my essence for the fire, but I enjoyed the acrid scent of a match. The flames began to lick along the edges of the logs, then the gentle shuffle as Gray moved away.

"Good night, brother," they said quietly as the door shut.

I leaned back on my heels, staying crouched near the fire. Gray didn't understand that some of the humans not only knew about us but welcomed us. Not in the strange religious fervor of the old country, where we were gods. Gods who only conquered or saved humans, I no longer remember those details. No, there were humans that were just as connected to the lands as we were. They held great power, yet their brethren beat them down instead of celebrating such a gift.

I knew I wouldn't leave *her* alone. I couldn't leave her to that fate. Gray would be forced to punish me, whether that meant taking my wings or forcing me into a cave chained to the walls. I would be meant to suffer under the hands of those worthless old *moths*. It would be worth it to set her free, even if it isn't into the embrace of my wings.

MELISSA

I held the chunk of ice to my face. If Bill knew I'd pulled that out of the old ice box, he'd give me a reason to need it more. Bill would be gone for the week; he and his brothers had taken off to a larger mine across the state. They'd stay in the housing there until the weekend when he'd come home, and we'd start this all over again.

My oldest, William Jr., or Will for short, watched me from across the kitchen in the early morning light. His dark brown eyes, much like his father's, scrutinized every inch of my bruised and swollen skin. Unlike his father, though, he cared about me. He'd tried to intervene again, my boy, who wasn't so small anymore. Bill recognized that he himself wasn't so young as to take on his almost adult son.

Will would be 17 in a few weeks, almost old enough to be drafted in another war that seemed to only take *our* sons away. Too many uncles and cousins were lost in the *last* world war, the men who never came back to our hills and lost in time. Will was smart enough to be at the top of his class. He had planned on going to college to study engineering. His veteran father called him a draft dodger. I whispered into his ear before bed, "*Hero.*"

The twins were loudly bickering in the living room. I hadn't expected to ever be pregnant again after Will, but those two came blazing into our lives 12 years after my first. I felt too old to be a mother to children that young, but here we were. They seemed mostly unaware of their father's habits and my *clumsiness*. Or maybe it was Will, corralling them at night like little sheep away from the wolf.

"You're going to be late for school if you two keep fooling around in there like wild things," I sighed as I heard something fall to the floor.

Will stood up and walked into the room. I heard the twins squealing and Will's soft, commanding tenor. As much as he liked pretending it put him off to hurry his brothers along, he had this smirk reserved for only them. They trampled into the kitchen, all arms and legs, cawing about wanting toast and jam.

"The last jam bottle fell and broke last night." Will directed Jacob to his seat with a firm hand. I nudged Matthew with my hip as I pulled away from the counter. I put down two bowls of hot oatmeal that were quickly accompanied by huffs of irritation. Will set down butter, sugar, and the last of some maple syrup. The twins buzzed with delight at their older brother for saving them from too healthy of a meal.

"Eat up, loves; you've a long day ahead of you." I opened the box to toss the melted ice back in.

"Ma, why'd we have to go to school?" Jacob whined behind me.

"Because you need to learn how to read, and I'm volunteering at the campus again." I didn't bother to look at him. He knew it was a lost cause. I'd been going up to the university two to three times a week since the spring, helping with special collections at the town's historical society. I was the youngest volunteer they'd and the only one who was well-versed in Appalachia *folklore,* as they called it.

"Yeah, Ja-Ja, you need to learn how to read," Matthew sing-songed. I sensed the smack before I felt it. Will's voice rumbled for them to stop, followed by the gentle scrapes of spoons against porcelain. I was staring beyond the yard into the trees that backed our property. I caught the outline of Will's reflection; he was watching me again.

I turned and smiled despite the bruising on my cheek. Matthew looked up, and it registered in his little face that I was injured. His eyes widened a little, and he quickly glanced at Will. Matthew fisted his spoon, knuckles turning white as he glared at his older brother. Jacob seemed to sense the tension and glanced between the two before settling on my face. His big hazel eyes were wide and sad. My little lambs knew more than I wanted to believe.

"I'm fine, boys, just bumped my face last night." I straighten out the front of my housecoat.

"Don't fib, ma. We know what he does," Jacob said darkly, his eyes still shining brightly as if he were about to cry.

"Well, I didn't say on what." I glared back at them. "What happens between your pa and I is just that, between us. I'll handle him. You understand me? Don't you ever go near him when we're... talking."

The twins blankly stared at me while Will's expression was unreadable. I couldn't tell if he was even listening to me. I could feel the anger tickling at me low in my chest. It was tight and hot. I wanted to scream at them. I wanted to break something to make my point clear. I felt my eyes get hot.

"You will promise me that right now. None of you, I mean *none* of you, will get in his way." The tears fell down my cheeks without permission.

Will walked over quickly and wrapped me in his fiercest hug. "I promise, mama. Don't cry. We'll be okay. He's gone for a week." He paused, saying quieter, "And if we're lucky, the mine will fall, and he won't come back at all."

INDRID

Gray's words haunted me as I watched him hit her again. She was strong, but *he* towered in his bulk, pushing her down to the floor. I'd never seen him force himself in her before, but she'd admitted that'd happened in the past. That they were married. That such an act is permissible among the humans. So is the hitting, except I didn't believe that.

The first of their younglings was preparing to leave their nest in a few short seasons. He came into the kitchen dangerously close to his raging sire. I could feel myself tense. If he hit the *boy*, I wouldn't keep my word to anyone; I'd attack. His sire was drunk and stumbled. He slurred some hideous words at the boy and went to leave the kitchen.

The boy, Will is what Missy calls him, followed his sire to the back where an old pickup and sedan sat. The man was trying to get into his truck, but Will grabbed him by his shoulders and spun him around, pinning him against the cab. He thrashed under Will's hold, hissing about the boy being a *worthless fairy*. While Missy was touched by essence, her children were not of the Winged Folk. I didn't think that's what his sire meant.

Will was thrown off by his father. He stumbled a few steps, giving the older man enough time to swing and connect with his ribs. Will went down hard; the breath was knocked out of his lungs. He gasped as his sire reared back like his youngling was something to be stomped underfoot. I felt my rage flood, and my essence let loose.

The older man slammed into the truck door, grunting as he lost his footing. He hit his head on a sharp corner of metal. I smelled the blood before I saw it drip between his swollen, dirty fingers. He smelled like death already, but that wouldn't take him soon enough. I'd have to intervene. It'd be painful.

Will stood up and backed away, clearly unsure of what'd happened. He sprinted back inside to his ma. Missy hadn't come outside. She wasn't at the window. I could still hear three heartbeats inside; she was alive. She was too injured to aid her youngling, though. I felt that ripple of heat through me again. I couldn't end him here. I couldn't *implicate* the youngling or his mother.

MELISSA

I felt him outside the other night, or more like his magic. As I laid on the kitchen floor, gasping for air, I heard them both storm outside. Will ran after his father to do God knows what after seeing him hit me, and then I felt that twinge in the air. Almost like the moment before lightning strikes beside you. I could smell it, too; apparently, it was unusual to smell things like water and electricity in the air. Tonight, I was sitting outside the old plant where we usually met.

Will hugged me that morning before he took the twins to their cousins so he could head off to high school. The little ones would stay with Mary until Will was done doing his delivery work. She'd feed them for me. She knows what Bill does to us. She knows I need to recover in my own way, among fading pictures and antiques. She's hinted that I have a lover out there, but I don't. At least, not in the way she thinks.

It was still warm enough that I didn't need to leave the engine idling. I sat in the dark. I should be afraid, knowing what I knew. The first time I came out here, I didn't believe in them. There'd always been the stories about the beings that were settled out here; I'd heeded my mawmaw's warnings as a child. As an adult, I'd become more reckless, and that's how I stumbled upon *the Folk*.

They all seemed to be bastards, but I've only met two. Eamon was apparently outside of his *territory* when we met. I wanted to go for a drive on the back roads one night. I realized something was following me through the trees near the old factory. At first, I thought it was a large animal, but it was moving too quickly and intently.

When I slowed to a stop, something else fell from the sky and into the woods. I heard hissing and what sounded like a language before two hulking creatures burst from the brush into the beams of my headlights. One was as bright as the moon, while the other blended into the night. The fairer one had blood-red eyes and massive black wings that looked like a moth's. It glared directly at me. The larger, darker-looking one punched the moon moth in the face.

More hissing back and forth before the smaller one backed up and took flight. Before my eyes and God's, the other monstrous moth changed into the form of a man wearing a suit and hat. He adjusted his jacket before walking to the driver's side window. I don't know what possessed me to roll it down – maybe it was his smile – but I did. There was some odd sense of peace I felt around him. I quickly realized it was a power the Folk had to calm humans. To lull them into a false sense of safety. I should feel scared, but I couldn't.

He told me his name was Indrid Cold and to please excuse that brute's behavior. I let him in the sedan while I parked us near a clearing in the trees. We talked for hours about the hills, the land, and the changes we'd all seen. He told me about his cabin that wasn't too far away from here in a quiet valley. I told him about the boys and Will. He kissed me gently and told me not to worry about Eamon or any of the other Folk. He stepped out of the car, and I felt that magic ripple through the air. He was gone.

I kept coming back every week for another kiss for months. Tonight, I sat here patiently waiting for Indrid to return. I knew he'd been around the house on more than one occasion. He'd seen the bruises on my wrists and arms. The last time we met, he had warned me about Bill's behavior, that it would have grave consequences.

I was lost in my thoughts until I felt the air shift and my door open. It'd been locked. He reached his hand in to help me out. I looked up at his beautiful face. It wasn't completely human, but it also wasn't terrifyingly foreign to me either.

He pulled me into his arms before caressing my bruised cheek. I wanted to hide it, but he'd already seen it happen. He kissed my forehead, taking in my scent.

"You were watching last night." It wasn't a question.

"Yes." His low, deep voice sounded strained.

"And you did something?" That was a question.

"He was going to harm the youngling, irrevocably so." His face looked saddened.

"You didn't kill him, though." I sounded disappointed, even to my own ears.

Indrid leaned down, finding my lips in a deep kiss. I could feel his tongue beg entry into my mouth. We stood there under the stars, gently caressing one another. I've never felt so wanted, so understood before this... being.

He broke away from my mouth, trailing kisses down my jaw to my neck. His longer fingers eagerly found every curve and dip of my body. I wanted him to explore me fully.

His mouth found mine again; he sucked on my bottom lip, giving it a gentle bite. I moaned into him. Wandering hands had unbuttoned the front of my pants. I wore them when I worked to avoid any incidents with ladders. I wished right now I hadn't bothered. Soon, I felt fingers reaching down to stroke me. He'd never gone so far before. His fingers pulled back the cotton of my underwear as long digits dipped into me.

He worked me, gently at first, slowly easing into a quickening pace. I was writhing and panting in his arms as he held me pinned against the sedan. I peaked too quickly, sagging in his arms as he pulled his hand away from my molten heat. He brought the glistening wet fingers to his lips, sucking each one clean slowly.

Fuck, this man knew what he was doing. I could feel him, steel against my leg, yet he made no move to find his own release. I leaned my head on his shoulder as he continued to hold me in the peace of the night. He kissed the top of my head, a soft purr escaping from his throat. There were brief moments when I remembered he wasn't human. That I wasn't sure if he even wanted me to think of him as a man.

Indrid tilted my chin up so we could see one another eye-to-eye. There was something predatory in that look. Again, a reminder that we were not the same. It did nothing to tamper my lust for him. *He will be the death of me.* Still, I smiled at him; he was one of the few brief joys I had outside of my volunteer hours and my boys.

"You are not my mate, but I do care greatly for you," he said quietly. I blinked, not knowing how to process that. "I need to take care of your *husband*, though, before he goes too far. He *will* go too far."

"Take care?"

I could feel the warning rumble in his chest. "I won't let him harm your younglings. I won't let him harm you." He stiffened, his arms suddenly feeling more possessive.

"But I'm not your mate," I said cautiously.

"No, but that doesn't mean I can't care for you and your nest. That doesn't mean I can't fuck you when you wish." Indrid smirked. "And I could smell that that was your wish tonight."

I had the decency to blush at the comment. He definitely had a way of saying things plainly. I appreciated that about my shape-shifting moth... lover. I straightened, leaning back more on the sedan than on Indrid. I studied him for a moment.

"What are you planning on doing?" I didn't expect him to answer me.

He adjusted his jacket but not the straining bulge in his pants. "Something horrible."

I cringed. "What would that be?"

"Missy," he said softly as he caressed my bruised cheek again. He seemed more distressed, and I knew it wasn't about murdering my husband. "Make me a promise?"

"What is that, Indrid?" I was curious as to what would unsettle this ancient creature.

"The suspension bridge close to your town. It'll fall before the winter solstice. Promise me you and your boys will stay away from it." He ran his fingers through my hair.

"Wait, the bridge is going to collapse? Indrid, I need to tell..." I stopped as he shook his head.

"The bridge drowning," he paused, as if thinking of the gentlest way to say it, "is not the worst thing that could happen. Believe me; it would be wickeder if we intruded on what is to come."

"I don't understand. Why would I let it happen?" I pulled away from him, horrified. At peak, the bridge could have dozens of cars on it. People would die.

"Because the last time someone was warned, thousands died instead of a few. People will cross the veil regardless. I wish for you not to be among them." He didn't try to reach out to me again. Indrid wasn't one to comfort. He shifted his left foot back as if to turn away. "Promise me, Missy. Stay away."

I nodded, not knowing what else I could do. Our meetings usually lasted hours, not minutes. He frowned at me; his eyebrows knit together tightly. There was something about that look that made my stomach clench and the rest of me go cold.

"Indrid... I'm not going to see you again, am I?" I could feel tears welling in my eyes.

"That is for the best, dear one." He sighed. "There are things I must do and not do. It will be easier for you not to see me again. You will never forgive me. I would never ask for it nor apologize."

"What'll happen to Bill?" I shivered, not wanting to know.

He shook his head as his human visage melted into his true form. He was beautiful like this. The monster of the wood. The demon. The devil. The mothman. I felt the buzz against my skin, and before I took my next breath, he was gone.

The tears that had been hanging on started to fall. I'd never again see my smiling Indrid. Was freedom from Bill worth that price?

INDRID

I followed him and the other men from his family to the mines. I'd spent many nights watching them from the trees. When away from their homes, they gambled, drank, hired prostitutes, and used drugs. Bill's poison came in the form of a bottle that'd lead to him losing at cards with increasing frequency. He also followed others into the woods for very specific companionship. Unsurprisingly, he always chose younger men to fuck and hurt.

His last victim was barely old enough to be considered an adult. Bill choked him, using nothing to ease his entrance, shredding the boy's most intimate parts as he fucked him. Eventually, the pounding became more fluid and smooth as blood eased the rough slide. When Bill left the woods, the boy's body remained crumpled in the leaves. He'd lost consciousness either from pain or lack of oxygen. I never saw him in the camp or with the other men again.

Tonight, Bill was deep in his cups of cheap whiskey at the bar near the mine camps. He'd played a few rounds of cards before he started searching for his victim to fuck and kill. I'd used a glamour that made me look young and relatively small. Bill liked his boys lean and soft. I'd decided on hazel eyes and dark blond hair. I needed to look attractive to a predator like him.

The place was dimly lit, smelling of body odor and desperation. His eyes eventually found mine as he made his way over to the table I was sitting at. I held an empty cup I'd picked up on my way in. I told the men playing cards that I didn't have enough coin to play and wanted to watch. They'd shrugged and said little to me after. He plopped down next to me, noticing my lack of drink.

"Can I fill ya up?" He smirked at what he thought was a smooth euphemism.

I smiled shyly and half-shrugged. "Don't got any extra money tonight."

"I hear ya; it's tight until payday. What'd a pretty boy like you spend all his money on? Whores?" He laughed annoyingly loud at his own jest.

I attempted to look shocked at the accusation. "Oh no, sir. I just started."

"Don't worry, boy." He nudged my shoulder with a lascivious wink. "There's still time for whoring. Let me get you a drink."

I handed him the empty mug. I had no intention of drinking. I also didn't give a shit about what he wasted his money on. I watched him head to the bar and get a refill, eagerly smiling as he walked back, his hands full. I stood up, dusting off the worn denim pants and a blue flannel I wore. Of course, the glamour was not dirty; I needed to act *normal* and have a reason to stand. I thanked him when he handed me the cup.

"Care for a walk?" I asked in what I thought was a polite tone.

The predatory look washed over his face in the low light. "That sounds like a swell idea."

We walked far enough away that I was sure no one would hear his screams or pleas. I imagined he was thinking the same thing. I made sure we came back to the same clearing he'd left that boy in all those weeks ago. If he noticed where we were, he didn't show any recognition on his drunken face. I led him back to a shaded spot, the ground covered in the underbrush that would soak up his blood well.

He leaned in, breath drowned in whiskey, and landed a sloppy kiss on my lips. It was all tongue and teeth. I should kill him for his bad breath alone. I shoved him back, keeping it playful. He smiled as he unbuttoned his flannel, showing a stained white undershirt. He was in good form – decades of surviving in hard labor does that to a man's body. He pulled his undershirt over his head. Dark hair covered his chest, trailing down his abdomen and into his pants. He unbuckled his belt, struggling with his fly.

I leaned into him, pushing him back against the tree. "I want you to fuck my ass." I giggled, his grin growing.

"Oh, sweet boy, I'm going to do that and so much more." He swayed a little on his feet.

"Suck me first." I play pouted. "Please?"

He huffed, clearly considering that this is what would get me into a more accommodating position later. "Alright. Only 'cuz you're cuter than most. I don't suck dick. Queers do that shit."

Interesting. I kept my face neutral. "You calling me a Fae?"

"I ain't calling you shit, now show me, or I'm heading back." He dropped to his knees.

Good boy. I smiled to myself as I pulled the single cock out. I made sure it looked large. I wanted this to be memorable for him. All of it. He sighed when he saw it, quickly taking in the crown and sucking hard. *Eager fucker.* He bobbed his head, relaxing his throat to take all of me in. I groaned for him. Something about the glamour dulled the sensation on my actual cock.

He sped up, fondling my sac and moaning around my length. The girth didn't seem to be a deterrent. I'd considered making it wider to crack his jaw and pop it out of place. That'd make for an interesting face fuck. I thought of Missy and the bruise on her cheek. The way Bill was going to stomp in his own offspring's head in a drunken rage.

I felt my finger grow into claws as I pulled his hair harder. The hands that had been resting on the sides of his head were now holding Bill tightly. He moaned louder around my aching prick. I started to slam into him, my pelvis meeting face. I fucked his throat relentlessly, feeling him gag around me. I quickly grabbed his jaw, squeezing until I heard an audible pop. He screamed in pain, muffled around my dick.

He was thrashing, trying to push me away as I pumped harder and faster into him. Missy was afraid he was going to hurt the boys one day. Truly hurt the boys. There was a darkness in her tone. Something too deep to be spoken. The young man sprawled under the trees came to mind. I dropped the glamour and pulled out, forcing Bill to look at my face.

He moaned in agony. In fear. I could smell the piss that soaked the front of his pants. He was shaking, jaw at an odd angle. There was blood where the side of his lips had torn toward his cheeks. Bruising was blossoming on his cheekbones and temples. Tears and snot ran down his face. The scent of abject terror filled my lungs. I could feel my teeth lengthen. My blood began to sing. Both of my cocks hardened to steel rods.

I bent down to his level. "You'll never hurt them again."

He shook his head, jaw moving in a grotesque fashion. I clamped his head in my vice-like grip and shoved my slightly smaller cock into his mouth. There was no risk of him biting.

He cried out, probably begging me to stop. I found my way to the back of his throat, and he involuntarily contracted around my length. My lower cock rubbed along his throat, scratching against the mangy-looking neck beard. With a claw, I slashed, giving both cocks a hole.

His jaw was in the way. I heard him gurgling on my prick and his blood. I dismantled what was left of his jaw and pounded in three times before pulling out and finishing in both hands. His body crumpled to the ground, twitching and smelling like piss and shit. I came blindingly hard, covering his mangled face with copious amounts of spend. I leaned back, enjoying the kill. I knew *they* were watching.

"Why didn't you stop me, *little bug*?" I asked, lazily stroking out the last bit of my seed.

"It was already too late for him," Gray replied barely above a whisper.

"Yes, it was." I put my dicks away and faced them. "So, now what? You take me away to be punished?"

"Indrid..." They ran a hand through their hair. "There are so many deaths that the humans would accept. This is not going to be one of them."

"That's the point. He was a horrible creature. Vile. This," I gestured to the cooling corpse, "was too good for him."

I saw movement behind Gray. They'd brought others to collect me and probably what remained of Bill. I frowned. I wouldn't fight them on this. The punishment was worth it for Missy.

Nael and her brother walked out into the clearing. Nael had a bag, her brother chains. I nodded, pulling my wings tight behind me.

"Do you think they'll rip all four off?" I gestured to my wings. "Or simply kill me like I fucking deserve?" I asked Gray as they grimaced at the corpse.

"Neither; I will ask for something more humane."

"Careful, *little bug*," I cautioned. "You might be punished, too."

I felt the iron lock around my wrists. The moon hung high above us, illuminating the bloody justice I'd given. Death was quickly setting in. Perhaps the human was closer to killing himself with booze than I'd realized. I still would've killed him.

It was going to be a long night with The Five.

Acknowledgments

Thank you to my partner of 13-years. My greatest love. My *Beloved*. To our child who will not be reading this book for a *very* long time because "it's for grown-ups and full of monsters." You are two of the strongest and most beautiful humans I've ever known. I love you.

Thank you to every person who helped me make *Song* real; Steve, Sierra, Kelly, Melanie, Kit, Lee, Delaney, Abrianna, Red, my patient editor (Editing by Sierra), Beta readers, and of course the artists that brought my cryptids and humans alive visually. Thank you for listening to me babble, ramble, and curse. Thank you for making my manuscripts stronger. Thank you for your support. Your excitement. Your generosity.

Thank you to every person in my life who told me to write.

And, thank you to every Indie Author who's become my friend & mutual. You inspire me every day.

IN LOVING MEMORY

Mrs. Low, my high school creative writing teacher, who after having me in her class banned students from putting heads in "the bucket" prompt. Sorry about that. I hope you knew how much of a lifeline your classes were for me. And, also, sorry the in memoriam is a part of a *monster fucking* book. You probably would've expected that.

And Steve, one of the last things you said to me was that I always made you proud and that you loved me. Doing what I love, even if it was hard, would've made you proud. Again, sorry about the in memoriam being in a monster *fucking* book.

Characters & Glossary

SPOILERS IF YOU DIDN'T READ THE BOOK

CHARACTERS

(Mostly an author's ramblings to keep things straight)

Ezra Williams cis-male (he/him): Six-foot-two, 190 lbs. 29-year-old doctoral student at the University. His focus is on modern poetry and he is failing, miserably per his committee chair. He was born in Pittsburgh PA and raised between there and Columbus, Ohio. His father and sister moved to California when Ezra went into his undergrad studies. Ezra's sister still lives in California and is his last living family member. His father died in 2018 from cancer, his mother when he was a teenager. Ezra died in 2022 and was reanimated by The Well into Winged Folk. Ezra was renamed Ezra of the Last Song and is a Keeper of Records and Histories.

Gray of the Winged Folk, Gray The Keeper of the Mist and Hills, gender diverse (they/them): Six-foot-nine, 270 lbs. Born in 1695, 325-years-old, born in the Appalachian mountains in what is known as present day Pennsylvania in the Allegheny Plateau. Gray lives in the Dark Wing territory (southern Ohio and Western WV/Allegheny

Mountains) as a Keeper of Whispers and Songs. They are known for being cautiously curious, generous, and friendly with the other Folk and peoples. Gray is fiercely protective that leads them to make errors in human social norms. Gray has an older brother Indrid, who is feral.

Indrid of the Winged Folk, also known as Indrid Cold, male (he/him/bastard): Six-foot-eleven, 295 lbs. Born in 1597, Ind was born in the swamps of modern-day Ireland. Indrid and Gray share the same birthing parent they call Modor, modern day word is "mother." Little is known how or when his Modor came to the new world. Indrid resides on the border of Dark Wing territory and is an exceptional bastard. Because of his antics with humans in the 1960s, Indrid has been required by The Five to stay near or within Gray's area for keeping. Indrid hates it and spends a significant amount of time being a complete terror about it.

Pooka the Basement Goblin, gender diverse (they/them): Pooka lives in Ezra's basement and eats all of the spiders, mice, and fleas. Pooka also enjoys eating broken glass, ash, and monster flavored cans. Ezra is unaware he has a roommate who does not pay rent. Pooka enjoys watching  Ezra sleep while they eat the empties in the room.

Richard Henderson, cis-male (he/him): 69-year-old. Is the longtime friend of Ezra's father (John Williams) and current mentor/parent figure for Ezra. Rich is an English Professor at the university. Rich is in his late 60s and genuinely no longer gives any fucks about what "looks good" to others. He will not be the first man to throw a punch, but he will be the man to end the fight. He has a history with Folk and Blood Born, however, his involvement has only been mentioned briefly in book one.

Addison Charles, gender diverse (they/them): Age not stated. Lives with Ezra in a rental home on campus. They previously completed an MFA while working in a youth center specifically for adolescents who were deemed unable to live in "traditional" foster care systems. Addi is passionate about equity and change in social services, especially when it comes to undeserved youth who are put at higher risk due to the state's "care" and judicial systems. They date sporadically, usually local witches. Addi is from West Virginia and is a treasure trove of knowledge related to Appalachia magic and lore. They were cast out from their Blood Born clan, it is unknown why. Addi is a death singer turned necromancer.

Missy Jones: 85-years-old. Lead volunteer for the archives at the historical society. Widower and former lover of Indrid Cold. Was a direct witness to the mothman sightings of 1966-1967.

Nick (Undergrad), cis-male (he/him): 20-year-old. A junior in his undergrad studying journalism. Born and raised in Cleveland Ohio, but plans on moving to Columbus after graduation. There is no other mention of his life/goals in the book.

James Allen, cis-male (he/him): late 60s. Is a horror show of a human. He is the primary antagonist in this story. He will get what's coming to him.

Josiah Simmons (AKA Josias Simking) born* 1880, was a notorious judge for the town from 1914-1943. He was called *the executioner,* who would stage photos of those who had been sentenced to death. Judge Simmons also required all deceased people be photographed before burial, no matter the state of their bodies. It was unclear where these photographs were stored until the estate collection was sorted. The historical society uncovered 112 executions as well as 40 documented unsolved deaths of those 16 were children.

Dr. Everhart, male (he/him): Age not stated. The Dean of English. His mistakes are plenty when it comes to Dr. Allen.

Emily & Sandra, cis-gender female(s) (she/her): Both in their 40s. English Professors who align themselves with Dr. Henderson.

TERMS

Essence: A source of power not readily available to all. As Gray explains it there are those that are of it and those who live in it. Most humans live *in* essence. Essence is also referred to as *magic* and *song*. There are other forms of power that are not directly from essence but are a corruption of that power source. Necromancy is considered a secondary form of magic, separate from essence.

Mitch's Moonshine AKA The Jersey Devil's Jizz is an infamously backwoods distilled liquor from a townie who enjoys *fucking up the kids* so they get the full college experience. This moonshine is the punkest thing you can drink that isn't whiskey from a plastic bottle. It will both put hair on your chest while taking years off your life. Story goes Mitch came to college in the late 90's from Jersey to pursue an MFA. He never finished the degree and he also never left.

The Well/Well of Essence/The Sentinel: The naturally occurring points where essence pools and can be drawn from. While not mentioned in Song, wells are often found at sites of great trauma, lay lines, and where tectonic plates have come together. The Sentinel is the physical form of the Well in this world. It takes shape as a tree that sometimes becomes sentient.

Simmons Estate: Josias Simking was a changeling born in 1692 to boogarts and traded to Puritans in Massachusetts Bay Colony. His birth was recorded in one of the many Bibles donated from the Simmons Estate to the Historical Society. It was noted that while there was an assortment of King James Bibles, there was one Geneva Bible that lacked any additional notations in the margins. It did not contain any photos or other items from the family. Josias Simking (Josiah Simmons) was executed by Gray of the Winged Folk sometime in the mid-20th century.

The estate had documents as early as 1800 noting the family came to the area in 1799. The last document in the collection was from 1947, a letter from a serviceman who was stationed on the South Pacific during WWII. The most notorious items in the collection were Bibles from as early as the 16th century through late 18th century, all printed in Europe. Only the Geneva Bible carried the family surname of Simking that later had "Simmons" entered after births and marriages in the 19th century.